Ann, Not Annie

Ann, Not Annie

SAGE STEADMAN

Mmhmm Books

Ann, Not Annie

Copyright © 2017 by Sage Steadman

MmHmm Books

1118 North Fairway Circle
Farmington, Utah 84025
www.MmHmmBooks.com

ISBN*: 978-0-9970565-6-3 (sc)*
ISBN*: 978-0-9970565-7-0 (ebk)*

"Let us settle ourselves, wedge our feet downward through the mud and slush of opinion, and prejudice, and tradition, and delusion, and appearance…till we come to a hard bottom and rocks in place, which we can call reality."
-Henry David Thoreau, *Walden*

Where I sort of introduce myself as the narrator.

Annie Julia Grey was one of my favorite specimens to research. She never once remembered the times I beamed down from my alien spacecraft, snuck into her bedroom, and probed her brain. She was a fretful sleeper, easy to wake, and I had to be careful when I extracted her memories so as not to rouse her. Once aboard my spacecraft, I watched her private thoughts via projector while eating a bag of Earth's candy corn, which I *cannot* get enough of.

Shit, never mind. Scratch that. That is literally the worst way to start a narration.

Let me try again.

Hi, and welcome. My name is…well, I'm not going to tell you, but what I can tell you is that I am an Earthling. I bleed red, I was born in the states, my parents are *Homo sapiens*, I have ten toes, I wear clothes, and I don't have an abnormally large-sized head… well, just a little, but the point is I'm not an alien. Who I am is less important right now anyway, so shelf your curiosity and just work with me. I am here to introduce myself as the narrator. And I'm sorry about the whole "alien" ruse; this is my first time narrating something and as you can tell, I suck at it.

The thing is, who I am is not that important because this story isn't about me. I'm just here to relay a story to you that was once shared with me about a girl named Annie, who, despite her best efforts, fell in love. That, after all, is what the great stories are written about: How people manage to find themselves in love. Well let me just say that *how* a person falls in love is more important than *who* they fall in love with, for to truly fall in love with someone else, you must first fall in love with yourself. The process a person goes through to break down his or her outer shell and let love in is often as miraculous as the mystery of falling in love. But I'm getting ahead of myself.

Many of these experiences I witnessed firsthand. I stood next to Annie and watched while her world fell apart and reassembled again. As I said before, the story is not about me and at this time my identity will remain anonymous. I can't promise to withhold my own additions or prejudices, but I'll do my best. So let me begin by telling you that Annie once insisted on being called Ann, not Annie. Those two simple letters at the end of her name seemed to change how she felt about everything in her world. They were the difference between bearable pain and unbearable hell. And I think I will begin the story with the unbearable hell.

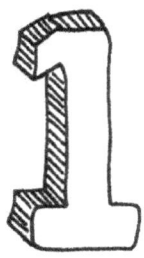

Detention blows.

Some people you meet in life are polite, respectful, kind, and docile. They smile at strangers because they know their smile will brighten another person's day, and it does.

Then there's Ann. An ill-tempered, loudmouthed, smart-ass who'd been sent to detention for the second time that day and the fifth time that week.

It was *Tuesday*.

She'd begun the day like any other. Lisa picked her up for school, and they got into an argument over which candy bar was better, Almond Joy or Mounds.

"Almond Joy, hands down," Lisa insisted. "You need the salt from the nut to balance out the coconut's sweetness."

"You just like nuts because you're a slut," Ann teased.

Lisa pinched the fat on the underside of Ann's arm, and Ann punched Lisa in the boob. After that they called a truce, and then Ann chucked both bars at a cheerleader in the parking lot, who happened to be Maggie Shirvey.

Did I love Ann for this? Yes. Is that wrong of me? Probably.

When the principal caught them, Lisa batted her beautiful brown eyes and played innocent. So Ann ended up in detention, alone. Lisa promised to take notes in their first-period child development class. So Ann hugged Lisa instead of punching her in the boob again.

Ann's second stint in detention was because she often spoke three decibels louder than most clinically sane people, and her idea of whispering was dropping her tone an octave—this coupled with a cursing problem—you get the idea.

So when she thought she had quietly said, "This B-minus is bullshit" after her sophomore English creative writing essay was returned to her by Mrs. Forchester, it was more like, "THIS B-MINUS IS BULLSHIT!"

It wasn't bullshit, because Ann hadn't written the essay. She'd bought it from the Internet without checking for spelling errors. Ann also made her comment no quieter than a jackhammer at a construction site, and school-mandated penance followed. Ann did detention like Whitney Houston did cocaine—frequently and without consideration of the consequences. The school's "no tolerance" policy regarding vulgarity used in the classroom didn't help either.

As Ann sat in detention for her umpteenth time, she thought, *I am a good girl. I've never been past second base with a boy even though in eighth grade Johnny Templeton really wanted to. I've never drunk or even looked at drugs. And I've never shoplifted with Lisa. And I refrained from vandalizing Mr. Sedgwick's apartment even though he's a prick for failing me in gym and he totally deserves it.*

Well, most of this was true.

Ann forgot about the time she and Lisa drank half a bottle of wine in the eighth grade. Ann was too tipsy to ride her bike home, so Lisa called Ann's mom for a ride. This was before the accident, when Ann trusted her mom to drive.

Ann reeked of alcohol and knew she would vomit at the slightest onset of movement. To remedy this, Lisa shoved an open jar of peanut butter under Ann's nose. "Smell it!" Lisa demanded.

"No!" Ann knocked the jar to the ground. "You know I hate that stuff! Are you trying to make it worse?"

Lisa picked up the jar and stomped her foot. "Do you want to vomit in your mom's car?"

"No." Ann held her stomach.

"Then smell it, you crazy bitch!" Lisa shoved the jar under Ann's nose again.

Ann took a quick whiff. "Oh god, it's so bad," she moaned.

After a few sniffs of the hideous, vile, putrid paste, Ann hurled red on a swath of lawn, just before her mom arrived. Then Lisa doused her in perfume. Ann's mom knew Ann had been drinking, but the natural consequences were enough so her mom didn't punish her further.

Despite Ann's insistent thoughts regarding her virtue, she still shared detention with her fellow outcasts while the Grey family social standing vanished.

The usual slackers joined Ann in detention. Stacey what's-her-face always insisted on wearing a tankini belly shirt with a push-up bra, and liked to obnoxiously bat her eyelids and flirt with teachers. If she'd had the decency to throw on a cardigan, then Ann wouldn't have to spend countless hours of unlawful imprisonment watching Stacey flip her hair and hoist her boobs repeatedly.

Then there was Mike. He was quiet and had an affinity for fire and things that exploded. Ann overheard two of her classmates say that Mike was in detention that day for wadding up newspapers and sticking them in the tailpipes of teachers' cars. Ann slumped in her chair as Mike discreetly etched a bomb into his desk with a razor blade.

Rumor had it he'd once told the high school guidance counselor he wanted to grow up to be the next Unabomber. Ann was certain if there were ever going to be a Glenwood High School shooting, it would be Mike who did it.

That never happened, I might add. In fact, Mike eventually attended Harvard Business School (his dad, a financial bigwig in New York, pulled a few strings—I'd say a whole orchestra's worth), and Mike became next in line to be vice president of a chain of grocery stores before his twenty-second birthday.

Ann absentmindedly drummed her fingers loudly on the desk. It was that or bang her head against it. Ms. Steinberg shot her a glance from over her gossip magazine, and Ann slumped back with a sigh.

"Don't you have homework to do?" Steinberg asked.

Don't you have lice to clean out of your curly rat's nest? Ann thought, before grabbing her notebook.

The odor-heavy Ms. Steinberg was the school's detainment officer. She sat behind an ancient, wobbly desk, manufactured sometime in the seventies, and read gossip magazines. Occasionally she stood in front of her desk and ominously slapped a ruler into the palm of her left hand. She waited, as if any minute a special messenger might burst through the door perspiring with excitement, to deliver the news that corporal punishment was lawful and say "By all means Ms. Steinberg, swing away. These infidels had it coming."

I've often wondered how people like Ms. Steinberg end up in school education. Did she used to like kids? Or has she always hated them and felt like high school would be the best place to nurture that hatred? Either way, Ms. Steinberg was a joke, and Ann liked to fantasize about tying Steinberg to a chair and escaping from detention. Ann closed her eyes and was entertaining the daydream when the door abruptly opened and the school's leading outcast (kind of like head mascot, but less reputable) sauntered in.

Now, I am of the firm belief that until you're eighteen it is your God-given right as a teenager to break rules, trespass on private property, and streak naked in public without subjugation to severe punishment.

This brings me to Danny Feller. You might say he was beautiful, hot, gorgeous, magnificent, sexy—pick which adjective you like, they all fit—and he was walking into Ann's detention. Now Danny didn't consider himself a bad-looking guy. He just wasn't into flaunting his awesomeness, but sometimes a person's awesomeness simply flaunts itself, even when you politely ask it not to. And I don't say all this to toot Danny's horn. I'm not really into tooting horns, anyhow, but here's the thing: At this particular moment, Ann Julia Grey was in denial about Danny Feller's obvious magnificence. (Tragic sigh.)

She looked up, locking eyes with Danny. She looked at him as if she were trying to produce a paralyzing lightning bolt from her eye sockets. Really, she was just grumpy. Danny sensed as much and tried smiling at her. Ann immediately grew flushed and glanced away.

Danny brushed his dark brown hair from his eyes as he looked for the misplaced detention slip. He rummaged through pockets, pulling out candy wrappers, random homework assignments, loose change, until finally he found the slip and handed it over to the model of patience, Ms. Steinberg, who was making loud, disapproving sighs. She snatched the slip with a tight frown as sweat formed at her hairline.

Ann watched Danny take his usual spot in the back left corner. He plugged his headphones into his iPod and began drumming his fingers on the desk. Ann noticed his solid hands: not too meaty, but not skinny either, and tanned from the summer. She noticed a slight tingling sensation in her knees as her stomach did back flips. She wrote it off as indigestion and turned back to her notebook. She grabbed a pen and started mapping out her detention escape plan.

Danny shared fourth period math with Ann. The last time he was sent to detention by Mr. Dutton was because he had picked up a pigeon from the open window.

I know, random.

Ann remembered the sudden look of alarm on Mr. Dutton's face when he spotted Danny holding a bird during lecture. "Feller, what are you doing with that pigeon?"

The class turned. Danny shrugged. "Holding it."

The class laughed. Mr. Dutton waved his arms in disbelief. "Where did you even get a pigeon?"

"The windowsill." Danny pointed with the bird. "I think Joey's wing is broken. We should call the vet." (Yes, he'd already named the bird.)

"We're not calling the vet! Put that thing outside before you get a disease!" Mr. Dutton insisted.

Danny refused and what followed was detention for Danny and no medical care for poor Joey.

Ann took a break from her drawing and reached into her backpack for Thoreau. She had started reading *Walden* upon her brother William's recommendation. She had only recently gotten around to borrowing the book from the shelf in his now-vacant room.

So far Ann liked the book. Even though she didn't always understand it. She definitely liked the part where Henry David Thoreau escaped to Walden Pond in Massachusetts. Ann desperately wished she could do the same. Except Ann wanted to get out of Glenwood. But she didn't exactly want to build her own wooden house and have nature as her latrine. Ann hated squatting to pee.

It wasn't the kind of book she normally read. She didn't understand many of the words and reading it often bored her to sleep. Still she read almost incessantly, searching for William in every passage she read, in hopes of discovering why he never came home after that day in December.

With Ann's nose in her reading she barely heard the sound of her name being called somewhere from the back left corner of the room.

Back. Left. Corner.

Her body stiffened. She glanced back to see Danny's toothy grin and crinkled eyes smiling at her. Ann shivered as she saw that he was holding up his copy of Thoreau's *Walden* to show her they were reading the same book.

Ann didn't blink. She wanted to blink. She wanted to smile, speak, nod her head, give him something other than a blank, idiotic stare, but that's all she mustered before she turned around and shoved the book down into her backpack, annoyed.

Despite Ann's loneliness, she had had a hard time letting people in ever since the accident, and if she was going to let anyone in, it sure as hell wasn't going to be Danny Feller. She'd be labeled an outcast for the rest of her life, and she had a little more ambition than that, or at least the old Ann did. Her life used to be apple pie perfect before it shattered into a million jagged pieces. Ann still held onto a morsel of hope that maybe someday things could be different.

Luckily she still had Lisa, even though Lisa had grown distant in the past few months. Not that Ann could blame Lisa for that, but she just thought Lisa would be more understanding since she knew what it was like to be different. Lisa's mom had committed suicide when Lisa was a baby. Lisa's mom had long suffered from depression, and when postpartum depression hit, it knocked her last bearing loose. Ann's mom wasn't dead or suicidal, but she was, as Lisa liked to put it, "A Woman Gone Mad." But Ann didn't want to think about that right now.

FOR THE REST OF DETENTION, Ann finished drawing her escape plan. She did not look back at Danny. Eventually the bell rang, signaling the beginning of fourth period. The class she and Danny shared.

She threw her notebook in her backpack and slung the straps over her shoulders. She had paused to pull her hair out from underneath her bag when pencils and loose papers fell from an unzipped pocket. She squatted to grab them and felt a warm sensation on her shoulder. It was a hand. A not-too-meaty, but not-too-skinny tanned hand that radiated the warmth of the sun.

Ann looked into Danny's eyes. With a slight smirk, he reached out his hand, which held a folded piece of paper. Ann stared, unsure of what it was, or what she was supposed to do with it. Then it registered that whatever it was, she should take it. She did, and Danny walked away, glancing back from the doorway with the same smirk.

Ann stared at the paper, realizing it was a note with her name scribbled on it. She tucked it into her bra and left for her next class. Ann had to remind herself how to make her legs move so she wouldn't be late for math.

The pain of Glenwood High and how it devours souls.

Ann dragged herself down junior hallway, running late for her next class. If she took a shortcut through senior hallway, it would save her some time and she might even make it to her locker to get her math book.

Ann stopped at the intersection between the long route down junior hallway and the shortcut through senior hallway and debated.

The problem with walking down senior hallway was that you weren't allowed to unless a) you were a senior, or b) you were dating a senior. All others were either suicidal, in which case the stroll was a blatant attempt to end his or her life, or they were clinically insane. Those who attempted walking the short stretch usually got publicly embarrassed whether it was being tripped, ridiculed, or kidnapped and taken elsewhere and having who-knows-what done to them. Even Stacey what's-her-face had got an elbow to the clavicle the week prior and ended up in a pile on the floor.

Danny was grabbing his math book from his locker in junior hallway when he caught a glimpse of Ann gazing down senior hallway with a pained expression on her face. He watched as she bit her lip. He recognized the sadness in her eyes that most people ignored.

Did I mention Danny was in love with her? Well, I'm getting to that.

"Annie Grey, hoping for an escort?" Ann turned her head to see her freshman English teacher and neighbor, Mr. Gibbs, smiling at her.

"Are you volunteering? You know those seniors have no mercy on teachers. They will probably eat you alive," Ann retorted.

"Annie you'll do fine," he said with a smile before smacking her shoulder with a stack of red-inked papers and walking off.

"It's Ann! Not Annie," she called after him.

Mr. Gibbs turned his head and smiled. "That's not what your mother calls you!"

Ann rolled her eyes. *Well my mom isn't exactly in her right mind.* She turned her attention back to Krissy Stevenson (A.K.A. String Bean on account of her waif-like figure) and watched her pluck her fake fingernails through Greg Arbertson's hair, as they stood lip-locked at his open green locker. The scene made Ann sick, but not for the reasons you might think. Ann wouldn't admit it, but she was jealous.

All Ann wanted was a normal high school experience. She wasn't sure what that meant, but she had a pretty good idea that it didn't involve detention or having to buy school reports instead of just writing them. Ann blamed the accident for her lack of normalcy and made her way down junior hallway.

Luckily Ann made it to Mr. Dutton's math class without getting a tardy slip. Just before the tardy bell rang, she spotted Mr. Jackson, hall monitor, bee-lining it to the boy's bathroom with a worried look on his face.

Ann reached the closed door and her heart skipped as she remembered Danny and the note. She wondered where he'd be sitting in class today, since they didn't have assigned seating. Ann didn't want to prolong her anxiety, so she dramatically swung the door open and marched in.

Mr. Dutton turned from the whiteboard to Ann.

"Ah, Annie Grey, nice of you to join us."

"It's Ann."

"Right. Ann, why don't you take a seat. Do you have a tardy slip?"

Ann shook her head, and glanced at the full classroom and the twenty-two pairs of eyes staring at her. Well, twenty-one and a half, if you don't count Stephanie Thompson's glass eye.

Once Ann saw that the only available desk was behind Grease-ball Bryce Singleton, she let out a deep sigh and trudged to the empty seat. Bryce smiled menacingly at Ann as he hung his letterman jacket on the back of her chair. Ann gritted her teeth and plopped into the seat.

There was a rumor that Bryce's parents forced him to do his own homework every night and then handed in his assignments for him, which is why he frequently failed math and was now the only senior in Advanced Algebra.

(It was also rumored that Bryce wore women's underwear and knew all the songs in *Phantom of the Opera* by heart. Most people found this hard to believe until Bryce became Brandy, after having a heart-to-heart with his overbearing father.)

Ann did her best to keep her thoughts to herself rather than blurting, lest she have another go in detention, which, by the way, she didn't think she deserved, but she swore Mr. Dutton had it in for her. This was because last week when Bryce Singleton yelled out that Ann was a lesbian, Ann was the one who was sent to detention for forcefully twisting Bryce's ear until he squealed in pain.

She did, however, forcefully twist his ear until he *squealed* in *pain.*

Ann pulled out her notebook and remembered the note in her bra, or what she liked to call "nature's pocket," and was waiting for the right moment to extract it. Ann developed breasts at an early age. She didn't flaunt her assets like some other girls. Mostly because she thought she was fat. I believe her exact words were "tubby." She didn't see that having a nice rack and curvy hips didn't make her "tubby," it made her a woman.

In retrospect, I suppose it might be difficult to develop early as a girl. Guys talking to your chest rather than your face is one thing. Then you're also surrounded by a bunch of girls with pre-adolescent bodies who wrongly think that no breasts and no ass are a good thing. Plus, if you own your sexuality at all as a teen girl you're a slut with a capital S. God, I'm glad those days are over. Not like adulthood is void of sexist platitudes, it's just easier to talk about. In high school, though, if you call someone out on their shit you get bullied. It's really a horrible time in life. Honestly, I don't even know why there is an entire genre of books dedicated to it. Completely overrated. Anyway, what was I saying? Oh yes, the note.

Ann's heart beat rapidly as she considered the folded piece of paper tucked in her bra. She turned her head to the back left corner of the room and was confused by what she saw: an empty desk. Ann glanced around the room and saw Danny wasn't there. Ann sighed with disappointment and reached for the note. She hadn't noticed Bryce had his head turned towards her and was staring at her as she did this. Ann was too mesmerized by her name on the note, scrawled in Danny Feller's handwriting.

Before Ann could open the first fold in the paper she heard Bryce whisper "lesbian" under his breath. Ann glanced up to see him rubbing his nipples over his shirt.

"Ann! Detention!"

"Mr. Dutton, I'm not doing anything!" she exclaimed.

"Yes, but the look on your face told me you were about to."

"Are you serious?" Ann said, aghast.

"I'm afraid so." Mr. Dutton hung his head between his shoulders, his hands rested on his hips.

Ann was fuming. She stuffed her notebook into her bag and stomped towards the door. Then she figured if she was going to get detention, she might as well deserve it. She spun on her heel, marched toward Bryce, and planted a hand across his cheek. Bryce shrieked and the class burst into laughter. Ann thought she heard Mr. Dutton mutter, "Nicely done" under his breath.

Ann walked out the door ready for another spell in detention with Ms. Steinberg when she heard Mr. Dutton order Bryce to detention as well.

"What? You're sending me to detention? Why?" Bryce protested.

"Because I'm starting to think you deserve whatever Miss Firecracker is dishing out."

The class erupted in laughter, and Bryce packed up his things. Mr. Dutton quieted the class and returned to droning on about logarithms.

Ann set off, ready for detention, while Bryce sulked behind her. Neither said a word. Bryce's footsteps landed with heavy thuds as they turned the corner toward junior hallway. Coach Watson emerged from senior hallway wearing his track pants and t-shirt, a whistle hanging from his neck.

"Coach," Bryce called.

Coach Watson turned to Bryce and asked him why he was out of class. Bryce told him he'd been unfairly sent to detention, and Coach reassured Bryce not to worry about it, but to follow him to the locker room and he would take care of it.

Ann shook her head. *Stupid jocks get out of everything.*

Ann opened the door to Ms. Steinberg's personal hell and tried not to dry heave when the putrid smell of rotten eggs hit her nostrils. Ms. Steinberg folded her arms in obvious disappointment when she saw Ann's face.

"So you made it a whole fifteen minutes before getting sent back here, huh?" Ms. Steinberg's voice sounded like a kindergartner's, which made Ann's hair stand on end. "Do you have a detention slip?"

"Mr. Dutton forgot to write one."

"He always forgets," she said shaking her head in disappointment. Ann was the only student there. She took her usual seat closest to the door.

"You're not staying here."

Ann looked at Ms. Steinberg, confused.

"I'm getting tired of seeing you, so I'm having you meet with the school counselor from now on."

Great, Ann thought as she stood without protest and slung her backpack over her shoulder. She didn't know which was worse. Ms. Steinberg or *Bob.*

School counselors (sigh), oh how they try.

Ann's shoulders sank as she moped toward the counselors' offices accompanied by Ms. Steinberg. She felt detention was better than seeing *Bob*, because he always tried to get her to open up to him about her "problems." Ann couldn't conceive how talking to a complete stranger about how much her life sucked would make her feel any better.

Ms. Steinberg escorted Ann to the offices and requested to the secretary that Mr. Mayfield come speak with Ann. The secretary called back to his office and then told Ann to have a seat while *Bob* finished with his other student. Ms. Steinberg smiled at Ann before walking away. She clearly gained pleasure by seeing another's suffering.

Ann anxiously tapped her fingers on her knees when she remembered Danny's note. She couldn't remember where she'd put it after she was sent to detention. She rummaged through her backpack in hopes it was there.

She found the note jammed in her notebook and pulled it out. She looked at what had caught her attention in class before. He had scribbled "Ann" on the outside of the note, not "Annie." She wondered how he knew to call her Ann when everyone else called her Annie.

She hated that name. Annie.

She remembered that Danny had whispered "Ann" in detention too. Ann's stomach began to get that familiar feeling of butterflies when *Bob* called her back.

"Annie, come on back." She looked up to see School-Shooting Mike exit his office. *Big surprise,* she thought, before realizing she was now in Mike's league when it came to being a troubled outcast, which made her want to cry.

Ann put the note into her backpack and dragged her bag into *Bob's* office. She preferred to call him Mr. Mayfield, but he insisted that all the students call him by his first name, which Ann hated.

Ann plopped in the chair opposite the desk, where she knew *Bob* would sit. Ann said nothing, but stared.

"Annie..." he said as he sat.

"It's Ann."

"Hmmm. Okay. Ann." He sighed and leaned forward, resting his forearms on the desk. "Ms. Steinberg and I are worried about you. It seems you've been spending a fair amount of time in detention."

Ann shrugged.

"I'm hoping that we aren't going to get a repeat of what

happened last year..."

Ann fixed her stare on the brown and green speckled tile floor.

"What's interesting about you, Ann, is that your grades seem to be holding up, you're very bright, it's just your behavior that's a problem." He sighed again and sat back in his chair. "And... I've noticed that things started declining since..." This was followed by an obnoxiously long pause.

Really, if he couldn't even talk about it, how was she supposed to?

"But it's been almost a year; I think it's time we make some changes."

We? Ann thought. *So nice of him to include himself when what he really means is,* YOU *need to change.*

"Mr. Gibbs vouches for you, thinks you're a great kid and so do I. Look, I'd rather have you in here if something's going on, than acting out in class and being sent to detention." Another deep sigh as he rocked forward again. "You know your brother came to see me after he graduated."

Ann glanced at him, confused. *My perfect brother William, who wants nothing to do with my family, came to* Bob, *the school counselor to talk about his feelings? Doubt it.*

"Look Ann, the offer's on the table. You can decide which you would prefer, repeated detentions for the rest of the school year, or hanging out in my office."

"So I have a choice?"

He hesitated considering. "Well, no, your detentions after today will be spent here." His head shook as if rejecting his own idea. "In my office."

Ann nodded with a mournful understanding.

"So, is there anything you'd like to talk about?"

Ann shook her head.

"Like why you got sent to detention today?"

Ann's head lolled back, she heaved a sigh, and launched into her version of the events (which didn't mention the note). By the end of her story, Bob's great advice was for her to ignore Bryce from now on and not let him get to her. Gee, thanks, *Bob.*

Bob released her with a pamphlet outlining the stages of grief. After she was excused, she paused outside his office and took a deep breath, hoping she could survive the day, let alone the school year. The clock above the school entrance said there were ten minutes of class left. Ann stopped by her locker and grabbed her notebook and a couple of books, then walked toward the north parking lot and Lisa's car.

Lisa's fourth period class was just south of the parking lot, so when the final bell rang, Ann knew Lisa would be at her on-the-verge-of-breaking-down Ford in seconds. Then she and Ann could cash in their get-out-of-jail-free card and leave school. Of course, if high school was the worst of Ann's problems, that might sound like a relief. But nothing felt simple in Ann's life, and Ann almost preferred an elbow to the clavicle in senior hallway to being home.

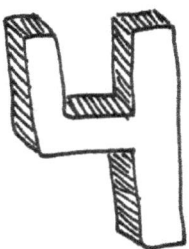

Being hip is overrated.

Ann kept her head down as she walked toward the double swinging doors that opened to the north-end student parking lot. She pushed past the first then second set of doors and ran smack into a pair of broad shoulders.

"Shit," Ann said, stooping to pick up the loose papers that had fluttered to the ground.

"You should really watch where you're going," a male voice answered from above.

"I could say the same. And don't bother helping me pick up my stuff." Ann slapped the papers together angrily. She immediately regretted the suggestion when the boy stooped and picked up the stages of grief pamphlet. Thanks, *Bob*. Ann hid her humiliation behind her hair while the boy she didn't have the courage to look at yet picked up her notebook that had flipped open to her detention escape plan. Ann, thoroughly embarrassed now, went to snatch the two items from his hand. She grabbed hold of the notebook and gave it a solid tug, but the boy didn't release his grasp. Ann finally looked up to see Jacob Waters smirking at her.

Ann's breath caught. Jacob Waters was the hottest senior in school. She had only talked to him one time before, when he came to pick up William for a party, but that was a year ago and she wasn't even sure if he remembered her.

"You're welcome," he said, releasing the papers.

"Thanks," Ann managed to say. Jacob smirked. Ann wanted to say something, drop Will's name or smile back, but it had been awhile since she'd smiled and it was as if her mouth forgot how. "So, uh, you know my—" Ann started to say when she was interrupted by a squeaky female voice calling Jacob's name from down the hall. Ann hated that she knew exactly whose voice that was from having to bear its obnoxious tone in Chemistry.

"Scavorski." Jacob stood. "Still need a ride?"

Her first name was Pam. As in "no-stick cooking spray." As in the stuff Ann was sure Singleton was inhaling on a daily basis.

Jacob slung his arm around Pam's shoulders and led her to his ostentatious red convertible. (I wasn't there, but I'm going to assume he probably had his shirt collar popped—yeah, he's *that* guy.)

"Guys! Wait up!" Krissy Stevenson called, walking past Ann. Her high heels punctured holes in Ann's loose papers. Ann grunted her annoyance. String Bean was dragging her boyfriend, Greg Arbertson along with her, fingers intertwined. Greg made an inaudible snide remark and Krissy started laughing. Ann figured it was at her expense.

"Ha. Ha," Ann muttered, knowing that anything Greg said

couldn't be that funny. Greg made Grease-ball look like a child prodigy on acid. Still she sighed, knowing that if there was ever going to be a chance to get in with Jacob Waters, she had just blown it.

The problem with Glenwood High was that most students believed that the school didn't have social cliques. Of course only those who belonged to *said* cliques believed this because they weren't aware of other breathing human beings that were in existence and taking up space and *did not* have *said* clique to belong to. Greg Arbertson, Krissy Stevenson, and Jacob Waters belonged to the "Totally Fabulous and Popular" clique that sat at the HEAD table during lunch. It was also known as the T.F.P. clique (always spoken with a high pitched sweet valley accent by Lisa and Ann, who had made up the nickname). Jacob was the unspoken leader of this group once William graduated. Most other cliques revolved around people's interest. Art, drama, sports, cars, band, skating, rodeos, dubstep (kidding, sort of). People were also connected within their religion, which Ann didn't have either. She did, however, learn to put lipstick on with her bosoms like Molly Ringwald in *The Breakfast Club*. She thought that would qualify her for something…But, no. She remained a clique-less, godless, outcast.

Ann finished gathering her things and walked towards Lisa's car, her eyes trained on Jacob. She wondered what it would be like to be in Pam's position, just once. To have the hottest guy in school lead you to his car with his hand placed on the small of your back as he opened the car door for you.

Jacob looked back in Ann's direction, smiled, and gave a head nod. Ann tried to smile, but it felt more like a scowl, so instead she gave a little wave. Suddenly she saw Bryce Singleton out of the corner of her eye. Jacob wasn't nodding to her after all. Ann's wave quickly turned into a wrist/arm stretch. She even yawned with disinterest for good measure.

"Lesbian," Bryce leaned and whispered in her ear as he passed.

"Shut up, Bryce!" Ann said punching him in the arm.

"Ow!" Bryce laughed and grabbed his arm. "Watch it, Miss Firecracker." He turned and sauntered off.

Ann sighed. "Shit." She stomped over to Lisa's car and climbed on the hood feeling skittish. The thing is, Ann had a thing for Jacob. I mean, every girl had a thing for Jacob, but for Ann it was different. She thought about him often. It was her secret shame, but she let it live because it was the only thing that connected her to the life she had before the accident, when she actually believed in the impossible. Her fantasies made her life bearable no matter how bizarre, embarrassing, or dark (in this case I'd say disturbing) they were.

Ann shamefully admitted to me one day that she did have a sort of boy fantasy involving the lead singer and occasionally the drummer of a rock band. I'm going to relay it to you here and add in a few of my own facetious details.

Scene: The lights dim, the steady thud of a drumbeat falls over the crowd, silencing them as searchlights fall upon a metallic drum set. Jacob Waters plays, the crowd screams (it's her fantasy, not mine), he's shirtless and wearing…spandex tights? (Maybe it's a Bowie thing.) His fists grip the drumsticks as he pounds on the drumhead; his heart pounds with every beat; his body pours with sweat; his hair becomes wild as he bangs his head with the music. The set ends and Jacob jumps onto his chair, leaps over his drum set and launches into the crowd.

If you're anything like me, at this point you might be wondering what this fantasy has to do with Ann. Well, you see, Ann is in the crowd. She's screaming and singing and dancing as the drummer plays, and when he jumps into the crowd, he finds her. He chooses her. Every girl in that room wants the rock star, and the only person the rock star wants is Ann.

Yes, she's embarrassed by this fantasy. Yes, she's going to kill me when she reads this. Yes, she finds the fantasy shameful and has already undergone extensive psychoanalytical analysis over why she has it (although the analysis was done by Lisa, who eventually summed up her analysis by saying, "Yeah, that's hot").

Personally, I've always been a bit wary of Jacob Waters. (The guy wears visors on purpose.) But to everyone else Jacob was charming, and I suppose he could easily make a pair of eighties rocker tights look sexy. And as Ann once put it, he had sex appeal, which was his main draw. The rip-off-my-shirt-and-pour-water-on-my-chest kind of sex appeal. (I stress, *her* words not mine!) But no matter how much Ann yearned for that life, she was certain she'd end up being labeled the disturbed outcast loser for the rest of high school.

"Shit, shit, shit," Ann muttered again, sinking her head into her hands. She was really starting to hate life, but at least she still had Lisa.

"Hey, bitch, get off my car, you're scratching the paint." Lisa was the only other girl in the universe who understood Ann.

Best friends.

Lisa pursed her lips as Ann remained sitting cross-legged on the hood of Lisa's retro Ford.

"Lisa, scratched paint on this hideous boat-car is the least of its problems."

"Hey, don't dis the Thunderbird," Lisa said, unlocking the driver's-side door with the key.

"Just drive with me on the hood, and if I happen to accidentally roll under one of the tires and die, you can tell everyone I jumped in front of the car."

"Ooo. You're in a darker-than-usual mood today. Although hearing my friend's bones crush under the tires of my car sounds super-perfect right now, I'd rather not. So would you stop moping and get in the car?"

Ann slid off the hood and waited for Lisa to climb into the car and unlock the passenger door by hand. Ann wrenched open the rusty door, climbed in, and slammed it shut with a loud clank.

"Buckle up." Lisa turned the key. The engine turned over several times before it finally started.

Being reminded to wear a seatbelt was one problem Ann didn't have. Ann pulled the seat belt across her lap and snapped the buckle. Lisa cranked Led Zeppelin from the CD player Lisa's father had installed in the car last year.

"Can we not listen to this?" Ann asked, agitated. "I don't think I can handle it today."

Lisa ejected the CD from the player and turned on the radio. She pulled out of the parking stall and into the line of cars waiting to exit the lot. Ann had about ten minutes before Lisa dropped her off, and Ann wanted to savor every minute of it.

"So, how was school?" Ann asked.

Lisa shrugged. "Good. How's Smelly Steinberg?"

"Odorrific."

"I couldn't stop staring at Mrs. Tingy's hump today in class," Lisa added.

"Of course you couldn't, that thing is an eye magnet." Ann laughed.

"It never gets old," Lisa agreed. "I keep wanting to tell her to stand up straight, but I think it's a disease."

"Ya think?" Ann joked.

"No," Lisa started, "I think she's a freaking alien. That's what I think."

Ann laughed. Lisa had a thing about aliens. Most of the time she just blamed stuff on them. Her first failing grade, mysterious bruises, the fact that Mrs. Tingy suffered from Kyphosis.

"So who gave you detention today?" Lisa asked.

"Mrs. Forchester, for swearing, and Mr. Dutton because of—"

"Grease-ball?" Lisa guessed. Bryce used *way* too much hair gel. He used so much one day that a blob of it dripped off his spiky tip and onto the desk. (At least we hope it was hair gel.)

"Bryce is such a dick," Ann said.

"Total douche," Lisa agreed. "Why does the radio suck?" The stereo was losing reception so Lisa resorted to banging on her dashboard with her free hand. "Damn aliens," she muttered.

Even though Lisa's dad could afford something better than the rusty tetanus trap Lisa was rolling in, he felt it was best to start one's driving career with a hunk of metal near death. The decision may have been swayed by the fact that the car could no longer make it over 60 mph. Lisa rattled the vintage radio knobs until the radio's static noise declined. Once she started singing to the next song, Ann stared out the window with mounting anxiety.

When Lisa pulled off Main Street and onto Ivy Lane, Ann's stomach churned. There were a few reasons why Ann didn't want to be home on this particular day.

1. Her room was messy and she thought she saw a big, black, furry, and possibly poisonous spider in a pile of clothes before she left for school.

2. Tommy, Ann's younger brother, made it his mission to annoy Ann, and

3. Meredith, whom Ann sometimes referred to as Mom, was as present as a Jew at a Nazi convention.

Lisa's clunker sputtered into Ann's driveway. Ann gave Lisa a hug before fighting with the door handle. With a forceful yank the door sprung open and Ann willed herself out of the car. Lisa backed out of the driveway and honked in the street before speeding away. Ann turned to wave and then sulked to her house.

Ann walked past the hungry red flowers cast into the shade by the red brick house looming before her. She rested her hand on the handle of the large oak door, and hesitated, nervous to enter whatever disaster lay behind it.

Home suck home.

Ann pushed the front door open with the weight of her right shoulder. The entryway had marble flooring, and a spiral staircase shot up to the right. To the left was the office that nobody went into since the accident. Turn right and you were in the living/family room. Ann crept into the room; her shoes left dirt on the white carpet. She peered over the couch. Empty. *Where is she?* Ann thought, trying not to panic.

She went to the kitchen. No one in sight. Not even Tommy. Her heart started to race. *Not again!*

Ann raced up the stairs, taking the steps two at a time. She followed the long hallway down to the master bedroom. She burst through the door and saw her mother lying on the floor, unconscious. Ann ran to her side and rolled her on her back. There was no vomit nearby, which Ann thought might be a good sign, but wasn't sure.

Ann shook her mother. "Meredith! Meredith! Wake up!" Meredith's lids opened as her eyes rolled out from the back of her head. Ann let go and gazed at the empty rum bottle on the dresser. Ann couldn't remember if that had been full this morning.

"Annie? What?"

Ann stood and muttered, "You're pathetic."

"Annie, what is it?"

"Nothing, Meredith, just wanted to make sure that I didn't have to pick you up at the bar before I started my homework." Ann stomped from the room and slammed the door shut.

Ann was never sure what she'd deal with when she came home from school. Meredith was most often in bed nursing a hangover or starting on the next one. Occasionally, she had a good day, which meant she had something she needed to do: lunch with friends (to keep up appearances), doctor's visit (anti-anxiety, anti-depressants, and sleeping pills), or buy groceries (putting random shit in the cart so it didn't seem like she was only buying alcohol). On those days, when she was slightly more sober (but mostly hung over), Ann came home to a person almost resembling the mother she once had —a mother who offered Ann a warm smile when she returned home. Those days were becoming fewer and fewer as the alcohol consumption increased.

When the accident happened, Meredith's drinking was heavy. She'd spend a few days really drunk and then manage her hangover by drinking more. Then she pulled herself together (sort of) and drank mostly at night when she thought no one would notice. It worked. For a while Ann thought she had stopped altogether, but then Ann found secret stashes around the house and realized Meredith was just hiding it better.

Ann stomped to her room across the hallway. It wasn't your typical run-of-the-mill teenage bedroom. No band posters, no magazine cut-outs, no pictures of friends. All Ann had was a plant that was trying not to die on her windowsill and tiny holes in the blue walls where posters used to hang. She tore them down after the accident. She couldn't bear to look at people who seemed so happy and fulfilled.

Ann plopped on her bed and pulled out her homework. She checked her syllabus and saw she had an assignment for child development, an essay regarding the stages of pregnancy. Ann pulled her textbook from the desk drawer and sprawled it open on her bed, flipped to the right page.

Ann was strangely grateful to have homework to do. It was a normal activity that distracted her from the anxious tension crawling up her spine and settling in her shoulders.

Later, she'd likely watch TV, even though she didn't have the attention span for it. She was easily distracted these days, as she replayed her past, present, and predictable dreary future. It was a montage of hopeless fury set to an indie-slit-your-wrists ballad.

There was a soft knock on the door. Ann yelled for Tommy to enter.

"Where's Mom?" Tommy asked.

"Where do you think?"

Tommy straddled the desk chair. "Did you see the gift I left for you this morning?"

"If you're talking about a large furry creature, I'm going to kill you."

"I couldn't resist."

"You suck."

At thirteen, Tommy still found fake insects to be funny. Ann rolled her eyes and focused on the essay, hoping Tommy would take the hint and leave.

"Well, I'm going skateboarding."

"Tommy, don't you have homework?"

"No."

"Liar."

"You're not my mom."

"Well someone has to be," Ann muttered. Tommy's grades had been suffering. She knew she couldn't convince him to do his homework right then, but thought maybe she could convince him to stay and eat dinner before coaxing him into doing homework. "Are you hungry? What if I cook spaghetti tonight? Maybe Mom will even feel up to eating with us."

"I think I'll pass. Besides I already had a bowl of cereal."

"Lame," Ann said, turning away.

"What?"

"Oh nothing, just leave me here with Mom." Ann knew if she couldn't entice Tommy to stay with food, she could always employ guilt.

Tommy wasn't fooled. "You've reached a new low, Ann."

"Psht." Ann denied. "You can go skate," she said, waving him off.

"Wasn't asking for your permission, Big A." An unfortunate nickname that Ann ignored.

"At least eat dinner with me. I don't feel like making a meal for one."

"I thought you said Mom would feel up to eating."

Tommy was catching Ann in her tangled web of manipulation. The truth was she didn't want to be alone or sit back and watch her family fall apart.

Ann sighed. "I was feeling hopeful," Ann lied. "But obviously that's not likely to happen, so how about humoring me a little?"

"Fine." Tommy relented.

One thing about Ann is that even on a good day she has a fiery wit to her personality that often turns sour when she hasn't eaten. You can imagine how fun that was for Tommy who, as a brother, was forced to live with her. He agreed to stay for dinner, because he knew if he didn't, Ann would forget to eat and become surly.

Since Tommy agreed to stay, Ann used the excuse to ditch her homework and prepare dinner (just as Tommy hoped). No jelly sandwiches or cold cereal for the Grey family tonight. Or at least what was left of the Greys. She fixed spaghetti with a meaty marinara sauce.

Tommy and Ann ate in silence. Neither of them saw Meredith, but at one point Ann thought she heard her crying upstairs. She eventually bribed Tommy into doing homework by promising him a trip to the skate park on the weekend. Ann didn't have a driver's license yet, or even a permit. The whirlwind of the past year kind of took precedence over every thing else. But she already knew how to drive and figured if she obeyed all the traffic laws she would never get caught.

Ann went to her room after dinner and finished her essay. She was already feeling exhausted and glanced at the clock. Eight p.m. She felt like collapsing into a coma and never waking up.

As Ann slid the essay into her backpack, she saw Danny's note. She didn't care anymore what it said. It couldn't change the fact that Ann felt completely alone.

She reached for the note. Unfolding it she saw a few lines written at the top: "*Walden* pg.7 lines 3 and 17." Ann rolled her eyes again, which she liked to do. A lot. She grabbed her copy of *Walden* and flipped it open to page seven and found the note's first line.

The mass of men lead lives of quiet desperation.

Ann counted down 15 more lines and read:

It is never too late to give up your prejudices…

Ann chucked her copy of *Walden* in the garbage and pounded her fist on the wall.

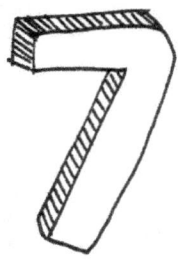

Girls that suck.

Danny Feller was missing from school the next couple of weeks. To make matters worse, he kept showing up in Ann's dreams. No, not like that (she wished). This wasn't a magic pony ride dream where Ann is cruising on a rainbow bridge mounted on a unicorn with Danny seated behind her sporting a very dapper knight's outfit. In the dream, she's trapped in detention with him while the room grows smaller and Ann's teeth fall out. She had the dream three nights in a row. The other nights she dreamed of drinking alcohol and riding rides at an amusement park, and then a few nights later she dreamed about the end of the world. (You can see why she doesn't sleep well.)

Danny's absence from school made Ann livid. She hadn't gotten over the note he gave her. And now she was missing out on opportunities to tell him off while the offense was still pertinent and fresh.

The lecture she was mentally rehearsing went something like this: *I know you think you're above high school and everything, so in keeping with your too-cool-for-school attitude, don't ever write me a note again!* Or, *I'm not prejudiced and don't talk to me about my stupid desperation, jerk-off.*

Some versions of the tell-Danny-off fantasy regrettably included Jacob Waters, wearing a knight outfit while watching Ann give Danny a severe tongue-lashing. Then, after Danny got thoroughly lambasted, he sulked away, while Jacob, entranced by Ann's verbal flogging skills, rushed to her side, scooped her into his arms, and kissed her passionately.

Ann mulled this over while she sat in chemistry class staring at the back of Pam Scavorski's blonde mop of hair, waiting for class to begin. Ann felt a stab of jealously as she thought how Pam was with Jacob Waters in the parking lot two weeks ago. Pam leaned over to whisper something in Krissy's ear. String Bean laughed, a little too loud, and relayed the joke to Maggie, who managed a smile. Ann was sure the school would come to a rumbling collapse of rubble if the cheerleading sub-clique didn't have *every* class together.

With all the possibilities of having chemistry class at a different time, why did Ann have to have it at the same time as these three girls? Flaunting their excitement as they flipped their hair, and smiling with their *perfect* white shimmering teeth as they talked about their *perfect* boyfriends and trips they took last summer with their *perfect* families.

I hate you, Ann thought. What could she do when someone was living the life she *should* have been living? Plus, Krissy's bird refuge of ratted hair made her three inches taller, and Pam's eyelashes were so fake and thick they looked like a black moth wing when she blinked. Those two facts alone offered Ann enough justification to dislike them.

Once the lecture started, Ann began sketching String Bean tied to a railroad track with an oncoming train speeding straight toward her. Ann was putting the finishing touches on her sketch when the teacher announced they were doing a lab. He then broke the class into groups of four, and Ann was assigned to work with the cheerleading trio. The sub-clique all looked at each other smiling, satisfied, forgetting that a fourth person was being forced to enter their sacred circle.

The teacher assigned the group to burner eight and the girls grabbed their notes and skipped over, so bubbly and alive in their cheer skirts. Ann ambled over in a slumped position in her flannel button-up and jeans; she was beginning to feel like a man. They slipped on their goggles, and Krissy exclaimed that hers smelled funny. She laughed obnoxiously loud at her own observation. *Kill me now*, Ann thought as she slipped into the over-sized goggles that made her feel like a fish stuck in a fishbowl. She did find comfort in the fact that the cheer group looked equally ridiculous in their goggles. They all resembled comic book villains.

"So you know how to do this, right?" Pam asked Ann.

Ann didn't know how to answer the question because Pam was literally holding the written-out five-step easy process in her hand. "Um, yeah," Ann answered.

"Perf," Pam said before turning back to Krissy. "So, as I was saying, I was like *seriously* surprised when he first asked me out. I mean *ohmigod*! Jacob Waters!"

Ann rolled her eyes; the only reason why Jacob would possibly be interested in her was because Pam was still considered "fresh dough" at Glenwood High, as in "easy to work."

"Jacob is the hottest guy in school now that William Grey's left." Ann flinched at hearing her brother's name. She glanced at Pam, who was grinning. Ann swears her teeth sparkled. Krissy nodded while Maggie faked a smile and shifted uncomfortably.

Gag me. Ann thought detention would be better than this, but she knew that meant she would have to talk to *Bob* again, so she was mindful to keep her tongue in check. Just because Ann hadn't been in detention since her visit with *Bob* two weeks ago didn't mean she could keep that kind of self-control going, especially as it was only first period and she had four more classes to survive that day.

"I think you're supposed to add the first solution to the second solution. That's step one," Maggie said, grabbing the vial to help Ann.

Great. Head cheerleader thinks she's helpful. Ann muttered a surly thanks and grabbed the chemical and handed it to Maggie, who poured it into the first vial.

The rest of the experiment went the same, with Krissy and Pam blabbering on about Jacob, over-analyzing every single one of his mindless words or actions to gauge how interested he was in Pam.

"Well, yesterday in the hall, he looked like he was in a really bad mood and then when he saw me his whole face, like, broke out into this huge grin." Pam was beaming.

"Ohmigod," Krissy said as if she had just spotted the most adorable puppy. "He's totally into you."

Maggie said nothing but focused on finishing the lab while Ann half-heartedly helped. Once the solutions were properly mixed in the beaker, Ann watched the solution's color turn from clear, to amber, to blue and back to clear again. "That was awesome," Ann muttered. "Yeah," Maggie agreed. The momentary camaraderie was strange, but nice. Ann gave Maggie an unsure smile. She tried to think of something to say to Maggie, but all she could think was, "So you're a cheerleader, huh?" She then considered making a clever observation on the Krissy Stevenson level about how bug-eyed she felt in her goggles, but decided that was too lame. *She used to know William, maybe I can ask her about him. Maybe they still talk,* she thought. "So," she began to say, but not being able to find the words she started flailing her hands and accidentally knocked one of the beakers filled with hydrogen peroxide onto the floor. It landed with a shattering explosion at Pam's feet. She scrambled back with a shriek.

"What the hell?" Pam spat.

The whole class turned to watch the scene unfold as Pam tore off her shoes and rushed to the emergency wash station and began rinsing. "What's wrong with you?" Pam exclaimed.

"Are you okay? What happened?" The teacher rushed to Pam's side and helped her rinse.

"She knocked a chemical on me!" Pam pointed to Ann.

"Omigod are you okay?" Krissy stroked Pam's arm, as if having disinfectant touch your cheer shoes was the worst thing that could ever happen.

"It was an accident, right, Annie?" The teacher asked.

Ann considered saying no. One, because Pam was annoying, and two, detention would be better than having thirty-two people watch her humiliation, and three because he called her Annie.

"It was an accident," Maggie assured the teacher before Ann could speak.

"You should be fine," the teacher said. "Everybody finish cleaning up and take your seats and write up a summary of what you learned." Krissy and Pam sat down while Ann and Maggie finished cleaning.

"Maggie," Pam whined, "I need you." Maggie stopped helping

Ann and went to Pam. "She's such a freak," Ann heard Pam say. "Why are you helping her?"

"I'm not," Maggie defended. "I'm just cleaning up."

Ann rolled her eyes and finished cleaning. She plopped down in her seat and instead of doing the assignment she started scribbling in her notebook while making a mental list of why she hated these girls so much. Before she knew it, she was writing the list.

Dear stupid cheer girls, this is why you make my chemistry class a living hell:

1. Because you're extremely annoying.

2. Your hair looks stupid.

3. You're self-absorbed.

4. You won't give another living soul the time of day.

5. Did I mention the hair?

6. You yell things like "How funky is your monkey!" in unison.

7. You wear too much make up.

8. You giggle instead of laugh.

9. Your mom's boob job is more real than you.

10. Other than being a vapid fake you're also dreadfully pathetic!

The rest of class was absorbed in chatter as they worked on the written part of the lab assignment. The teacher had his back turned toward the door as he bent over a student's desk explaining the equation. Pam glanced back throwing Ann some classic mean-girl-shade and Ann saw the perfect opportunity and went for it. She grabbed her backpack and discreetly ducked out.

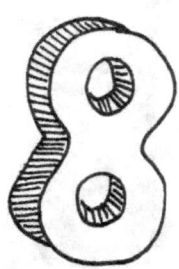

Still hating life and loving it.

Ann made it to fourth period math unscathed. She had been getting to Mr. Dutton's math class as fast as she could without running in the hall, or cutting down senior hallway, also known as the hall of death, so she could pick a seat at least five feet away from Grease-ball Singleton. Ann sat in the back left corner, pulled out her notebook, and worked on the earlier sketch of String Bean while the rest of the class filed in. Ann was so absorbed in her sketching she didn't notice the figure hovering over her until he spoke.

"You're in my seat."

Ann recognized the voice. Her body froze as her heart sped up and her knees weakened. What was the speech she had prepared for this moment? Something about him being a jerk-off? She couldn't remember. Ann could see his hand out of the corner of her eye as it moved towards her desk and rested gently on it. She didn't look at him. She didn't even speak. She wanted to, but even the English language seemed to be foreign to her at this moment.

"Do you mind if I sit next to you?" Danny asked. Ann managed a nod and a quick glance at his handsome face before returning to her drawing. She hoped that would be the end of their one-sided exchange.

"I like your drawing," Danny said. Ann closed her notebook mid-sketch. "Is there something wrong?"

Ann shook her head.

"Can I get more out of you than head movements?"

"You know these seats aren't assigned?" she said. It was something to say.

Danny smiled, "Yeah, I was just kidding. Did you read my note?"

Ann nodded with clenched teeth. If her heart hadn't been racing due to *other things*, it definitely was racing now.

"Well what do you think? Thoreau's great isn't he? I love how he describes things, don't you?"

Ann's resolve to be mad at Danny weakened. Maybe the note hadn't been meant as a message to her. Maybe he just wanted to share his favorite passages or something.

"Nod if you agree," he said.

Ann quickly nodded and let a sigh escape her lips.

Danny took the seat next to her and pulled out a notebook. Ann returned to her sketch. Just before the tardy bell rang, Danny set a folded note on the corner of Ann's desk. She held back a smile and picked it up.

"Ya know," Ann finally found courage to speak, "people don't have to pass notes anymore. Nowadays I think they call it texting," she said, touching her pocket and realizing her phone wasn't there.

"Yeah, I don't have a cell phone," Danny said.

"Serious?" She didn't believe him.

"Yep," he said.

"Did you used to have one?"

Danny shifted uncomfortably. "Yeah, it's just not my thing anymore, I guess." Ann could tell he was holding something back.

"Well, doesn't matter, looks like I left mine at home anyway," Ann said. Mr. Dutton called the class to attention and she unfolded her note from Danny.

You want to hang out sometime?

Ann repressed a smile and bit her cheek as she considered his question. On one hand, she did need a life outside of the ongoing Grey family tragedy. On the other hand it was Danny. Sure he was (extremely) attractive, but he seemed a little intense, which kind of scared Ann. She could tell he was an all-or-nothing kind of guy, and Ann didn't want anyone getting too close.

From the corner of her eye she saw Danny pulling out his math book and splaying it open on his desk. Then she saw him covertly plug in an earphone, tuck the chord behind his ear, roll up the volume on his iPod, and begin softly drumming his fingers on the desk. Instead of answering him, Ann focused her complete attention on her doodles and tried to let the world fall away. This worked for about five seconds.

"Annie Grey you're wanted in the principal's office," the intercom blared. A sudden wave of nausea poured over her as her heart anxiously thudded. She didn't know what this was about, but didn't like the sound of it. Ann gathered her things and made a swift exit. She felt a little more at ease once she entered the empty hallway. She decided to take her time and enjoy the solitude as she trudged down the hall to the principal's office. She hoped this had nothing to do with *Bob;* but then again, there could be worse things.

She walked through the open glass doorway to the main desk and announced herself to the receptionist. "Hi, I'm Ann Grey."

"Oh yes, Miss Grey," the obese lady sitting behind the desk said. "Let me see what we have for you." The lady stood and went to the corner desk and shuffled through some papers. It was hard not to notice how her ass had molded to the shape of the chair's seat. Ann shuddered at the thought of her ass being cube-shaped someday.

"Oh, here it is," the woman said, holding up a pink slip for Ann to see. "It looks like you are to call your mom immediately, some sort of emergency at your house." The woman smiled despite delivering bad news.

Ann's throat closed off as she reached for the school phone and dialed her home number. The phone rang without an answer. *Great.* Ann thought. *She's probably choking on her own vomit and I'm going to have to call an ambulance for her.*

Ann hoped that wasn't the case when finally on the billionth ring, her mom answered.

"Hello, this is Meredith Grey."

Ann could tell her mom was trying hard not to slur her words. "Mom, why did you call me?"

"Oh, yes, hello, Annie dear. I was wondering if you could tell me how to work this damn blender. Every button I push does nothing."

"What are you trying to make?"

"Oh, never you mind dear, just tell me how to get the blender working."

Ann's mom had various stages of drunk. The first, or beginning stage, was always accompanied by a sort of panicked desperation. The second stage, after she had loosened up a bit, was what Ann referred to as the Audrey Hepburn stage where her mother was a classier drunk. The third stage may or may not include uncontrollable laughter before the fourth stage in which she passed out. Then there was Ann's personal favorite: stage five, where she'd wake and start crying and then cycle back to stage one.

Meredith was currently in the second, Audrey Hepburn, stage. When Meredith was in the Hepburn stage, alcohol appeared as a simple prop in her life, instead of the weapon she used to obliterate all feeling. Ann imagined her mom wearing her silky robe over her silk pajamas and smoking a cigarette with her hair slicked into a ponytail. "Well, Mom, did you plug the blender *in* to the outlet?"

The other line was silent for a moment before Ann heard a sharp giggle from her mother. "Oh Annie dear, you are so clever. See you after school, darling."

Click.

Clever? Ann thought. *Who says that?*

She never called her "clever," or "Annie dear," or "darling," in any of her other stages of drunkenness.

Ann scowled, grinding her teeth before slamming the phone on the receiver, making the receptionist jump in her seat.

"Sorry," Ann muttered when the woman stared at her with startled disbelief.

The woman smiled cautiously back. Ann dragged herself from the office.

Now what to do? Ann didn't exactly want to return to class, but she didn't want to have a full hour by herself to dwell on the unholy mess that had become her life. As she debated what to do, her thoughts were interrupted.

"Annie Grey, just the young lady I was looking for. Meet with me in my office?"

It was *Bob*. He smiled at her with worried eyes. It resembled the look a father would give his daughter. Ann shuddered at the thought of another one of *Bob's* office visits, but her choices were limited. Before she entered the doorway, she hesitated for a moment and thought she saw a familiar face out of the corner of her eye staring at her from behind a brick pillar in the commons area. Ann blinked hard and figured she must be going crazy. She entered the office and plopped on the available chair. *Bob* leaned against the desk.

"I will get straight to the point, Annie." Ann cringed at the sound of her name being slaughtered. "We're worried about you."

Here we go.

"Frankly you and I both know that your adjustment to high school hasn't been great." He folded his arms and stared down at her. "And lately, as we've tried to involve your mother, we're getting little response from her."

Ann's throat tightened. She knew she had to think of a lie, a really good one, or her so-called-shitty-life would look like something straight out of *Hellraiser III*. Minus the gateway to another dimension and hell on Earth, and all that, but you get the idea. The last thing Ann needed was to be shipped off to some foster care because of a negligent mother.

"Well my mother is quite busy. She's an avid gardener, you know?" *Or at least she used to be.*

"And she always wants to make sure everything gets done and looks perfect for us kids." *Which also used to be true.*

"And..." Ann sighed. He didn't look convinced. *She's a single mother for hell-sakes Bob, give her a break*, she begged silently.

His eyebrows softened and he nodded his head. "Yes, I'm sure there's quite a bit to do and not a lot of time to do it."

"I can take care of myself."

"That's what I'm afraid you don't understand, Annie. You can't. You can't do this by yourself."

Ann got a lump in her throat the size of a tennis ball. A lump that held a hundred muted sobs and a thousand tears that Ann was sure as hell not going to let out, especially not in front of *Bob*.

"I just want to reiterate that I'm always here for you, Annie, if you ever need to talk."

Ann said nothing but swallowed her tears.

"Think about it, Annie, and keep in touch, okay?" His voice was softer now. Ann swallowed hard against the lump in her throat that felt like sand paper and stood to leave.

"Hey, and you've been doing a lot better not getting detention. I'm proud of ya. Keep it up, okay?"

Ann nodded, and left.

Ann was shaking when she stepped into the commons. She rubbed her hands against her forehead before letting them fall to her sides. She closed her eyes and sighed deeply. She wanted to crumple to the floor and dissolve, but knew she had to stay strong.

She thought about asking Lisa to come over and help her with math; that way she wouldn't have to be alone. Not to mention she was well on her way to failing that class anyway, and could use the help.

Ann opened her eyes and before she could walk to the girl's bathroom, she felt a hand latch onto hers and tug her towards the exit.

Hello beautiful.

Ann followed the tug on her arm. Danny grinned as he pulled her to the exit. Ann heard Ms. Steinberg yell, "Where do you think you're going, Mr. Feller?" just before the front doors slammed shut. *Danny must be escaping from detention,* Ann realized. Ann began running, no longer being pulled behind Danny. She tried to pull her hand from his tight grip but was unsuccessful. Danny's hand wound around hers and she could tell he wasn't letting go.

They ran through the north parking lot, keeping an eye out for Mr. Jackson, who patrolled for kids cutting class. Danny led Ann around the north portable and behind a large tree.

Not until they were safe behind the tree did Danny let go of her hand. She took it back and glanced around haphazardly.

"It's okay. As long as we don't make a lot of noise they won't look for us back here."

"Were you in detention?" she asked loudly.

"Shhh," he said, inching closer to her with a smile. "Don't you know how to whisper?"

Ann rolled her eyes and repeated the question, this time trying to speak softer, but really she just spoke lower.

Danny laughed, "Yeah. You?"

"The counselor's office."

"Hmm," Danny said, unchanged.

"Why were you in detention?"

"I got caught listening to my iPod."

"That's it?"

"And I called Mr. Dutton an animal killer."

"Oh," Ann said, alarmed. Danny didn't seem like the type to be purposefully disrespectful to a teacher. "So why didn't you just stay in detention?"

"I needed some fresh air," Danny casually said as he hung from one of the tree branches.

"So why haven't I seen you in school lately?" Ann blurted. She bit her tongue as soon as she said it, wanting to play this cool.

"You tell me your secrets and I'll tell you mine," Danny goaded.

Ann rolled her eyes and folded her arms tight across her chest.

Danny conceded. "Fine, if you don't want to say, then I'm allowed to have my secrets too."

"Fine, like I care. I was just wondering."

Danny plopped on the ground and pressed his fingertips together as his brow creased. He looked like he was either deep in thought or plotting Earth's destruction.

"Ann? Let me ask you something?" Danny motioned for her to sit.

She sat a few feet away from him.

Danny scooted closer so they were facing each other. Ann could almost taste the mint on Danny's breath. She tried to hold her breath, knowing it probably smelled like the burrito she ate for lunch.

"So do you come here a lot?" She was nervous and didn't know what to say. They both laughed.

"Sometimes." He smiled. "So, I wanted to ask you..." He paused.

"What?"

"Um, I'm not sure how to ask you this." He drummed his fingers on his knees.

Confused, she looked at him and waited.

"How are you?" he finally said.

"That's your question?"

"Mmmm, yeah."

"I'm okay."

"Just okay?" he asked, concerned.

"Geez, you're as bad as *Bob*."

"Who?"

"The school counselor," she explained. "If you must know I'm...kind of shitty," she admitted.

He waited for her to elaborate.

"I mean, how can you not be shitty when you're here." She motioned to the school, trying to brush off her momentary lapse of honesty.

"Why do you hate it here so much?"

"Is that a rhetorical question? I mean, it's high school."

"Yeah, I guess. I actually think I know why you hate it here. I was watching you the other day in the hall staring at Krissy Stevenson and Greg Arbertson. It was like you were...sad, but angry. That's one of the reasons why I wrote you that note."

Ann flushed with embarrassment. "Wow."

"What? I said the wrong thing, didn't I?" Danny blanched.

"You just told me that you wrote me a note in order to inform me that you have been watching me and deduced that I'm desperate," Ann said plaintively.

"Oh my god, I did, didn't I?" Danny covered his face with his hands. "I'm so moronic. I can't believe I just said that."

Ann managed a laugh at seeing Danny's embarrassment.

"You have to understand," he went on to explain, "I can be impulsive sometimes, and I just do and say things without thinking. Can we just start over, pretend that never happened?"

Ann rolled her eyes.

"Please say you forgive me," he said grabbing her hand with both of his and pulling it to his chest.

Ann laughed, "Okay, I forgive you. If you buy me a donut," she added.

"Of course. What kind?"

Ann considered, "Chocolate."

"A girl of my own tastes," Danny said.

"And I want sprinkles on mine."

"Like multi-colored sprinkles, or just one color?"

"Hmm," she considered. "Let's go with any color, to make it easy on you."

"Sounds great, I'll deliver it to your doorstep on a silver platter."

"You will?" Ann smiled. "When?"

Danny considered, then laughed, "Probably when you least expect it." Ann smiled. "Okay, so all is forgiven?" Danny asked, letting go of her hand.

"Forgiven." She couldn't even remember what they had been

talking about before the donut. Oh yeah, her desperation. (Real smooth, Feller.)

"Awesome, okay." Danny scooted closer. "So, how are you?" he said, tapping his fingers on her knee.

Ann smiled, amused. "I'm fine. How are you?"

Danny shrugged, "Good. I'm good."

"Good," she pursed her lips and nodded. Whenever a conversation went dry, Ann seemed to fill up the space with an abundance of facial expressions. As they sat in continued silence, Danny gazed at her with interest, watching her go from shy to bored to uncomfortable all in the matter of a few expressions.

Danny may not have realized he was in love with Ann at this time, but he definitely knew he liked her. The first time Danny had noticed her, *really* noticed her, was after school one day last year. She was cleaning out her locker, stuffing a bunch of disorganized loose papers into her backpack, when one fell to the floor unnoticed. Danny retrieved it once she left and saw it was one of her sketches. He considered giving it back to her when he saw her next, but something made him hold on to it. It was one of her darker drawings. A classified ad of an unidentified suicidal person seeking someone to put them out of their misery, followed by a drawing of Ann presumably answering the ad. It was gruesome, funny, and beautifully ironic. That's when Danny realized she was different, (and possibly emotionally disturbed). He had wanted to say something to her, but—what? Ann wasn't the only one who liked to keep people at bay.

You know how some people develop addictions to manage their overwhelming emotions? Some people become alcoholics, coke fiends, potheads, pill-poppers, over-eaters, sex addicts or meth-heads. Well, Ann seemed to have a similar addiction to anger, he concluded. Feeling angry served the dual purpose of keeping others at a safe distance while drowning out all other competing and overwhelming emotions. Danny recognized this in the horrific, yet wistfully funny and amusing picture Ann had drawn, because he had once been there too.

"Wow, you're really close," Ann said, finally. Danny didn't realize he'd unconsciously been leaning toward her.

"Is that okay?" Danny asked, his heart pounding. He thought about kissing her. He'd never done anything that spontaneous before. (Really, it's true.)

Ann couldn't speak so she nodded. Danny leaned in closer, letting the moment carry him. He reached up and pushed her hair behind her ear. Ann's heart fluttered. She didn't make eye contact with him but could tell he was staring at her with his beautiful brown eyes. Danny's fingers glided down Ann's cheek and it felt like a thousand feathers brushing against her naked skin. He lifted her chin so her eyes met his. Ann looked into Danny's eyes, afraid he might be staring into her soul. Danny smiled at her and leaned in closer. He moved slowly. His lips gently brushed against hers sending chills through her body. Just before Danny's lips could lock with Ann's, an alert went off in Ann's brain.

Danger!

Like a red flashing sign.

Of course there was no danger, except for the danger of Ann letting her guard down and falling in love. But Ann's version included getting hurt and experiencing the most excruciating pain a person could ever feel.

She jumped to her feet like a jolt of electricity had shot through her. "I can't," she blurted, and then ran.

"Ann wait!" Danny called.

She bolted towards the north parking lot. Danny called after her, so she sped up until she could no longer hear him.

She scoped out the cars in the parking lot, looking for Lisa's old clunker. Feeling disoriented from the almost-kiss, Ann couldn't remember where Lisa had parked.

Finally she spotted it on the south end and marched toward it. She noticed her classmates were flooding from the doors. School was out. She sighed in relief as she slowed her walk toward Lisa's car.

Lisa was fiddling with her keys, looking mellow and confident as usual. She began rattling the lock in the driver's side door, and Ann jogged the rest of the way, wanting the refuge the hunk of metal provided.

"Hello, Annie darling, how was your day at school?" Lisa said, smiling.

"Oh don't get me started, Lisa, you'll never believe what my mom did today. She called the school to ask me how to use the blender."

Lisa laughed, then abruptly stopped. Her eyes widened. Ann felt a tap on her shoulder. She swung around and saw Danny.

"Hi," Ann said awkwardly. As if they hadn't almost kissed sixty seconds ago.

"Hey." Danny smiled. "Look, sorry about that." He gestured to the portable. "I know we don't know each other really well, but I was wondering if you'd give me a chance and get to know me," he said with a pleased grin and soft eyes. Not like he was begging, nor was he demanding. It was more like he knew what was best for Ann, and if she wasn't so damned stubborn, Ann might see that Danny Feller could be good for her.

She stared at Danny, bewildered, as he slid a note into her palm, softly touching the back of her hand with his fingers. Ann kept her self-control, even though her body wanted to pounce on him like a cheetah (which is what she should have done, if you ask me). Danny smiled then. And I've been told that Danny had the kind of smile that radiated a light you wanted to bathe in. The kind of smile that breathed oxygen into a room. The kind of smile that reflexively made everyone around him smile. Ann watched him walk away, her lips pressed together in a hard line, refusing to smile.

She turned toward Lisa who glared back at her, astonished. "What the hell was that about?"

Self-control is overrated (but I can respect that).

"Ann, what the hell? Why was Danny Feller talking to you? Begging you for a chance?" Lisa demanded as she cranked the circa 1980's steering wheel that lacked power steering, and turned onto Main Street.

"I don't know. The psycho's stalking me," Ann said. She wished she had remembered the "don't write me notes" lecture she'd been reciting in chemistry.

Lisa darted around the next turn, not bothering to slow down. Ann tensed and clung to the dashboard. She remembered the note in her hand and slid it into her pocket, hoping Lisa hadn't seen the exchange so she could read it later in private.

"Seriously, slut, what are you keeping from me?"

"Lisa, I'm not in the mood. Can we just drop it?"

Lisa stayed quiet the rest of the drive home. Ann was glad when Lisa stopped pressing the subject of Danny Feller, which lasted about, oh, five minutes, until they were sitting at Ann's kitchen counter drinking iced tea and snacking.

"Ann, you have to tell me, when did this thing with Danny start?"

"Lisa!" She bit into a piece of red licorice. "Nothing's going on! I barely know him."

"Ann, stop acting like you're not interested in him. I've never seen your face look so flushed before. It was almost embarrassing for me to watch you two be so...so..."

"What?"

"Intimate." Lisa popped a grape into her mouth. "That exchange was kind of steamy. But I guess everything would be with Danny Feller."

Ann looked down. She could feel her cheeks turning red again.

"Ann, it wouldn't kill you to have a little fun, or at least get a little action."

"You really are a whore, aren't you?" Ann laughed.

"Whatever, I saw you blush. Just because you haven't done anything doesn't mean you're not a slut on the inside."

Ann rolled her eyes. "Please. I couldn't be a slut even if I wanted to."

"You could," Lisa insisted. "Remember Horse Face?"

Ann laughed. "I've tried to forget."

"You're like ten times hotter than her, and sluttier."

"Thanks?" Ann said quizzically.

Tommy slumped into the kitchen and grabbed a glass from the cupboard. "Will you stop calling each other sluts and whores?"

"Why?" Lisa asked, amused.

"Because..." Tommy replied with a shrug, "It's... degrading."

"I can't figure out if your brother is really smart or really weird," Lisa said.

Tommy rolled his eyes. It was probably a Grey thing. Lisa and Ann watched Tommy grab the carton of orange juice from the fridge.

"How old are you these days, Tommy?" Lisa asked, patting the stool next to her inviting him to sit. He didn't.

"I'm thirteen," he deadpanned.

"You got a girlfriend?" Lisa's eyes widened with intrigue.

"No," Tommy said, taking a swig from the carton.

"No!" Lisa said faking shock. "Why not? Aren't you interested in girls?"

"Yeah," Tommy said, "I just don't see the point in dating until I'm, like, nineteen."

Lisa burst into laughter and Ann smiled. That was Tommy. The only thing that could make the scene better was if Tommy was wearing glasses and had a comb-over instead of a faux-hawk and a band t-shirt.

"Is it true, Big A?" Tommy asked, interrupting Lisa's laughter.

"Is what true?" Ann asked.

"That there's someone interested in you at school?" Tommy said. "I overheard your gal-pal here mention it," he said, pointing to Lisa. "Ya know, just before she called my only sister a slut."

Ann shook her head and glared at Lisa. "No Tommy, it's not true, Lisa was just exaggerating."

Tommy slumped into his shoulders. "Well, maybe you should give it a chance, go out on a date or something."

Bewildered, Ann turned to look at Tommy. He just shrugged, "Except minus the slut part, so not cool," he added before he gulped down the rest of his juice and set the empty carton on the counter.

"You know who's not watching enough TV?" Lisa joked to Ann.

"Tell me about it," Ann said. "He's either on his skateboard or playing video games."

"I do other things," Tommy said defensively.

"Like what?" Ann asked.

"Wouldn't you like to know!"

"Eww!" Ann shrieked. "I'm not talking about that, you perv!"

"That's not what I was talking about, Ann!"

"Simmer down!" Lisa said, flapping her hands in the air like she was ready to take flight.

Ann and Tommy stopped and looked at Lisa, who turned to Tommy. "We all have needs."

"Gross!" Tommy yelled.

"Lisa!" Ann threw a licorice at her head.

"I'm going skating." He grabbed his skateboard and slithered through the sliding door.

"Stay close," Ann called after him.

"Your brother is sweet, Ann. Sweet, but weird."

Ann agreed. Since when did Tommy take an interest in her social life?

"He's definitely acting strange," Ann said.

"It's the alien implants," Lisa said matter-of-factly.

"I wish those implants helped him with his homework. I can't get him to do it."

Lisa cleared her throat. "I didn't know that was your job."

Ann bit the inside of her cheek and thought, *It is now.*

"So where's your mom?" Lisa asked.

Ann cringed. "She probably knows you're here and is trying to sober up so she can come down and act like a normal human being.

We may even get dinner out of it."

"Oh really, home cooked?"

"Please. Take-out," she said, annoyed by Lisa's ignorance.

"That's too bad because your mother is quite the chef."

"Used to be."

WITHIN TWENTY MINUTES Meredith was downstairs acting pleasant. She almost seemed sober, but Ann knew she was probably cycling back to stage one. Or perhaps she was building a tolerance to alcohol. Her mom was definitely trying too hard to actually be a mom.

"Lisa, so good to see you," Meredith said, smiling, before rotating her stiff body towards Ann. "So how was your day?"

"Good," Ann muttered, not making eye contact.

"How was school?"

"Fine."

Meredith smiled. The grin looked plastered on her face and seemed to be wavering.

"Well, I'm pretty tired, I think I might be getting sick. I don't feel like cooking dinner. Should we do take-out?"

Lisa snorted and Ann hid a smile. Meredith picked up the phone and tried to remember the number to the local Chinese restaurant. "I'll just get the usual then," she said after she had finished dialing.

Ann kept her gaze downward as she picked at a speck of unidentified food that was stuck to the countertop. She remembered when she used to come home from school and her mom would be out in the garden, tending to the tomato and zucchini plants. Her mom had always worn a beautiful smile so large that her eyes disappeared into thin slits. She used to hug Ann and tell her she loved her, before asking how her day was. At the time it didn't seem special, it just seemed normal. That was life. Ann had never thought it would change.

Ann and Lisa helped Meredith set the dining room table. The silence was uncomfortable between Ann and her mother, but Ann figured anything she had to say to her mom was worse than the silence. So she let Lisa do the talking.

"Mrs. M, I love what you've done with your flower bed out front, it looks really good."

"Oh, I actually hired a company to take care of my yard for me."

"Really?" Lisa feigned surprised. Lisa knew Ann's mother hadn't touched the flowers in over a year.

"I bet you miss being out there in your garden, with your plants and your flowers," Lisa said casually.

Meredith forced a smile and Ann glared at Lisa, who innocently smiled back. The doorbell ringing interrupted the awkward exchange. Meredith excused herself to answer it, and Ann left Lisa to finish setting the table while she went to retrieve Tommy. He was behind the garage practicing tricks on his skateboard where the grass met the cement.

"Tommy, come in and eat. Mom ordered take-out." Tommy's eyes lit up. Ann knew what he was feeling: excited. This was always quickly followed by disappointment. It wasn't often Ann and Tommy felt that they had a mom again. But occasionally, in moments like these, it felt like the possibility was there, and it was hard not to hope. But it never worked. The excitement came, almost like a gut reaction and then made Ann angry because she knew it never changed anything. Her mom was different. And nothing was going to change that.

Love & suffering.

Lisa and Meredith were organizing the food on the table when Ann and Tommy came back inside. Ann took the chair closest to Tommy and Lisa sat next to Meredith. The Greys weren't much for religion, so they skipped saying Grace and began piling food on their plates. Lisa wasn't much for religion either, but she was spiritual. If you call having séances to conjure spirits a spiritual practice. Lisa closed her eyes, steepled her fingers, and blessed her meal before eating.

Ann noticed her mom didn't seem to have an appetite. She poked at her orange chicken with a fork but only took a few bites. Tommy shoveled his food into his mouth like any growing boy before excusing himself from the table.

"Did you even taste your food?" Ann asked.

Tommy just rolled his eyes. It was definitely a Grey thing.

Ann decided to attempt a conversation with Meredith. "So, uh, Mom, have you heard from William lately?"

Meredith looked up from her uneaten meal. "Not lately, no."

"Well, do you know if he's coming home for Thanksgiving?"

"Oh, well, that's a ways off. We don't have to worry about that right now."

"I just was wondering if I get to see my brother," Ann sulked.

"Well, he might have other plans. He is young, and out having fun. We can't expect him to come home."

Ann gritted her teeth while her eyes, threatening to roll, mentally screamed, *Hold me back! Hold me back!*

"You used to say family was most important," Ann said tersely.

Meredith shifted in her seat and ignored the comment.

Ann looked away and gave in to the eye roll. She hadn't seen her brother since last Christmas. At that time Meredith had attempted to skate the fine line between functionally drunk and plastered. She occasionally slipped up and went too far. Ann knew when her mom was really drunk because her eyelids drooped, her speech slurred, and her head seemed too heavy to hold up. It was one of these drunker nights when William and Meredith got into a fight. Ann came home after shopping with Lisa to catch the tail end of the argument. William stormed out and Meredith locked herself in the bedroom.

That night Ann dumped all the liquor down the drain only to discover that Meredith had some in hiding. A bottle of gin in her underwear drawer, malt-scotch in a shoebox under the bed, whiskey shoved behind the garbage can in the bathroom. Ann emptied those bottles too, and placed them back into hiding; she couldn't wait until her mom discovered them empty. Ann was hoping for a confrontation. She wanted her mom to feel ashamed, or at least angry that her stash was gone. Ann waited for contemptible fireworks to explode between them, for hurtful bombs to be thrown, and words of blazing arrows to be exchanged.

Meredith said nothing. She pretended she needed to run some errands and instead went to a bar. She was going to drink one way or the other, and there was nothing Ann could do about it. The message was received loud and clear. Her mother did not care what her daughter thought about her, or what she was doing to her family. All she cared about was getting drunk, and no one could stop her.

"Well, I'm pretty tired, I think I'm going to go to bed early," Meredith said before making her exit. She didn't even bother to help with the dirty dishes. So Lisa and Ann cleaned up by chucking the dishes into the dishwasher before retreating upstairs to Ann's bedroom, where Lisa sprawled on the bed like a cat.

Ann thought about Danny's note in her pocket. It felt like it was burning a hole in her jeans. She considered sneaking away to the bathroom to read it. She wasn't sure why she didn't want to tell Lisa about it and briefly wondered if her secrecy was reaching a new level of mental.

"Ann, your room is depressing, the walls are so bare."

"Yeah, so what's your point?"

"My point is, no wonder you're so depressed," Lisa said.

"Have you ever thought that my walls are bare because I'm depressed not that I'm depressed because my walls are bare."

"Well, *duh,* Ann. I figured that much out, but maybe if you livened up your room a little, it would help."

Ann shrugged and thought, *Or maybe if my dad wasn't gone and my mom wasn't drunk.* She would never say that to Lisa, though. She knew Lisa was just trying to help.

"I have an idea," Lisa said, springing from the bed and out the door.

"Don't leave me," Ann said, sounding more desperate than she wanted to.

"I'm not leaving you, I'll be right back. Just wait here. I've got a surprise," Lisa said with big eyes.

She shut the bedroom door behind her, and Ann heard her go out to her car. Ann sat at her computer and logged on to her e-mail. No messages. Ann wrote a quick e-mail to her brother.

To: brother_who_abandoned_his_family@collegerules.com
From: desperate_sister@lifesucks.com
Subject: walden

i started reading *walden*. thanks for letting me borrow it. it's been really good so far. i was wondering if you were planning on coming home for thanksgiving? i know tommy misses you. maybe we'll see you then?

-ann

Lisa returned just as Ann clicked send. Lisa held up a can of red spray paint, a black marker, and a picture of her and Ann at the beach. "So what exactly is your plan?"

"We're going to decorate." Lisa said.

"Spray paint is for vandalizing, not decorating."

"Psht. That's what you think," Lisa said, shaking the bottle.

"Where did you get the spray paint anyway?"

"You know my wood dresser?" Lisa said. "It's red now."

Ann nodded. If she hadn't been feeling so apathetic, she might have protested. Lisa finished shaking the bottle and stood on Ann's bed, spray-painting the word "LOVE" on the wall above where Ann slept. Ann rolled her eyes and grabbed a black marker adding an equals sign at the end of "LOVE" and writing "suffering," so the message read "LOVE = suffering."

"Well, that's not exactly what I had in mind, but it could be therapeutic." Lisa shrugged.

"Since when do you use words like *therapeutic*?" Ann asked.

"Since five seconds ago when I decided I'm going to be a psychologist."

Ann snorted.

"Hey, don't knock a sista's dreams," Lisa replied.

Ann flopped on her bed and watched Lisa make a polka-dotted pattern on the wall adjacent to the bed. The red paint dripped from the polka dots.

"My wall looks like it's bleeding now," Ann said.

"Well, if that's how you see it, psycho."

"Would you stop with the psychologist bit? It's not how I see it! The wall looks like it stabbed itself and is now bleeding to death," Ann said, annoyed.

"Well that's an interesting glimpse into your psyche," Lisa said. "And speaking as your personal therapist, I think it would be best if, when you're having suicidal thoughts of stabbing yourself, that you try to think of rainbows instead."

"Rainbows?" Ann said hugging a pillow.

"Yeah," Lisa said, standing back to look at her wall art. "Ya know—happy, bright, refreshing, the calm after the storm, God's gift to the earth."

"Or the aliens' gift," Ann added.

"Course," Lisa agreed. "Can't rule that out."

"So your advice to a suicidal person is to think of rainbows?" Ann chucked the pillow at Lisa's head.

"Hey." Lisa ducked. "This shit don't come cheap. Besides it worked for the gays."

Ann laughed. "Glad I'm not suicidal, because that is the *worst* advice ever."

"Speaking of rainbows," Lisa said lying next to Ann, "I've been thinking about you and this thing with Danny Feller."

Apparently rainbows and Danny are one and the same. "Oh yeah? Enlighten me," Ann said, sarcasm dripping from every word.

"Well, just because your mom is an alcoholic doesn't mean you can't have a life. I mean this is Glenwood. Most mom's here are in-the-closet pill poppers."

Ann managed a smile.

"I need a thumb tack," Lisa said, jumping up from the bed.

"Why?" Ann asked.

Lisa pulled the photo from her back pocket and waved it for Ann to see. "I'm going to put this picture of you and me up. It's not a very flattering photo of you, but I look hot," she teased, "and I thought it would be good, since the picture was taken before...well, when you were happy."

"Whatever," Ann said, grabbing a thumbtack from her desk drawer and handing it to Lisa.

Lisa hung the photo of them next to the word *LOVE* that she had spray-painted.

"Hey speaking of aliens I dreamed about them last night," Ann mentioned.

"Really?"

"Yeah, it was disturbing," Ann added.

"What do you think that means?

"That we talk about aliens too much."

"I was going to say that aliens were probing your brain, but..."

Ann snorted.

"You should look that up," Lisa added, "like in a dream dictionary. Here," she said tossing the spray can to Ann, "I'll do it. You decorate." Lisa sat at the computer and pulled up a web browser and did a search.

Ann glanced from the spray can to the wall several times before tossing the paint can in the garbage. "What does it say?"

"Um," Lisa hesitated.

Ann stood behind her and read it.

Aliens: Fear of losing family. See also: Neglect, feeling disconnected.

Lisa cleared her throat, "Well, my dear, speaking of aliens, I think it's time for me to go home." She stood up and grabbed her backpack. "I DVR'd a UFO documentary I want to watch tonight."

"What about math?"

"Do you really want to study right now?"

"No," Ann said. She wasn't ready for Lisa to leave.

Lisa grabbed Ann for a hug. "I'll pick you up in the morning for school and then we'll hang out this weekend, okay?"

"I thought you were going out of town with your father on business."

"Oh shit! That's right. Sorry, Ann, I'll make it up to you." Lisa pulled away and kissed Ann on the lips. "Hey by the way, your wall looks like it's bleeding," she added.

"I know!" Ann said throwing her arms up in the air.

"It really does," Lisa said through a mouthful of laughter.

"Bye," Ann said, shutting the door on Lisa.

"Love you," Lisa called through the door.

"Love you back," Ann yelled.

She stood in her room like a statue and listened as Lisa climbed the stairs, yelled goodbye to Tommy, and shut the front door behind her with a clunk.

Ann sighed and turned toward the mirror and paused, examining her features. She never liked the way she looked. She never disliked it either. It was just, sometimes, when she looked in the mirror she'd think, "Is that really me? Is that what I look like? Is this how other people see me?"

She looked at her nose and concluded it was definitely too wide and needed to be smaller, pointier, elegant. She wondered if it would be totally lame to get a nose job. She thought her lips were thin when they should be full. Her eyebrows were supposed to rise in a sexy arch and instead were flat and linear. And her hair was drab brown when it should be—I don't know—lustrous?

She sunk into her chair and checked her e-mail. No messages. Ann wrote another e-mail to her brother.

To: brother_who_abandoned_his_family@collegerules.com
From: desperate_sister@lifesucks.com
Subject: help

will,

mom hasn't gotten any better. i'm starting to lose my mind, and i hate this. i wasn't expecting high school to suck. i was expecting to have fun. to not have to worry about anything. instead i feel like i'm babysitting mom and tommy. i need you. i can't do this on my own. please. at least come see us on the weekends. you're not that far. it might even help mom to see you. maybe you can talk some sense into her. think about it. no, don't think about it. just do it!

-ann

Ann didn't click send this time. She saved the draft to send it in case things got worse. Ann thought about flopping onto her bed and passing out, but wasn't sure if she could sleep. She started stripping down anyway, hoping she could shut her racing thoughts off tonight.

As Ann slid off her jeans, the note from Danny fell out of the pocket. Ann grabbed it and sighed. She was so stressed she hadn't even remembered to read his note.

If things were the way Ann felt they *should* be, she would have read the note as soon as she got in the car with Lisa. And that's all they would have talked about for the rest of the evening. Then Ann would have taken Tommy's advice and gone out with him. Then, when Ann fell asleep at night, she would fantasize about kissing Danny Feller while he wore a knight's outfit and she wore a corset that flattered her figure. And she would have trouble sleeping due to butterflies, instead of bad dreams.

Ann unfolded the note, and read the first line.

You are beautiful Ann. But it's not just your beauty that interests me. Read Walden pg. 167 the last paragraph. It reminds me of you.

Yours,

Danny

Instead of feeling butterflies, Ann felt sick. She didn't know Danny and what she did know wasn't reputable. He was an outcast, a troubled, angst-ridden nobody. Could she trust him? Never mind that Ann was also an outcast and a nobody. All Ann focused on was her concept of normalcy. If things were just normal, she would be happy. And Danny Feller, although sexy and mysterious, was anything but normal.

Ann pulled her copy of *Walden* from the garbage and turned to the designated page and began reading.

I went to the woods because I wished to live deliberately, to front only the essential facts of life, and see if I could not learn what it had to teach, and not, when I came to die, discover that I had not lived.

Ann cringed, thinking this had better not be another coded message reminding her of how much she sucked. She continued reading despite herself. She skipped down a couple of lines to a sentence her brother had underlined.

I wanted to live deep and suck out all the marrow of life.

Ann thought she definitely wasn't sucking the marrow out of life. No, she was simply sucking. She skipped a few lines and read further.

...to drive life into a corner and reduce it to its lowest terms, and, if it proved to be mean, why then get the whole and genuine meanness of it...

Ann read the sentence several times, not understanding it. If life proved to be mean, why would you want to get the whole genuine meanness of it? After all wasn't that what anti-depressants were for?

She slammed the book shut but didn't throw it away this time. Instead, she tucked it away in her backpack and finished undressing. Not caring to brush her teeth, she climbed in her bed. She had reached for the light switch on her lamp when she heard a knock at the bedroom door. Startled, she pulled the covers tight around her body and yelled for the knocker to enter.

"Hey, I just wanted to say goodnight," Tommy said.

"Did you have fun skateboarding?"

"Yeah."

Ann didn't know what to say. It was rare for Tommy to bother Ann after 9 p.m. He stared at her for a minute, then said goodnight and left. Ann sat for a minute, worried about Tommy and wondering if she should go talk to him. She chose to ask him later if he needed to talk about anything. Then she turned off the light switch, pulled the covers over her head, and breathed.

What the hell is Thoreau talking about?

When Ann woke the next morning she looked up the meaning of her dream online.

Tornado: Living with someone with mood swings.

"Tell me something I don't know," she grumbled. She hoped her mother wouldn't be awake. Her day always seemed to start off on the wrong foot when she had to be in close proximity to her mother in the mornings. Luckily her mom was still asleep when she left for school.

She walked into Mr. Gibbs' classroom feeling low. She didn't know how long Lisa was going to put up with her depression. Even though Lisa had always been a supportive friend, Ann could tell her patience was fading.

Fact: Lisa rarely went on business trips with her father. Fact: Lisa stated that she—and I quote—"hates going on his boring business trips." And now? She went every chance she had. Ann figured Lisa was starting to hate her and she couldn't blame her. She kind of hated herself too.

But Danny's note had sparked something in her. Made her think. She figured Mr. Gibbs was the only adult she could talk to without wanting to strangle.

The classroom was empty. Ann sat cross-legged on Mr. Gibbs' desk and told herself not to snoop through his desk drawers. Before the temptation could become a reality, Mr. Gibbs walked through the door carrying a stack of papers.

"Annie." Mr. Gibbs greeted her as if he was expecting to see her there.

"Hey," she said, trying on a smile, before sliding off his desk.

"What's up?" he asked.

"Well..." Ann hesitated. "I had a question for you. Do you have a minute?"

He glanced at his watch. "Looks like we have a few minutes before the first bell rings. What's on your mind?"

"Well, I've been reading *Walden* and I read this part in it that I don't really understand. I thought maybe you could explain it to me?"

"Sure. Which part?"

Ann slung her backpack off her right shoulder and began shuffling through loose papers to find the book. She grabbed it and flipped it to the exact page number.

"There," she said stabbing her finger at the sentence.

I wanted to live deep and suck out all the marrow of life.

"Annie—"

"Ann," she corrected.

"Right. Ann," he said, and Ann thought she almost saw Mr. Gibbs hold back an eye roll.

"This is about living life to the fullest. Taking risks, having no regrets."

"But what about this?" she said, moving her finger to the following sentence.

...to drive life into a corner and reduce it to its lowest terms, and, if it proved to be mean, why then get the whole and genuine meanness of it...

"Thoreau was all about living in reality, even if reality were mean, he wanted to embrace it."

"But why?"

"Because reality is all we've got. It's life itself. It's not that Thoreau wanted things to be bad, it's just that he believed in embracing life and in embracing life you have to embrace the bad with the good."

"That," she shook her head, "doesn't sound very fun."

"Ann," he said more softly. "What else do we have?"

Ann shrugged.

"What else can we do? Deny it? Ignore it? Run away from it? It doesn't make it any better. Sometimes we have to accept that life is the way it is and try to embrace the things about it that make it good. The good comes with the bad. If you can't embrace the bad you can't embrace the good either, so you find yourself pushing it away."

"No I don't," Ann retorted.

"I didn't mean *you* Ann. I mean people… in general."

"Oh," she felt stupid.

"Done with the lecture?"

"You were just answering my question."

"I know. But...I worry...about you."

Ann wanted to run. But her feet wouldn't move.

"If you ever need anything, I'm just around the corner, so let me know."

Hmm. Do I need anything? She wondered. Besides the fact that she needed a mom, a dad, and an older brother, she was doing just fine. Oh, but she did need a ride home from school; she refused to take the bus. Every time she was forced to, she swore the smell of feces and body odor clung to her for days.

"You think I can hitch a ride home?"

"Yes," he said, "but only because we've been neighbors longer than you've been my student. But next time you'll probably need to take the bus. School policy."

She nodded. "Thanks." The first bell rang and students began filing into the classroom. Ann took that as her cue to jet.

"Oh, Ann?" Mr. Gibbs said, stopping her. "I just remembered I'm leaving after third period."

"I have a work-study fourth period so it's no problem," she lied.

Mr. Gibbs nodded, satisfied, not knowing Ann would really be ditching gym class. Worst. Class. Ever.

Panic attack? Nice.

In Ann's words, life had become "a pile of rotting garbage." The final insult was when Lisa ditched Ann for a business trip with her Dad. Ann didn't have a dad. She couldn't remember the last time she let those three letters strung together slip from her lips: Dad. She thought about this as she rode silently in the car with Mr. Gibbs. That Mr. Gibbs was a dad. Something she wanted and didn't have.

They reached a familiar intersection. Ann's heart began to pound. The light turned from yellow to red and Mr. Gibbs punched the brakes. Ann's breath quickened. She turned to see a sign outside a vintage home-turned-business that sold antiques and other pawned goods. "Check Out Our SALE Items and Halloween Selection Starting October 5."

Her stomach lurched when she read the date. The car rolled forward as the light turned green. She tried to fight the developing sickness that exploded like a parasitic thought. *I don't have a dad.* The words bounced among her racing thoughts as the world closed in on her. All life seemed to drain and swirl away from her as she starved for the suddenly unobtainable feeling of safety. Air stopped entering her lungs, the flowers and butterflies disappeared and all that remained was a feeling of impending doom.

"Annie, you okay?"

Mr. Gibbs' voice sounded like a whisper in the background. Ann reached for the door handle. She had to get out. Now! She felt so hot, so weak, so fragile, so claustrophobic, all at once.

"Annie?"

Her heart slipped into her throat. She couldn't answer him. His worried tone made her sicker, more panicked. He was a father.

The car screeched to a stop. Ann didn't notice it was because she had flung the car door open. She tumbled from the car and onto the side of the road. She choked out her breath and wound her fingers in the tall grass. Her chest hurt. She was going to die. Her whole body shivered. This was the end. No air was entering her lungs. It was over. Ann surrendered to her demise.

After a moment, a warm hand rested on her back. It was a gentle hand, a father's hand. The anxiety was gone. She had not expired.

"Annie, you okay?" Ann rolled on her back. Mr. Gibbs hovered over her looking concerned, just like a dad. Except this time it didn't bother her.

She had known this day was coming. She'd been dreading it for months, and she'd done her best to ignore it. To forget it in hopes she could pass right over it and never have to confront this day or the well of feelings that lurked beneath.

"Annie, what is it?"

"My dad died a year ago today." This was the first time she'd ever said it out loud—that her dad was dead. The relief offered in finally speaking those words was brief and was quickly consumed by a carnivorous pain alighting from her chest. She tried snuffing out the overwhelming sensation of grief by holding her breath.

Mr. Gibbs' face fell. "Annie, I'm so sorry. I forgot."

Dangerous tears burned under her eyelids, but she wasn't going to cry. She couldn't cry. She had to be strong.

"It's funny," Ann said to me once, after all this had happened, "the things I remember about that day." October fifth, the day her father died. Ann was still adjusting to being a freshman. She was getting used to walking down the halls with people looming over her. Not that she's short. Just before, in middle school, most boys hadn't gone through the usual growth spurt, and now that they had, she was getting used to their relative size, their muscles and their facial hair.

She was worried about how her high school experience was going to play out. Who would her friends be? Would she get invited to homecoming? Would she ever have a boyfriend? What activities would she get involved in? These were the thoughts that pressed on her eager mind. Ann knew that what people thought of her in the first few weeks of school was crucial to how she'd survive the next four years.

That was before October fifth.

On October sixth all she could think about was what she could do to remove the hollowness from her mother's once-effervescent eyes. And the ache in her own chest.

"Annie, what can I do for you?" Mr. Gibbs asked.

"Just take me home. I have to get back to my mom."

"I will," he nodded and helped her back into the car.

"Oh, and Mr. Gibbs?"

"Yeah."

"It's not Annie. It's Ann."

Mr. Gibbs shook his head with a smirk and muttered, "Good hell," before driving on.

A very unwelcome visitor.

Mr. Gibbs pulled his Volvo into Ann's driveway. She wanted to give him a hug and pretend he was her father. She glanced at him. He hugged her with his eyes. She pulled herself from his car and went inside.

"Meredith!" she called, once the front door clunked shut.

Silence answered.

Ann checked the garage: her mom's car was gone. Ann stormed into the kitchen, scared and angry but not surprised.

Meredith usually drank at home, but whenever there was a birthday or anniversary, she left. Like if she didn't, her head might explode. Lisa usually drove Ann to the bar, where Ann had to coax her mother out to the car and drive her home in her mother's car.

So really, Ann had known she wouldn't be home. Meredith, Mom—whatever the hell you call a distant alcoholic mother—was gone. Ann paced between the kitchen counter and fridge when she spotted a note dangling from a heart-shaped magnet. It was in Meredith's handwriting. *Went to Cloverdale to run errands, be back soon.*

Ann scoffed. Her mother didn't have the guts to just say she had gone to visit her husband's grave. She instead referred to the town he grew up in outside of Glenwood where they buried him.

Ann stormed to her bedroom wondering why Lisa chose this weekend of all weekends to ditch her?

The first time Meredith sneaked out to the bar was after Ann dumped her liquor supply. Meredith was later picked up by the police for "disorderly conduct" and was escorted home at two in the morning. Luckily, the officer had let her off with a warning.

Ann plopped her things on the desk. She'd wait for Tommy to get home before looking for Meredith. A trip to the gravesite meant Meredith would later stumble into a bar. Ann desperately wanted to call her uncle Joe. He'd been a permanent fixture in the house until the accident. When he was over he'd often spend a considerable amount of time hiding in a closet, bathroom shower or pantry, waiting for the right moment to leap from his hiding place and scare the sack out of whomever came across his path first.

One time she and William plotted revenge. With pots and wooden spoons in hand, they skulked in the shadows behind Uncle Joe's parked car and watched as he said goodbye to her parents from the doorstep. When he came around to the driver's side door, Ann and William sprang from their hiding place clanging their pots and screaming. The look on Uncle Joe's face was absolute terror. Ann loved it. Their dad had a good long laugh. "Looks like you've finally been beaten at your own game," he crowed.

Ann would rather live with her uncle Joe than with her mom, but she knew Meredith would freak if she ever did that. Especially since it was Joe whom Meredith blamed for everything.

Ann logged onto her e-mail, hoping to hear back from William. She had one message. Her heart leaped. She clicked on it to discover a penis enlargement advertisement. False alarm.

Stupid penis freaks, Ann thought.

Stupid William.

Stupid Lisa.

Stupid Mom.

Had it really been a year since her father's death? She remembered the night as if it were yesterday. At the same time, it seemed that it happened a decade ago. So much had changed.

She had been asleep when Meredith came and shook her awake and told her that Dad was in the hospital and that she was going to see him. Ann sat up, confused

"It was a car accident," Meredith explained. "He went out to pick up Uncle Joe. I have to go, William is staying here," she said, then rushed out.

Three hours later she was escorted home by a police officer. Dad was dead. Ann knew it when she saw her mom's sunken shoulders as she drifted toward the front door. Ann couldn't hear her mom say it, that Dad was dead. She locked herself in her bedroom and refused to come out until the next afternoon.

The worst part about her dad's death was that Ann didn't cry. Maybe a few tears, but never gut-wrenching sobs. She never gave in to the sadness or basked in it with abandon. Maybe it was because Meredith seemed to be feeling all the grief, and there wasn't any room left for anyone else's feelings. William had to plan the funeral. Ann never realized before how weak and dependent her mom was. She came to believe that that's what love did to people, made them limp and powerless. Somewhere along the way, Ann made an unconscious decision never to fall in love.

Now, Ann denied the intrusive memory any more of her attention and wondered if Mr. Gibbs took in lost adolescent souls as she rested her head on the pillow, exhausted. Her eyes closed and she dreamed of eating spaghetti. She took a bite and felt something hard in her mouth. She panicked and spit out a tooth. She looked at it in disbelief. She set the tooth down and took another bite of spaghetti. Her teeth continued to crumble with each bite. She wanted to stop eating but had no choice. She kept eating and her teeth split and shattered onto her tongue.

"ANN?"

Her lazy eyes peeled open.

"Ann, you okay?" Tommy asked.

"What does it look like? I'm fine. Just tired," she shot back, quickly waking.

Tommy sighed. "Oh," he said, silenced.

Ann felt a pang of guilt. "What is it, Tommy?" she said more softly.

"I was going to go to Cliff's house and spend the night. I'm just worried about you."

"What?" *Worried about me?* "Tommy, go. I'll be fine."

"You saw the note?"

"Yeah, I saw the note. She'll be back soon."

"Ann it's already nine o'clock."

She looked at him, confused.

"You've been sleeping for a long time. I didn't want to wake you, but then you were sleeping for so long I wondered..."

"Wondered what?"

"If you were okay."

Ann understood his meaning. "No I'm fine, Tommy. I would never do anything like that."

"I know. I was just worried."

"I haven't been sleeping well is all."

"What are we going to do about Mom?"

"I've got it taken care of. Don't worry about it. Have fun at Cliff's. I'll let Mom know..." She couldn't finish her sentence. *Let Mom know what?* That her son had gone somewhere? As if she'd notice.

Ann wished she had someone to call other than Lisa. All the friends or acquaintances she had before the accident disappeared shortly after the funeral. It wasn't their fault. Their lives were moving forward and Ann wasn't ready for that. Nobody wanted to hang out with the girl with the dead father. If you did, you started to notice how flippantly things are said regarding death—"I'm so embarrassed I wish I was dead," or "I was so mad I could have killed him." Once this was realized the conversation grew strained, until someone finally suggested watching a movie. Then it took two hours to find one where no one died. Eventually, they had all drifted off, except Lisa.

"Sure you'll be okay without me?" Tommy asked.

Ann straightened, pursed her lips and smoothed her hair with her hands. "Fine. Just get out of here, Tommy."

"Okay, but..."

"But what?"

"Promise me you won't get mad?"

Oh great, now what? Ann thought.

"Tommy, just tell me."

"I let your friend in."

"Huh?"

"Danny? Your friend... He's downstairs. We've been playing video games."

Ann's heart lodged in her throat. She tried to choke out a reply but all she could manage was a cough.

"Don't be mad. He's really cool."

Ann felt sick. "He's here?"

"Yeah."

"How long?"

"I don't know, awhile."

"How long?"

"Since about seven-thirty, I guess."

"He's been here almost two hours playing video games with you?"

"Yeah. Look, Ann, just go down there and hang out with him. Don't worry about Mom right now."

"Damn it, Tommy," she spat. She wanted to yell at him. Did he really think she wanted to play house with Feller and pretend nothing was going on? She was a peeled apple burning in the sun, too raw to muster the strength to yell. She didn't need this right now. "Tommy, just go to Cliff's, now, before I kill you. Okay? And I'll figure the rest of this out."

Tommy nodded. "I'm sorry."

Ann softened. "Me too."

"I'm just tired of this shit. What if for a night, just tonight we forget about all the crap and pretend it never happened?"

Ann attempted a smile, "That would be nice."

"Just, go crazy or something." Tommy shoved his hands in pockets and gazed at the floor.

Tommy wanted the same thing as Ann—to have a normal life. A surge of anger ran through her. "Fuck this, you're right." She shook her head. "I'm so sick of feeling this way."

Tommy nodded. There was a long pause before either spoke. "Forget about Mom. She can't keep doing this to us, ya know?" He kicked Ann's shoe on the floor.

Ann didn't like seeing Tommy like this.

"Go." Ann smiled at him. "Have fun."

Tommy managed a slight smile.

She turned away from him and anxiously brushed her fingers through her hair.

" 'Kay. I'll just be at Cliff's."

"Sounds good."

"Ann," Tommy started. "Why does your wall look like it's bleeding?"

Ann rolled her eyes. "Lisa."

Enough said.

Tommy lingered a moment longer as Ann finished smoothing her hair. "See ya," Tommy said. She listened as Tommy descended the stairs, said goodbye to Danny, and shut the front door behind him. She was alone in her house with Danny Feller.

She glanced in the mirror to check how she looked and concluded she looked like shit. She ran a comb through her long brown hair and applied lip-gloss. Better.

She couldn't think about Danny downstairs waiting for her or she'd get too anxious and come off sounding weak and pathetic. She just had to go down there without thinking and deal with him. Somehow.

She pulled her shoulders back before marching out of her

bedroom and down the spiral stairs. She saw the top of his head as she approached the living room. He was playing a zombie-killing videogame. She glided up beside the couch and cleared her throat.

"Ann!" He jumped from the couch with a toothy grin and put the game on pause.

"What are you doing here?" she asked, arms folded.

"I came to play video games with Tommy."

Ann glared at him, confused.

"Ann," he said softly. "Come on."

"What?"

"Why else would I be here, if not to see you?"

Ann's resolve to be a bitch weakened, as butterflies fluttered around her heart and made her whole body feel it was tingling.

"Well, now's not a good time," she heard herself saying. Was that what she really wanted?

"Yeah, I know, Tommy told me the whole story, and the way I see it, I'm a godsend right now?"

Tommy and his big mouth, Ann thought.

"Oh yeah? Why's that?" she asked tersely

"Well, you have a missing, possibly drunk, mother, and I have a license and a car."

"I have a car," she retorted.

"Yes, but you don't have a license, do you? So it seems that my being here is meant to be."

Ann sighed. "How convenient for me."

Maybe Danny could help her. It made her livid, but he was her best option. The last thing she needed right now was for her mom to get picked up again and this time land in jail.

"What else did Tommy tell you?" Ann asked.

"Nothing, just that your mom liked to go out and drink occasionally, and we would probably have to go find her."

Ann relaxed. At least Danny didn't know the whole tragic saga. Some privacy remained intact.

"So, shall we go?" he said with excitement as if they were kids going on a treasure hunt.

"Yeah." Ann was somewhat relieved to let Danny take the lead. "Let me just grab a jacket." She ran back upstairs to her bedroom. She checked herself in the mirror again and felt like an idiot for even bothering, since she hadn't changed in the past five minutes. Then she grabbed a black hooded sweatshirt from her closet and met Danny downstairs. He was waiting for her at the front door, jingling his keys in his pocket. "I have something for you," he said once she was facing him.

"Yeah?" she said surprised.

Danny pulled his hand out from behind his back revealing a chocolate donut with sprinkles, sitting on a pink napkin. "Sorry it's not on a platter."

Ann smiled. "Looks like you're officially forgiven."

"Good," he smirked and handed her the donut. She happily took it, feeling hungry.

Danny smiled, grabbed her hand and pulled her out the door.

Driddled-aged munken women and other spoonerisms.

Ann had a pretty good idea of which bar her mom was visiting. The place she usually went was just outside of Cloverdale, near where Uncle Joe lived. Ann wondered if her mom went to that bar to work up the courage to give Joe a piece of her mind.

Ann hadn't seen Uncle Joe since before the accident, because Meredith banned him from attending the funeral. She missed him, just as she missed her dad, William, Meredith. She seemed to have lost everyone she cared for most that day.

"So where are we headed?" Danny asked.

Ann was still flushed from the feeling of Danny's fingers intertwined with hers. Danny had held her hand on the way to his car and hadn't let go until after he opened the car door for her and she sat down. She placed the donut in both hands now, in an attempt to fill the empty space that letting go of his hand had created. She gave him directions to the bar in Cloverdale, Danny said he knew the place, then shared the donut with him. Despite Danny's working hands, he insisted that she feed him.

"Do you have music we can listen to?" Ann suggested.

"Nah, I don't really feel like listening to anything right now," Danny said.

Ann offered him a bite. "That's strange, you're always listening to your iPod at school."

Danny finished chewing. "Yeah. Most the time it's because I'm somewhere I don't want to be."

"Are you saying you want to be picking up my mom from a bar right now?"

Danny shrugged. "I want to be with you."

She blushed and turned away. "How did you find out where I lived?"

"The school phone book." Danny drummed his hands on the steering wheel.

"Do you want the last bite?" Ann offered.

"No, you have it."

"Are you sure? I'm about to devour it!" she said, opening her mouth.

"It's all yours," Danny laughed.

She popped it into her mouth. "Mmm." She chewed. "The last bite always tastes the best."

"What! Why didn't you tell me?"

Ann shrugged. "I thought you knew." She laughed. "It tastes the best because you know it's the last, that it's almost gone, so you appreciate it more."

She was at ease with Danny. Almost by accident she tasted a

blip of happiness and it scared her. She shut off and went quiet, running through an array of facial expressions—happy, nervous, concerned, melancholy—before landing on irritated.

"So are you going to make stalking me a habit?" She was kidding, but sounded accusatory.

Danny shrugged. "I just wanted to see you."

"Why?"

"Why not? You're..." he searched for the right word, then settled on "interesting."

"Really? Is that it? Or is it because I am the only girl you see, since you spend most of your time in detention."

"I can tell by your tone that you're trying to insult me, but you do realize you just insulted yourself, right?"

"Shit," Ann covered her face with her hands, "I did, didn't I?" She managed a sad laugh.

"Ann, I'd like to get to know you, but that would be a lot easier if you'd let your guard down a little."

Lisa had said something similar to Ann on more than one occasion since the accident. Ann knew it was a problem she had, but it was a problem that was working for her at this moment. She didn't know if she could survive without this barbed wire fence of protection she had wrapped around herself.

"Um, I guess you're right. I'm sorry," she muttered.

"Really?" Danny said, surprised. "I didn't think that would actually work. Can I have that in writing, before you change your mind?" Ann shoved him and his beautiful grin made her feel warm all over.

"So..." Ann said, searching for a conversation topic.

"So," Danny said, glancing at her.

Ann felt suddenly self-conscious of how dry her lips were. She reached down her shirt and grabbed the lip-gloss from her bra. She glanced at Danny, who was grinning ear to ear. Ann turned scarlet and slipped the lip-gloss into her pants pocket and laughed. "So what do you do when you're not looking for drunken middle-aged women?"

"What do I do when I'm not looking munken driddle-aged women?" Danny pondered.

"Munken driddle-aged?" Ann says.

Danny laughed. "It's a spoonerism."

"Huh? Are we speaking the same language?" Ann asked. "Or are you really an alien?" She was suddenly serious.

"No," Danny laughed. "Maybe," he reconsidered.

"So, is this a recent disease you've developed that affects your speech, or have you had it your whole life?" Ann teased.

"I've been doing spoonerisms since I was a kid. Sometimes I don't realize I'm doing it. It's when you switch the consonants or vowels in two words."

"Hmm," Ann said.

"Like, dappy hay for happy day, or mancake pix for pancake mix. That's one I came up with this morning at breakfast."

"Or fexican mood," Ann chimed in, reading a Mexican food sign they were passing.

"There you go." Danny grinned.

"Um, what were we talking about?" Ann laughed.

"You asked me what I like to do?"

"Right."

"Well, you should know that looking for drunk older women is my favorite pastime, and I'm actually really good at it. I've learned how to lure them out of the bar with red licorice and eighties ballads," he said, tapping a rhythm with his fingers on the steering wheel.

Ann laughed.

"Works every time."

Ann shot him a glance.

"No, actually I practice a lot."

"Practice?" Ann asked.

"I play the drums for this band, Atticus Finch. We play about once a month in the city. Most of the band members are older, in college."

"Atticus Finch? As in..."

"*To Kill a Mockingbird*."

"How did you get hooked up with them?" Ann asked.

"I saw an advertisement online for a drummer and went and auditioned."

"That's cool," Ann said. She briefly considered Danny as the lead role in her fantasy. (Sorry, Waters, but Danny's the real deal, except no spandex. NEVER spandex.)

"You should come to one of our shows," Danny said.

"What kind of music do you play?"

"Progressive rock, I guess."

"I *love* progressive rock," she said.

Danny smiled, taking in her beauty.

"How do you feel about jazz music?" Ann asked

Danny shrugged, "Not my thing."

Aghast, "You're a drummer and jazz is not 'your thing.'" She marked the last phrase with air quotes. Danny smiled. "All the great drummers are jazz musicians."

Danny laughed. He loved how intense she was, how one moment she could be playful and smiling, the next passionate and feisty. "Well..." Danny shook his head. "I disagree."

"Well, my father would disagree with you," Ann said.

"Is that what your dad played? The drums?"

"Saxophone. He was a nerd."

"Whatever. Sax is badass."

Ann smiled. A memory of her father flitted through her consciousness. The time he played a slow, melodic tune on the saxophone in the misty rain of the yard on a summer's night, surrounded by the patio's twinkling lights. She remembered peering out the window and feeling like she was catching a glimpse of another world. One that was timeless and majestic. She touched his saxophone after that as if she were touching the hand of God, wishing to hold onto that feeling forever. For a moment she held that memory close to her and for a few fleeting seconds it was as if her father had never left her.

Ann was used to burying memories of her dad. Whenever she talked about him in front of Meredith, her mom would either burst into sobs or snap at her. Ann didn't want to cry over every memory she had of her father. Sometimes thinking of him in happy ways was the only thing that gave a bit of warmth to her day.

"So is that what you want to be when you grow up?" Ann asked, changing the subject.

"What, a musician?"

"A rock star?"

He shrugged. "I don't know."

"Your stage name could be Fanny Deller."

Danny grinned. "Hot."

"I'm going to start calling you Fanny," Ann said.

"Fine with me," Danny shrugged, "as long as I get to call you Grannie.

"Gran," she corrected him.

Danny laughed. "So do you know what you want to do after high school?"

"Haven't a clue." Whenever the counselor asked her that question, she always sarcastically told them she wanted to be a gymnast. Never mind that Ann hadn't willingly entered a gym in the past five years, nor did she have any skills in gymnastics. Poor girl couldn't do a flip on a trampoline if it got her back stage passes to her favorite concert. The fact of the matter was she didn't know, so she figured that guess was as good as any she could give them.

For a moment she had forgotten to feel sad or angry about everything she had lost. It wasn't as if she had forgotten that her dad was dead; she only abandoned the sadness long enough to remember what it felt like to be her—something she hadn't felt in a long time. But then it was too late to loll in the feeling because they had reached their destination.

"There's my mom's car. Pull in here."

Danny did as Ann instructed without saying a word. She thought about how her uncle Joe lived just a few blocks away. She wanted to call him. He would know what to do. He could help. But she knew it wasn't worth the drama.

Danny took the parking space next to her mom's car and Ann sighed.

"You're ready for this?"

Ann nodded "Thanks for the ride." She took off her seatbelt and climbed out of the car.

"I'll just follow you home then?" Danny asked.

Ann paused before shutting the car door. She planned on Danny dropping her off, but not him following her home and wanting to hang out. There was no way in hell he was going to hang out at her house with her and her drunk mother on the anniversary date of her dad's death. No. Way. In. Hell.

"Danny, thanks for the ride, but go home."

"Why?"

"Because..." She couldn't answer him. She couldn't tell him

that she felt too vulnerable, too scared, too lost.

"Why, Ann?"

Ann shook her head, fighting back the tears.

"Danny, you don't know me. Just leave me alone," she said, slamming the door in his face and treading toward the bar's entrance.

"I know your dad died a year ago today."

Ann spun around to see Danny standing outside the car door.

"How do you know that?" she said, fighting back tears.

"I remember when it happened. I've always noticed you," he explained. "I noticed you on the first day of school." He paused as the information sunk in. So Danny had known about her all along. "Let me just be your friend. I'm not going to hurt you."

A lovely sentiment that may have swayed any less hardheaded girl, but all Ann said was, "Go home, Danny," before she walked into the fug stench of the bar.

The idiot mother.

Louis was bartending that night. Ann was glad she didn't have to explain her situation to the guy working the door. "Dale," Louis called from behind the counter. "She's okay to come in."

Dale shrugged and let Ann pass. She muttered a "thanks" and approached the bar. There were people playing pool on a rundown table and a few others sitting at booths nestled in a dark corner. The only music came from a jukebox at the end of the bar that was messy with peanut shells. Needless to say, the place was a dive.

"You know your mom can take care of herself," Louis said.

"Where is she?" Ann snapped.

"She's fine. We'll call her a cab."

"No. I'm going to take her home."

"Ann, you're just a kid."

"Louis!" She gave him the death look. A glare she'd perfected the past year while playing mom to Tommy. The look let the other person know who was in charge. "Where. Is. She?"

"She's in the back talking to the guys."

"By talking you mean gambling?" she asked, curtly. Meredith sucked at gambling but was always generous with her bets.

Louis shrugged. "It's her life."

"Yeah, that affects me." Ann stormed behind the counter, past the EMPLOYEES ONLY sign, to a secluded room with couches, a table in the middle, and a desk to the right. Five people sat at a table, four men and her mother.

"Mom, you idiot," Ann said.

Meredith looked up groggily from her deck of cards to her daughter.

"Oh, Annie. Everyone, this is my lovely, darling daughter, Annie."

The men grunted, and one reached out his hand for Ann to shake. She rolled her eyes and ignored the offer. He awkwardly took his hand back.

"So, Meredith, what's your bet going to be?" one man asked.

Ann rushed to her mother's side and yanked her arm. "Mother, we're leaving."

"But Ann, I'm in the middle of a game of twenty-one."

"Mom, you're playing poker, not twenty one. Let's go."

"No wonder I'm losing." Meredith burst into laughter. Ann slung her mom's purse around her shoulder and yanked her to standing. Meredith took a swig of her drink and left the empty glass at the table.

"Later, boys," Meredith said with a sloppy wave as Ann tugged her toward the door.

"Bye," the men called after her. " 'Til next time."

Ann held her mother's elbow, steadying her as they left. Louis hollered a goodbye as they walked out. Ann rolled her eyes, irritated that he didn't seem to mind that her mom was too drunk to drive.

Danny's car was gone. This offered Ann a small relief. She didn't want him to see any of this. She propped Meredith against the hood of the car and fished for the keys in her purse.

"I can't feel my arm," Meredith muttered. Maybe she was worse than Ann thought. Ann watched as Meredith's eyelids grew heavy. By the time she got the keys out of her mom's purse and unlocked the car, Meredith was hugging the hood. Ann helped her mother into the car by shoving her onto the front seat and slamming the door in her face.

Once Ann got in the driver's side and adjusted the seat she wished she had shoved her mom into the back seat.

"Mom, stop touching me. Mom. I have to drive. Stop touching me!"

Is it bad to wish your mom were drunk to the point of passing out? Ann thought.

"You are my sunshine, my only sunshine," Meredith sang off-key in her drunken haze.

Ann slapped her mom's hand and pulled the car from the lot.

"Remember when I used to sing that song to you, Annie?" Her words were slurred.

"No, I don't," Ann said brusquely.

"That's right, because you were just a baby so you wouldn't remember."

"Mom. Please just shut up. If I'm going to drive us home I need you to shut up."

Meredith started to protest and Ann cranked the stereo volume. Meredith lay back in her seat and closed her eyes.

HER MOM WAS ASLEEP by the time Ann turned the car onto their street. The last time she had picked her mom up it was the Fourth of July. Picnics had been a big thing in the Grey family.

It started as a daddy-daughter thing, but eventually included the family and later became a tradition. On the Fourth of July, they picnicked at Hyde Park. They stayed all evening, hanging out to get a good spot to see the fireworks. That was when life was perfect.

This year William made up some excuse that he needed to look for apartments and Tommy went to Cliff's house. They were his new family. Meredith went out drinking. The traffic was so horrible that night that Lisa and Ann had waited until it was past midnight to get Meredith. Not letting Lisa's dad know what they were up to, they planned a sleepover.

That night Meredith didn't sing lullabies. She just cried. "You know my husband's dead," she had said, as if Ann were a complete stranger. "I'll never love anyone but him."

Ann was grateful this time that Meredith was unconscious. She figured she could pull into the garage and let her mom sleep it off in the car.

Ann pulled onto her street and saw Danny's car parked outside her house, blocking the driveway. He sat on the front stoop listening to music. Annoyed, Ann parked behind him. He stood and slipped the headphones off.

Ann wondered what he was thinking. Did he really believe she would be happy to see him after she told him to take a hike after using him for a ride?

Ann jolted from the car.

"What are you doing here?" she sneered, stomping toward him.

"Ann, chill, I just want to help."

"You've helped enough, now leave!" she said, waving him off.

"Ann..." Danny sighed.

Meredith opened the side door and yelled, "Annie" before she fell onto the grass and started laughing. Ann rushed over to her, wishing desperately that Danny would leave. But he didn't. The stubborn fool wouldn't. Instead he walked over to Meredith, and knelt down beside her.

"Who are you?" Meredith asked.

"I'm Danny."

Meredith responded with a "humph." Ann was too embarrassed to make eye contact with him.

"Let me help you," Danny offered Meredith, just before cradling his arm around her back and helping her rise. "Let's get you in the house." Ann grumbled and slammed the car door behind them. She watched as Danny half-carried her mother to the house. Ann snagged the front door for Danny, and he moved Meredith into the sitting area and laid her on the couch.

"She'll be okay," Danny said.

"How would you know?" Ann said with contempt.

"I have a mom too," he smiled wryly. Meredith snored.

Ann shook her head. Danny knew nothing about her life, or what it was like living with an alcoholic parent. Her self-pity was the one thing she had left, and she wasn't going to let Danny take that from her.

"Well, I'm sure your mom doesn't do this on a daily basis."

"No," Danny sighed, "she doesn't. But I thought your mom didn't either."

"She doesn't," Ann lied. "By the way, do you have a problem

respecting another person's wishes?"

"Only when that person is lying to herself."

Ann looked startled. "Excuse me?"

"I know what it's like to lose a father and you're not fooling me."

"Did your father die?" Ann said, softer now.

Danny shook his head, but couldn't find words to speak. He gazed down at her hand and reached for it.

Every time he touched her she felt the tension in her body melt. It reminded her of being at the beach, listening to the soothing crash of the waves and drinking in the warmth of the sun. She could feel the layers of herself falling away. Her guard was disappearing and beyond it lurked feelings of a mournful isolation. This forlorn feeling of grief rested at the apex of Ann's heart and she felt it pulse through her body with every heartbeat. With the feeling came a restless longing and desire to need someone, which shuddered to the surface of her skin and took hold of her. These feelings frightened her, but being with Danny made her feel safe. For the first time in a long time it felt okay to be sad, without pretending.

"Are you okay?" Danny asked, sensing a change.

"Um," she didn't know what to say. Her standard response was to shrug her shoulders, or say, "fine," just to get people off her back. But she didn't feel like continuing the charade.

He grabbed her shoulders and pulled her toward him. She wrapped her arms around his waist and rested her head on his chest. A few tears escaped her eyes. She pulled away and wiped them with the sleeve of her jacket. Danny took her other hand in his and rubbed the back of it. When she had the courage to make eye contact with him, she saw something different in him. She couldn't find the words to explain the connection that was forming.

But she didn't have to. Danny felt it too.

"Let's go somewhere else," he said.

"Why?"

"I don't want to disturb your mom."

"An interplanetary war wouldn't disturb my mom right now."

Danny locked eyes with Ann, and she saw an intense hunger in his gaze. She felt a sudden surge of heat course through her body. She looked away, irked that her hormones were getting the best of her. At least that's what she blamed it on. Her hormones, not the fact that she hadn't been touched by anyone, not even her mom in a long time and she was yearning for affection. She was yearning to be seen.

"Okay," she said as Danny glided up the stairs, not releasing his grip on her hand. He led her straight to her bedroom as if he'd been there before. Ann was in a trance as Danny shut the bedroom door behind her and led her to the bed where they sat next to each other.

"Does your mom let you have boys in your room?"

"I don't know. You're the first one."

"Oh," he said, a bit startled.

Ann blushed. This was the closest she had ever been to a boy. Besides Johnny Templeton in eighth grade, but he was so clumsy and slobbery that Ann figured it didn't count.

"My dad didn't die," Danny said, still holding Ann's hand. "I wish he had died. That would have been easier to deal with. He just left."

"Oh. I'm sorry." She wasn't sure if that was the right thing to say. She hated when everyone had said they were sorry after her dad died. As if their being sorry made it any better. Now, here she was saying it and sounding lame.

"You have a lot of Led Zeppelin CDs." He gestured to the

bookcase.

"Yeah, it was my dad's favorite rock band. My mom didn't want those CDs around, but I couldn't get rid of them."

Danny unlatched his hand from hers. She noticed her hand was sweaty, so she wiped it on her pant leg as Danny looked through her CDs. "Can I play one?"

"Sure." Her stomach churned.

Danny grabbed the Led Zeppelin IV CD that had "Stairway to Heaven" on it and slipped it into the player. "I like your room, by the way. It's different."

"Oh," she said, embarrassed. "You mean the spray paint? It was Lisa's idea. She thought my room was too depressing so she wanted to liven it up a bit."

"By making the walls look like they're bleeding?" Danny joked.

Ann smiled and made a mental note to kill Lisa.

Danny sat next to Ann on the bed, his body almost touching hers.

"There's something I have been wanting to tell you."

"Okay," Ann said.

"Remember when I was gone for a couple weeks and you wanted to know where I'd been?"

"Yeah."

"Well, I was at my grandma's funeral."

"Oh, I'm sorry."

I'm saying it again. Ann thought to herself. *I sound like such an idiot.*

"Thanks," her apologizing didn't bother him. "Well, that's not all. I saw my dad there. I haven't seen him in almost five years. I uh, kind of started a fight with him."

"Really? Like, you punched him?"

Danny nodded.

"Huh. You don't seem the type."

"What do you mean 'the type?'"

"I don't know," she said, blushing. "You know the stereotypical no-neck, too much testosterone, picking fights and being, ya know...aggressive?" *What am I even saying?* she thought.

The expression on Ann's face made Danny laugh. He looked away. "There's a lot you don't know about me."

Ann nodded, uncomfortable.

"When I saw him I just got so angry and before I knew it I was saying things I didn't mean." He shook his head. "Or maybe I did mean them."

Ann shuddered, knowing how that felt.

"I see myself in you, though." Danny locked his eyes with hers. "I used to be a lot like you."

Ann found that hard to believe.

"I wanted something different with my life, but I was so angry and confused after my dad left that I was looking for it in all the wrong places. But now I've become more comfortable with myself and with life. I wasn't expecting to feel that way toward him. Just so many emotions came flooding back. It was like everything I had wanted to say to him when he left came pouring out."

"When did he leave?"

"When I was twelve." He adjusted on the bed, brushing his fingers through his hair. Ann watched him, not knowing what to say. "So, that's my secret."

"Hmmm. Well you seem to already know my secrets," she said.

"Not all of them. I was wondering…"

"Yeah?"

"Remember when I told you I had seen you watching Krissy Stevenson and Greg Arbertson?"

"When you admitted to being a stalker?"

Danny's mouth formed a lop-sided grin. "Yeah, that time. I only mention it because I remember how sad you looked and you never told me what was going on. I'm curious?"

Ann sighed. "I don't know, I really can't stand Krissy Stevenson, she's so..." Ann paused. "Her life is perfect and..." She felt inane saying it out loud. She searched her brain for more eloquent words. "It would just be nice to have things so easy."

"You think Krissy Stevenson has it easy?"

"She's rich, popular, likely to get into any college she applies to, she has two parents, a boyfriend. Yeah, she seems happy."

"Maybe she is. You never know, though. Sometimes having it all can be a curse too."

"Doubt it," Ann muttered.

"Well, the good news is you have something she doesn't."

"What, an anger problem?" she admitted with a laugh.

"You do have a sense of humor. I knew it was buried in there somewhere."

"Whatever. Just tell me what I have that she doesn't, besides tame hair."

"Make that two things you have."

Ann laughed. "Come on, tell me."

Danny shrugged. "Perspective."

"That's it?" Ann's brow furrowed. "Perspective?"

"Yeah. It seems that around here so many people are so ignorant sometimes. It's like they're missing the big picture, they think the world revolves around them."

Ann understood, but at the same time she didn't. She still wasn't happy with life the way it was. She still hated Krissy Stevenson because Krissy had everything she didn't. Ann just wanted things to be the way they should be. Ann was flattered that

Danny saw her as being deeper than the hollow shell she felt she was.

"Like Thoreau, in *Walden*," Danny added.

Ann shook her head, not following.

Danny explained: "Thoreau saw society as being superficial, people so focused on appearances that no real relationships could be formed. He saw nature as his neighbor. It can be messy, wild and unpredictable, but it is also real."

"Thoreau wanted reality," Ann chimed in, reminded of the conversation she had with Mr. Gibbs earlier that day. It felt like their chat had happened weeks ago. It had been a long day.

"Yeah, do you have your book? I'll show you."

Ann got up and grabbed her backpack. She shook the contents of it onto the floor and retrieved the book from the pile. She offered it to Danny. His fingers caressed the back of her hand as he took it from her. Ann's arm began to tingle. She had to admit this new sensation felt better than the one produced by her usual stonewalling tactic.

Danny flipped through the pages of the book, before landing on one. "See, look here," he said, pointing to a passage. Ann walked up beside him and tried to peer over his shoulder. "Do you have a pen?" he asked.

"Sure." She grabbed one from the dresser. Danny underlined the passage before reading it out loud to her.

Thoreau's words came to life: " 'Yet I experienced sometimes that the most sweet and tender, the most innocent and encouraging society may be found in any natural object.' " Look, I will show you another one. I think its page..." Danny said, muttering to himself, "Yep, right here. 'Society is commonly too cheap. We meet at very short intervals, not having time to acquire any new value for each other.' What do you think?"

"I like," she said, rather than shrugging, which was what she was about to do. Her head sort of felt like it was spinning. It had been awhile since she'd last eaten a real meal. Danny ripped the page from the book.

"What are you doing?"

"Oh sorry. I wasn't thinking. It just felt this passage deserved to be on your wall."

"Oh, okay," she said.

"Do you have something I can hang it with?" Ann retrieved a pushpin from her desk drawer for Danny, who hung the torn-out page next to her dying plant.

Too bad William wasn't around to see them massacring his book.

Ann had an idea. "What about this?" she said, holding up a black marker. "Then we don't have to keep tearing pages out of the book."

"Perfect," Danny said, brushing his dark hair out of his brown eyes. He grabbed the marker from her and gazed at the walls, looking for a good spot to write. Good thing Meredith was too complacent to care about Ann's new wall décor. Danny decided on the area just above Ann's computer desk. He scrawled a *Walden* quote on the wall. His handwriting was surprisingly clean. Ann stared at him, feeling surreal. She had forgotten about her mom downstairs unconscious, about Lisa ditching her, and about her dad's accident. She was alone in her room with Danny Feller. Never in a million years would she have guessed this. She wasn't sure how to feel about it.

Scared?

Frustrated?

Excited?

Danny finished and hopped over to where Ann stood near the

edge of the bed.

"What do you think?"

Ann read the words he'd written:

I went to the woods because I wished to live deliberately, to front only the essential facts of life, and see if I could not learn what it had to teach, and not, when I came to die, discover that I had not lived.

"It's awesome," she said, heart pounding. How was she going to explain a night like this to Lisa? She turned and looked at Danny, her eyes meeting his gaze. He began to caress her hand, her arm, her cheek. Ann's body was surging with energy and she needed a release. She pressed her lips against his. They moved in sync together. Danny's hand moved to her stomach and her whole body flowed with heat.

She felt so protected in his embrace. She wasn't feeling angry or scared anymore. Even when Danny tore up her brother's book she hadn't been angry. Instead, she felt naked, but in a good way.

As they kissed, Danny began to notice Ann's kisses morph from unrestrained passion to a riotous desperation. She was no longer pouring her soul into him, but asking him to suck the poison out of her as she tackled him to the bed.

Rejection's a bitch.

Ann straddled Danny on the bed. He was startled, but let his lips continue to speak to hers as they kissed. Ann pushed further and harder, until desire swallowed her whole and everything she'd been running from was swept away. *This is it*, Ann told herself. *I am going to lose my virginity to Danny Feller, in my own house, on my bed, on the anniversary date of my dad's death.*

The thought hung gloomily in the air above her. Hot tears swelled in her eyes, but Danny's touch was like a thousand kisses against her skin, and it pulled her from her grief. She traced her hand along the bare skin just above his buckle. He quivered at her touch. She could have fallen into him and cried, but she hated her tears. She hated the girl she used to be. So innocent, naïve, weak...hurt. She told herself she was stronger than that. So, too bad her dad wasn't alive to barge in on them and give Danny the third degree and be overbearing and protective. So, Ann didn't have a dad. She resolved she would have this night. She buried the tears as her anger and excitement rose.

Ann's kiss grew fierce as she bit Danny's bottom lip. Her hands held fistfuls of Danny's shirt. She began pulling his shirt off, when Danny stopped her.

"Ann," Danny said, gasping for air. "I can't do this."

Ann stared at him, confused.

"What do you mean?"

"Sex. We can't..."

"You don't have a condom?"

"No, it's not that...I just..."

Humiliated, Ann climbed off him and turned away. A hollow empty pain was forming in her chest as the thought occurred to her that he probably just felt sorry for her.

"Ann I didn't mean it like that."

It was too late. The bricks to the wall had already been laid within a matter of seconds. Now that invisible wall stood between them.

"Danny, just go away."

"Why?" Danny asked.

"Why?" Her anger rose. Because you came in here being pushy, and then as soon as I gave you what you wanted, you tossed me aside!" Ann yelled. The shrillness in her voice startled her. She knew she had to calm down, to get away from him. She stormed out of her room. Danny followed, calling after her.

"Ann, that's *not* how it is and you know it," he said.

Except, that's not what Ann heard, what she thought she heard was, "That's just how it is and you know it."

Ann raced down the stairs and flung open the front door, not caring if she woke Meredith. "Get out!" she screamed.

"Ann," Danny said, pleading with her to understand, "I just know that we're both in a vulnerable place right now; I don't want you to do anything you might regret later."

"You're right! And neither do I. That's why I want you to leave!"

Danny looked at her, defeated. Ann looked away from him, arms crossed firm over her chest, pleading for him to give up and leave so she could be alone. So she could feel safe again in her shell. But then a part of her wanted him to stay. To not give up on her, to see she was just scared and hurt. But it was too late. Ann's guard was like the Berlin Wall, and despite its destruction in 1989, hers wasn't coming down any time soon.

And Danny left.

Ann slammed the door behind Danny and sank to the floor. A few tears dropped on her cheeks. She wouldn't allow any more. She couldn't. She worried that if she cried she'd lose herself, *really* lose herself and never come back. In her mind this proved her theory right. He didn't want her. He just felt sorry for her. She wasn't desirable enough even to sleep with. She was pathetic.

"Annie?"

Ann quickly wiped the tears from her cheeks and sprang from the floor.

"Mom?"

"Did I hear the door slam?" Figures. She'd missed the screaming but was awakened by a friggin door closing.

"Yeah. Are you feeling okay?" Ann said, changing the subject.

"I feel like I've been spinning in circles is all."

Ann wanted to feel sorry for her mom. She had lost her husband, but what about her kids? Did her children mean nothing to her?

"Annie, I'm so sorry."

Great, Ann thought. She wasn't going to be spared the crying part of her mom's drunken spree.

"Yeah, Mom. I know."

"No, really Ann, I've been stupid. It will never happen again, I promise. They say the first year is the hardest and it's done now. I'm done, I promise."

Ann turned away and rolled her eyes. "Good night, Mom." She heard her mom whimper, but nothing else. She climbed the stairs to her bedroom and locked the bedroom door behind her. She grabbed the marker from the dresser where Danny left it and ripped off her shirt and began coloring her chest black with the marker. Forcefully dragging it across her skin.

Anger.

Hurt.

Sadness.

Loss.

She went to a blank space on her wall and wrote, "Times I have heard the *It Will Never Happen Again* speech by Meredith Grey." Then she counted silently in her mind before etching seven hash marks below it. Seven times she had heard different variations of the same speech. And every time, nothing changed.

The deplorable Jacob
Waters.

After the incident with Danny Feller, life went on in the Grey household as usual. Ann heard nothing from William. It was getting colder outside. Lisa returned and was impressed with the Danny Feller story and the new decorations in Ann's room. Of course, Lisa was disappointed by the fact that nothing had happened between Ann and Danny. Ann was angry that Lisa didn't realize what a jerk Danny was and how he had totally made her into a charity case. Their conversations echoed and warped in Ann's mind as they played on repeat: *You remind me of how angry I used to be. And you're interesting and totally pathetic. And let me take care of you so I can avoid my problems and feel good about myself. And let's form a club for kids without dads. And wouldn't that be great?*

Ann's mission was to escape further embarrassment by avoiding Danny. All she had to do was not get detention and not go to math. Besides, if *Bob* made good on his threat, detention would no longer be suffering through Ms. Steinberg's stench. It would be staring at *Bob's* bald spot. Nobody wanted that, not even Bob. So getting detention was out of the question.

Instead of going to math, Ann hung out in the bathroom near senior hallway. It had worked all week. She spent the time occasionally doing homework, mostly doodling.

Except today was different. The bell rang. Ann was already in the bathroom. A few lingerers rushed the door to get to their classes while Ann checked herself in the mirror, analyzing what she would change about her face or body if she were ever to get plastic surgery. She looked at her supposedly ginormous nose and thought, *Oh yeah, definitely getting it done. No question.* She saw her boobs and ass as different matters entirely.

Before Ann could get to degrading her entire self-image and stabbing it into a box marked "Next Step: Bulimia," Pam Scavorski came in sobbing. Startled, Ann stared, unsure of what to do. *Should I leave and give her some privacy? Should I ask if she's okay?* Ann shifted uncomfortably.

"Please leave," Pam said. Her head hung between her shoulders over the bathroom sink.

Ann grabbed her backpack and left. A familiar knot grew in her stomach. Something about the way Pam looked, hovering over the empty sink. She wasn't just sad, she was in despair. Like her life had crumbled around her, and she was unable to pick up the pieces.

Ann didn't realize this at the time, but looking back she recognized that in the jumbled confusing of all her emotions, she too felt lost. She wandered without a compass or map. She grabbed onto anything that seemed sturdy, anything that could hold her up. And in this moment, what was holding her up was Jacob Waters.

"Are you okay?" Jacob asked. His arm wrapped around her waist as she steadied her legs. In her rush to leave the restroom she had turned the corner, and her face slammed into his broad chest as she tripped over his foot. She was seconds away from face-planting when he caught her.

Ann blinked twice to make sure she was seeing straight. "Yeah. Fine."

"Are you sure? You must have been in a hurry." Jacob let his arm linger on her waist.

"Yeah, I'm fine." She adjusted her backpack. Jacob blocked her path.

"You have a habit of not watching where you're going," he said.

Ann smiled awkwardly, wishing he hadn't remembered their earlier encounter with the grief pamphlet. Thanks again, *Bob*.

"You going to class?" Jacob asked.

"No." Ann wondered why he was still talking to her.

"Me either." He grinned. "I'm actually looking for someone; do you know Pam Scavorski?"

"She's in the bathroom," Ann said impatiently.

"Oh you saw her? Is she okay?"

"If you mean bawling her eyes out, then yeah, she's fine."

"Oh," Jacob said, startled. "Did she say anything to you?"

Ann shook her head.

"Well, I just broke up with her. We'd only been out a few times. But she's taking it really hard. I feel kind of bad. It's just she's not really my type, ya know?"

Ann tried not to roll her eyes. *Isn't your type—hot, blonde, and stupid?* Everyone knew Waters had a reputation for being the biggest player in school.

"She'll recover," Ann said, trying not to sound too sarcastic, but wanting Jacob to get the hint. Jacob nodded with a slight smile. Ann took this as her opportunity to turn and leave.

"You know I remember you?"

Startled, Ann turned back. "Huh?"

"You're William Grey's sister. We've met before at your house."

Ann blushed.

"Remind me of your name again?"

"Ann."

"Right, Ann," he said grinning, looking her up and down. "I hear you have a nickname for yourself?"

"I do?"

"Yeah, my buddy told me about you. Miss Firecracker, right?"

"Uh, yeah. I guess that's me." She glanced at the ground, embarrassed.

"Why don't I ever see you at any parties?"

Ann wanted to say, *Because I'm never invited you stupid, man-whore.* But instead she coughed on her own spit.

"Are you okay?" Jacob said, resting his hand on her back.

"I'm fine," she said, trying to close her throat off so she could end her humiliation.

"Do you need some water?" he asked, concerned.

Ann shook her head and stopped coughing. "No, I'm good."

"Okay...well do you want to hang out sometime?"

"Sure," Ann said before realizing what she was saying. Hang out with Jacob Waters? This was exactly what she always wanted, right? She wasn't sure what she would do with him. She didn't exactly fit in with his crowd.

"Great." He smiled and shoved his hands into his pockets. "Well how about today, after school, are you free?"

"Um."

Jacob's eyes looked intently into hers. She was in a stupid love trance. *Jacob Waters.* Ann mused. *Super hot, hottie. The guy you have embarrassing fantasies about wants to hang out with you.*

So what if he was a player. Ann didn't mind. She wasn't looking for a relationship. She would settle for just having something to do besides take care of her mom and Tommy.

"Can I pick you up at home? We're all going out for pizza, and then there's a rival football game tonight that we're going to."

Pizza?

Football?

Yes, Ann considered these activities "normal" things that "normal" teenagers did that Ann had never considered doing since the accident. Ann didn't even know it was football season. She was completely out of touch with high school sports. She used to know when William was playing, but now...

"Yeah I'd love to. You still remember where I live?" she smiled flirtatiously.

"Of course. See you tonight." He smiled and walked away.

Ann took a deep breath, as she remembered how to walk.

Holy shit. Jacob Waters?

"Are you shitting me right now?" Lisa said, astounded. The car wobbled as Lisa skidded the old Thunderbird around the next corner. Ann held tight to the dashboard and slid into the door.

"Of course I'm not."

"Ann, they will eat you alive."

"Which I am well aware of."

"I think you have to have some sort of Barbie Makeover to hang out with them. You could be Skipper."

"I'm not hanging out with the cheerleading trio. I'm just hanging with Jacob."

"Why would Jacob be interested in you?"

Ann took the comment like a knife to the aorta. "You are being such a bitch right now."

"Me? A bitch? Ann, first you turn down Danny Feller—"

"Danny turned me down!"

"Whatever. Then you're completely okay with being absorbed by Jacob Waters and his lemmings. They feed off the souls of the weak. You're like lunch meat to them."

Lisa was just jealous. This is what Ann always imagined her high school experience to be like, and she was finally getting it, and now Lisa couldn't even be happy for her. Maybe Lisa was worried about being left behind, which was definitely not the case. She was going to ask Lisa to come. She needed her friend with her. She'd die if she had to make small talk with the cheerleading triplets. What could she and String Bean possibly have in common? Then, what if someone brought up the accident and her father? She definitely was not walking into this without her best friend.

"Then come with me? It might be fun."

"Fun?"

"You're not even curious what it might be like?"

"Not in the slightest. I have my own life, I don't need to obsess over someone else's."

Is that what Lisa thought Ann was doing? Ann's muscles flexed and tightened. She couldn't be angry with Lisa, she was the only person Ann had left.

"Seriously, come," she demanded.

"Why are you even interested in Jacob?" Lisa asked.

Ann scoffed. "Are you joking? He's freaking gorgeous."

Lisa shrugged.

"You cannot deny that he's hot, Lisa."

"Yeah, but he's, like, too hot."

"What?" Ann asked, incredulously.

"It's like I'm reading one of those teen romance novels you

used to love where the guy is gorgeous and older and out of her league and he's got dark hair and piercing blue eyes."

"Dude, his hair is, like, a dirty blonde color." Ann argued, deciding to ignore the "out of her league" comment.

"And then there's always a love triangle with a mysterious misunderstood outcast."

"No there's not."

"And everyones white, except for the token black side character they throw in to not seem racist."

Ann rolled her eyes and smirked, "Hey, Danny's like, half Italian or something."

"Still white." Lisa shrugged.

"And I'm, like, an eighth Guatemalan. Or is it Costa Rican?"

Now it was Lisa's turn to roll her eyes, "Well, I'm a quarter Japanese so, I win."

"You're so annoying." Ann smiled.

"And there is an overarching lesson that corresponds with the main character's English assignment," Lisa continues.

"Will you stop!" Ann laughed.

"I'm just saying, you've become a cliche."

Ann laughed, "So as I was saying about this super hot white guy I'm about to go on a date with tonight."

"Are his eyes stormy? Do they remind you of the ocean?" Lisa joked.

Ann laughed and punched her in the arm.

"Ow!" Lisa squealed.

"Will you just come tonight?" Ann begged.

"Maybe I have plans." Lisa said, rubbing her arm.

"Plans?" Ann doubted.

"Yeah, I'm busy."

"Fine," Ann huffed and dropped it at that.

THE REMAINDER OF THE DRIVE WAS SILENT. "Are you sure?" Ann asked again once they were in her driveway. "It could be interesting?"

"No, thanks," Lisa said.

Ann pouted and slammed the door. Not out of anger, more to make sure it would latch, and okay, maybe a little bit of anger, but she was trying not to let it show. She sulked as she watched Lisa peel out of her driveway onto the road. Well, as much as she could peel out without losing a car component. Ann didn't know why it was so important to have Lisa there. It was a date, after all, wasn't it? Having Lisa there would only make it weird. Ann shook off her nervous energy and entered the house. unconcerned about her mother's condition, or whether Tommy was doing his homework. She didn't know when Jacob was going to be there. He said after school. Was that in five minutes or five hours? Either way, she figured she should get ready just in case.

She ran to her room and chucked her bag on the floor before glancing in the mirror and concluding she looked like a twelve-year old man-boy. (Seriously. Her words, not mine.) She tore off her t-shirt and jeans and searched her closet for a nicer top. It had been so long since Ann had cared about what she looked like she wasn't sure if she had anything decent to wear.

She thought about what the girls in the T.F.P. clique wore. Usually their tops were skin-tight and accentuated their cleavage. They were matched with skin-tight jeans or a mini skirt. Ann didn't have anything close to that.

She settled on the tightest pair of jeans she had, a V-neck sweater that didn't show enough cleavage, which was probably a good thing, and her Mary Jane shoes. She usually wore her hair straight and flat. She had never learned to use a curling iron and she definitely didn't know, or want to know, the secret to the web of hair other girls would be sporting. So she ran a brush through it and called it good.

Ann didn't wear much makeup, either. Her mom never wore much, and her brother William insisted she not get in the habit, saying natural girls were more beautiful. So, since all Ann owned was mascara and lip-gloss she applied it in globs.

All of this took about ten minutes. Then she was left sitting at her desk biting her nails. It was a habit she wished she could stop, but found it too soothing to bother.

She thought about Jacob Waters picking her up and tried to imagine what she would say to him. She saw herself gliding out the door. Happy. Smiling. Confident. Jacob would smile back, and they would feel comfortable with each other as she had felt with Danny for that brief moment. Then she would hop in his convertible, and she would feel...free.

The clanking of dishes in the kitchen pulled Ann from her trance. She wanted to tell Tommy about her date. She knew he'd be happy for her. Ann entered the kitchen and saw Tommy sitting across the kitchen table from Meredith.

"What's going on?"

"Oh," Meredith said, looking at Ann in surprise. "We were just wondering about you. What do you want for dinner?"

Ann was stunned, Tommy was smiling. Meredith was dressed, her hair done and everything. Despite this she still looked sick, even frail. Her face was blanched, with dark moons hanging under her eyes and tiny red spots that looked like broken blood vessels dotted her cheeks and nose. She used to be so beautiful.

When Ann's dad had met her on a blind date, he thought she was the most beautiful woman he'd ever laid eyes on. He was so quiet and awkward. Nothing between them clicked. Meredith wasn't sure why she agreed to another date as she was sure they had nothing in common. "But I must admit there was something about him," Meredith had told Ann. "I could just tell he was an honest and caring man. Plus, even with his glasses, he was kind of cute," she admitted. "And once I got to know him he made me laugh, and then before I knew it I was in love, and I knew there would never be another man for me."

When Ann's father quit his job at the bank and opened the restaurant, her parents relationship grew strained. Ann had heard them fight on several different occasions about how he was never home. Dad kept telling her to give it time. They finally came to a truce when Dad promised Meredith he'd hire someone to take over for him so he could spend more time at home. He was never able to make good on his promise. The fatal accident, his dying and all, ended that.

"Where have you been?" Ann knew Meredith hadn't made herself presentable for them.

"The doctor's," Meredith said.

"Why?"

Meredith got up from the table and pulled ingredients from the cupboards as if she were seriously going to prepare a meal for them. Ann looked at Tommy, confused. He just shrugged and announced he'd be out back skating and to let him know when dinner was ready.

"Mom? What's going on?"

Meredith glanced to the sliding door that Tommy had slid

through and shut it behind him before addressing Ann. "The doctor put me on Antabuse today."

"What's that?"

"It's to help me quit drinking. I can't keep living like this," she said, dispirited and sinking into her shoulders, avoiding eye contact with Ann. "I've tried to cut back, but maybe I should just stop."

It was weird for Ann to be talking to her mom like this. It was as if her mom saw her as the adult and not the child. At least she wasn't talking to a bad version of Audrey Hepburn.

"So, you're serious?"

Meredith finally made eye contact with Ann. Her eyes were red around the rims. Ann couldn't tell if she was about to cry, had just cried, or only had dust in them.

"Well it isn't going to be easy. That's why I will need you to help me take care of things."

Ann rolled her eyes. She *had* been taking care of things. Practically *everything*. "Mom, what the hell do you think has been going on here? I'm the one holding this family together while you get wasted every night."

"Oh, Ann, it's not that bad. Alcohol barely affects me."

Ann's body surged with anger to the point that she thought her head might pop off, or blow smoke through her ears.

"Mom, you're a drunk! You're worse than Joe, and if Dad were here he wouldn't even bother to take care of your sorry ass because you're pathetic!"

Meredith froze.

Ann wanted it to sting. She wanted to hurt her mom like she'd been hurt.

Meredith stood like a statue with her back towards Ann. "I will never be like Joe," she said, resolute.

"Mom, you already are. Joe killed dad. Now you're killing us."

Meredith's face fell. Ann knew she'd struck a chord, but she was too pissed to care. She grabbed her jacket from the hall closet, and slammed the front door behind her.

Yappy dogs and burnin' onions.

Ann bolted down the street, charged with enough adrenaline to run a marathon. She covered four blocks before she was able to calm down.

Shit! She remembered that Jacob would be arriving anytime, and there was no way she was going back in that house right now. No. Way.

Mr. Gibbs' red brick house was two down from hers. If she stayed there, she'd see Jacob's car pull up. She jogged back and approached Mr. Gibbs' door, wondering what she would tell him. Before she could change her mind the door flung open.

"Ann. Hi."

"Uh. Hi."

"What can I help you with?" He had an inviting smile. She shifted on her feet and stared at the ground. She couldn't think of anything to say, except for maybe the truth.

"I got in a fight with my mom."

"Oh," he said. "Come in."

That was it. Easy. No questions. No prying into her personal life, and no worried looks that made Ann want to puke. Within minutes she was chopping vegetables in the kitchen. Her eyes burned as she hacked into the onion. She stepped back, blinking hard, and heard a yelp. A small, fluffy dog scrambled around her feet. She ignored it and went back to slicing. The fight with her mom replayed in her mind. Her stinging eyes watered with tears. She took in a cool breath and finished the onion. She stepped back and heard another yelp. *Deep breath.*

"You poor thing," Mrs. Gibbs handed Ann a towel to wipe her eyes. "I should have told you to cut the carrots." Ann wiped her eyes. "You can put the onions in the pot, I'm going to make the dumplings," Mrs. Gibbs said.

"Dumplings?" Ann asked.

"Yes we're making dumpling soup. You've never had it?"

Ann shook her head.

"It's an old family recipe of mine. I think you'll like it."

"Thanks, but I don't know if I'll be here for dinner."

"Oh?" Mr. Gibbs said.

"Yeah, uh, someone is coming to pick me up...at my house. But since I'm at your house, I've been keeping an eye on the road just in case they show up."

"Well what time are you expecting them?"

"I'm not sure."

"Well, if not today then some other time," he said as if it were a possibility. As if Ann would start having dinner with the Gibbses.

"Yeah. Definitely." Ann was feeling more at ease.

"Sit down, Ann," Mrs. Gibbs bustled through the kitchen. "Only the dumplings are left and I'll do those."

"Are you sure I can't help?" Ann asked.

Mrs. Gibbs wiped her hands on her apron. "You can get the eggs out and crack two of them into that glass bowl right there so I have them when I need them." Ann went to the fridge, more mindful of the dog running eager circles around her. She liked being here. It felt like what having grandparents might be like. Ann mom's parents had passed away already and she rarely saw her Dad's parents, who lived in Florida.

"So how is Thoreau?" Mr. Gibbs asked.

"Oh, it's good. I guess." Ann cracked an egg. "I haven't been able to read it straight through. I've kind of been jumping around." Ann thought about the last thing she read while hiding in the school bathroom. "Right now I'm reading where he's explaining this kind of ant war that he's observing. The black ants are against the red ones. It's...I don't know..."

"Go on," Mr. Gibbs encouraged.

Ann grabbed a spoon from a drawer and fished an eggshell out of the bowl. "It makes me wonder if there is someone out there sometimes observing us and watching people tear each other apart and, I don't know, never doing anything about it."

"Hmm, it's possible," Mr. Gibbs said. Ann wasn't sure if Mr. Gibbs was religious or not. "I remember that part. I thought it was fascinating how determined the red ants were, even though they were outsized by the black ants. Whatever they were fighting for, it must have really mattered to them."

"Or they were just ants and it was completely instinctual," Mrs. Gibbs said, smiling.

"Honey, we're trying to be philosophical here."

Mrs. Gibbs grinned ruefully. "Well, darling, I don't think the ants matter as much as it matters that Thoreau noticed the ants."

"Oh?" Mr. Gibbs said, raising his eyebrows at Ann.

"What do you mean?" Ann handed the bowl of eggs to Mrs. Gibbs.

"Well, most of us don't notice the small things in life. We're too busy running from one place to another, getting carried away by our thoughts, completely unaware of anything else going on outside us. But if you stop and really pay attention and presence yourself, you notice things you didn't before and you start to see your world differently."

"Can you tell my wife's a psychologist?" he asked.

Mrs. Gibbs chuckled.

Ann smiled, "I feel like my problem is that I'm always noticing the world outside of me." Ann felt the sudden sting of high school oppression.

"Wasn't it Thoreau who said, 'It's not what you look at that matters, it's what you see'? Mrs. Gibbs added.

Ann shrugged. It reminded her of something Danny had said to her the night they picked up Meredith—that her experiences gave her a different perspective from everyone else. He had hinted that in some way this unique perspective was somehow more valuable than if she'd never suffered through the things she had.

Ann pushed the memory into the shadows. She looked down at the dog that had been under her feet since she got there, pining for her affection. She didn't even know its name. "What do you call her?" Ann picked the dog up and set it on her lap.

"Oh, that's Maddie," Mrs. Gibbs stirred the soup.

Ann felt Maddie's fuzzy curls with her fingers as the dog relaxed in her arms. She glanced out the window and saw Jacob

Waters' car turn the corner. She jumped out of her seat and Maddie fell to the floor, landing with a yip.

"Sorry, I have to go," Ann raced towards the door, flung it open and dashed towards her house, turning back to see Mr. and Mrs. Gibbs staring at her, smiling and waving goodbye. It was storybook weird and Ann liked it. "I'll come visit again sometime," Ann called, knowing she meant it.

The Jacob Waters date.

Part 1: Pizza.

Ann's imaginings of how it would be when Jacob arrived didn't exactly turn out as planned. Big surprise. Ann caught Jacob just as he was about to ring the doorbell to her house. Out of breath and clumsily charging towards him in her Mary Jane shoes she must have been a fabulous sight. Luckily, Jacob didn't see because his back was turned to her.

"Jacob!"

He jumped back. "Shit, Ann, you startled me," he laughed.

"Sorry," she said, hiding her face behind her hair and feeling stupid. Jacob laughed.

"Where were you?" he asked.

"Oh, I was just over at Mr. Gibbs' house asking him about an assignment I have due in my English class. He isn't my teacher, but he was helping me and...yeah."

Ann was bad at lying, and tended to ramble whenever she tried it. Jacob laughed and Ann blushed, cursing her body for being against her.

"Well, you ready to go?"

"Sure," she said and followed him to the car. He opened the car door for her. She climbed in and waited for him to come around to the driver's side, latching her seatbelt in the meantime. Jacob got in, neglected to put his seatbelt on, and turned the car on. The speakers blasted a rap song, making her jump.

"Do you have any progressive rock?" Ann yelled over the music.

"Who's that?"

Ann shook her head and mouthed "never mind" as the car sped away. Ann quickly learned that although convertibles look cool and sexy that in reality they are the opposite. Her neatly combed hair instantly flew into a wicked snarl while stray strands clinged to her lip-gloss. It was getting cold outside and Ann had left her jacket at the Gibbs's house. Jacob tried to remedy this by blasting hot air at her, which sort of worked. By the end of the evening he put the top on the convertible and Ann was sublimely grateful.

He parked at a local pizza place that Ann had never been to before. Jacob rested his hand gently on the small of her back as he led her into the restaurant. There, the T.F.P. crowd waited, according to Lisa, to feed on the souls of the weak. Ann thought it might very well be true, but hoped for the best.

The interior walls of the dim restaurant were covered with graffiti and band posters. An old jukebox in the back played a combination of 70s and 80s rock bands. Ann spotted Krissy

Stevenson's hair and Greg Arbertson waving for them to come and sit. Jacob led her to the table and pulled out a chair for her. She looked at the floor, not ready to make eye contact with whoever was there. She prayed Grease-ball wouldn't be there. She didn't need to be called a lesbian tonight.

When Ann finally found the courage to look up, she saw that Singleton, unfortunately, was sitting at the table but was luckily on the other end. Maggie Shirvey was sitting next to Krissy and Greg. Pam Scavorski wasn't there, and there were several other seniors that she didn't recognize wearing letterman jackets. Jacob didn't introduce Ann to the group. Awkward. He sat across from Greg and they started talking about sports. Ann shrunk in her chair.

"Ann, it's good to see you."

Maggie Shirvey was speaking to her.

It's good to see me, huh? She thought. *Since you've been ignoring me in chemistry ever since I accidentally bleached your friend's sneakers. At least you got my name right.* "You too." What else was Ann going to say? *Thanks for ignoring me in chemistry even though I sit right behind you.*

"How's your brother?"

Oh. Here it comes, Ann thought.

"He's good. Busy. But good." *So busy he doesn't even bother having a relationship with his sister anymore.*

Maggie smiled and nodded. "You're brother was a good friend. I miss him."

I'm sure you do, Ann sneered. "Yeah, me too."

"Waters, you going to introduce me to your date?"

Ann blushed.

"Oh Terrell, this is little Annie Grey."

Little Annie Grey, Ann thought. *What am I? His baby sister?*

Ann held back the inevitable eye roll as Terrell reached his hand across the table to shake Ann's. She remembered Lisa's comment about the "token black side character" and stifled a laugh.

"Just call me Ann."

"Nice to meet you, Ann," Terrell said, smiling. He was handsome, like the rest of them. His dark brown eyes and soft smile put Ann at ease. She knew she needed to act confident or they wouldn't respect her. She tried to pull up some of the hatred she had for Danny, but couldn't seem to find it. She was too scared at the moment to be angry. But Singleton helped change that, as she overheard his grating voice at the other end of the table.

"Dude, that English test today totally raped me." He announced, Maggie squirmed in her seat, Arbertson laughed, and Ann threw up in her mouth.

"What did you just say?" Ann blurted. She quickly regretted it.

"Oh Miss Firecracker, lovely to see you."

Ann rolled her eyes. She didn't want to be seen as a total bitch, but apparently it had been working for her so far.

"Did you just use a serious crime against women to make a joke about how you're such an idiot you can't pass English?" Of course Ann didn't say this, even though she *really* wanted to. Instead, she plastered a smile on her face and told herself to chill out and have some fun. Bryce was just joking anyway, right? She needed to just relax.

"Dude, Bryce, you're such a dick sometimes," Terrell said, punching Bryce in the shoulder, Bryce laughed, but shut up. (Years later Bryce, er-hem, Brandy, would write a letter of apology to Ann, and reference this night in her letter).

Ann smiled at Terrell, grateful someone at least said something. He smiled back and quickly turned away as Jacob rubbed her shoulder and chills went down her spine. She suddenly forgot about Terrell, Bryce, the comment, how to breathe.

Ann hadn't really thought about the obvious until this moment: that Jacob may want something from her, like something physical. If this really was a date, was she going to end up like Pam Scavorski, crying in the bathroom a week from now? Ann wasn't going to let that happen. She was going to tell Jacob exactly where she stood so there wouldn't be any confusion. She just wasn't sure she had the courage to do it.

She wondered how she was able to completely chew out the super-hot-and-sexy Danny Feller, the guy that made her lips numb when she thought about him, but uttering a one syllable "no" to Jacob seemed terrifying?

Seriously.

I guess this was Ann's one chance to belong to something. Belong to a group, a clique, even if it was the T.F.P. crew, it didn't matter. Besides, these are William's people. Carefree, happy and ready for a good time, and that's all Ann wanted. A good time, where she could forget about her dead daddy and stupid mom and neglectful brother and blah, blah, blah.

ANN EASILY STAYED CONSUMED with her own thoughts since Jacob ignored her most of the night except for the occasional flirty touch. He was talking with the rest of the guys about the football game they were going to tonight. Ann eavesdropped on the conversation enough to learn that their intention for going was to get an idea of the home team's strategy because they were playing them next week. Ann rolled her eyes, thinking they were taking high school football a tad too serious.

The pizza arrived and Ann was starving. She didn't want to seem too eager, so she waited until everyone else had a slice before she began to reach over Jacob for one.

"Oh, I'm sorry, Babe, did you want a piece?" Jacob asked, turning towards Ann.

"Uh, yeah."

"Let me grab you one," he said, smiling as he grabbed Ann's plate. "What kind do you want?"

"Pepperoni."

"Okay, coming up," he said with a gorgeous smile. Ann smiled back as Jacob grabbed a piece of pizza and set the plate in front of her. "You don't mind that the guys and I are talking, do you?"

"No, not at all," Ann lied, though she told herself it was the truth. She thought if she had to talk to Jacob all night she'd eventually make a fool of herself, so being ignored was a pleasant alternative to possible humiliation. Jacob smiled and turned back to the guys. He didn't ignore Ann completely. He'd throw his arm around her shoulder, rub his hand on her back, and sometimes let his hand linger on her upper thigh. But he wasn't doing it in a "hey, I'm purposely touching your thigh" kind of way, it was more he just needed a place to rest his hand and her thigh happened to be open and available.

Ann's stomach spun with every casual touch. She thought eating pizza right then might not be such a good idea. She wasn't sure if it was normal for her to feel so sexually nervous around Jacob that the mere thought of kissing him made her want to hurl. But it did. For now, she wasn't going to think about it. Maybe she'd address the issue in the car on the way to the game. She'd tell Jacob what was up, and if he didn't like it, then she would vomit on his seat before leaving the car. That seemed fair.

Ann nibbled on her pizza and watched in astonishment at how

Maggie and Krissy ate. They didn't even take bites from the piece of pizza itself but instead tore off smaller pieces and took *even smaller* bites from them. Ann shook her head, wondering if they were going to excuse themselves later to barf in the bathroom. (String Bean, yes. Maggie, no.)

She eavesdropped on the triplet's (minus Pam) conversation.

"O*migod,* Maggie you would have loved this dress, I'm *so* getting it for winter formal."

"That's great. You'll have to show it to me."

"So do you know who you're asking?"

"To winter formal?" Maggie said somewhat surprised. " I don't really feel like going."

"What? No way. You have to be there or it will be super lame."

Maggie laughed. Ann hadn't realized before how different Maggie was from the rest of them. She seemed just as uncomfortable to be there as Ann was. Maybe Maggie and she were more alike then she had thought. Maybe this was what Mrs. Gibbs meant by noticing the small things.

"I'm sure you'll be fine without me, Krissy."

"No, I won't. Homecoming sucked without you. You have to come. You can go with Bryce."

Ann watched Maggie cringe but String Bean was too excited to notice. Ann laughed at the exchange and Maggie glanced over at her. Ann smiled at Maggie, thinking they could be friends. But Maggie didn't smile back. She instead glared at Ann as if she were going to break her in half.

Oh shit. Ann thought, losing the smile and becoming suddenly interested in her pizza. *Was Jacob the person Maggie wanted to take to winter formal?* Ann thought. *And here I am on a date with him and she hates me. Great.*

Ann was eager to leave after dinner. Jacob turned his attention back to her as he led her through the restaurant and out to the car. His touch made her shiver.

"Are you cold?"

"Uh."

"You are. Here take this..." Jacob draped his jacket over her shoulders, rubbing them in the process. "There, is that better?"

"Yeah, better," Ann said. Jacob opened the car door for her. She slid into the seat and tried to force herself to stop shivering now.

No wonder Jacob Waters was such a player, he was charming and a total gentlemen. And when he smiled... How was Ann expected not to swoon?

She wondered if this was why he had such a bad reputation. Maybe it wasn't his fault. Maybe girls were falling in love with him, and then feeling heartbroken when he wasn't as interested in them as they were in him. She still wanted to talk to him, and his being so sweet made Ann feel a little more at ease.

Once the car swerved onto the main road, Ann tried yelling over the music. "Jacob."

He turned down the music. "What's up?" He seemed harder, less charming, he wasn't smiling, and Ann began to lose her nerve. But what else was she going to say now she'd gotten his attention?

"You know I'm not Pam Scavorski?"

"What do you mean?"

"It means I'm not going to bat my eyelashes at you and be enamored with everything you say and give you whatever you want."

"I know. That's why I chose you."

"You *chose* me?"

"Yeah, because you're not like the other girls, you're different. A firecracker."

"Okay. So you do know that you're not getting into my pants

just because you took me out for pizza?"

"Ann, chill. Of course not. Who do you think I am?"

Ann rolled her eyes this time and made it obvious.

"Why are you rolling your eyes?" Apparently he was unaware of his own reputation. "Look," Jacob said, "if it makes you feel any better I promise not to get into your pants at all."

Ann looked at him, unconvinced.

"Ann, look, we don't have to do anything if you don't want to. Okay? Just relax and have some fun," he said, smiling and cranking up the volume on the stereo to signal the end of the conversation.

Fun huh? That's why Ann was doing this, right?

Ann figured what the hell and put her hand on top of his that was resting on her thigh, feeling insecure that her hands might feel too dry. But Jacob didn't seem to mind. As he interwove his fingers with hers, Ann suddenly felt that she was on fire. *Yes*, she thought, *this was what she was supposed to be feeling at fifteen: nervous, with your basic high school insecurities and raging hormones. Not depressed, angry, moody, and volatile.* Ann felt so normal it was weird and she loved it.

Part 2: Football.

Ann didn't know a thing about football. Sure she used to support her brother, but she never really paid attention to the game. She was usually too busy goofing off with Lisa to really care. It was hard not having Lisa there.

When they first arrived, before they could find a seat in the stands, three guys from the rival school threatened to "beat the shit out of them." Their chests were all puffed up like gorillas on the nature channel. Jacob and Bryce retaliated with their own slew of threats. It made Ann feel like they were in the wild. Finally the alpha male (principal) came and broke it up. He let Jacob and the group stay but told them they had to behave.

After all the hubbub and death threats that never escalated into anything other than a bustle of testosterone-inspired talk about how they could have totally "kicked their asses," it started to get boring. Ann sat between Terrell and Jacob and paid more attention to the cheerleaders than the game. All the bouncing and smiling and cheering rolled up into one pointless activity that involved short skirts. The whole cheerleading culture completely miffed Ann. In trying to understand it, she looked up the history of cheerleading once, only to discover it used to be an all-male activity in which they actually led the crowd in cheers.

Ann stared at the cheerleaders so long her vision blurred and she summed cheerleading into one word: frivolous. And she figured there was nothing wrong with frivolity except when it included Lisa, her bedroom wall, and a can of spray paint.

"What do you think of the game?" Terrell asked Ann.

"Oh, I don't really understand it."

"Really? With Will as an older brother?"

Ann blushed, feeling moronic. "Yeah, I went to his games, but I never paid attention."

"Well do you want me to explain it to you?"

"Uh, yeah, sure."

Terrell explained the game to Ann, who nodded and said "uh-huh" in all the right places, but truthfully didn't care about the game. She was just glad someone was talking to her.

After Terrell explained the game to her they left, not staying for the second half. Jacob placed his hand on Ann's lower back, so low actually, that it might be more accurate to say he placed his hand on her upper ass, as he led her to the car. His casual touch lit her body on fire. She liked it, but was having a hard time getting used to it.

"Later, Waters. See ya, Ann," Terrell called.

"See you in math, lesbian."

"Bryce, you really are a dick," Terrell said as he put Bryce in a headlock.

Everyone else murmured goodbye as Jacob helped Ann into the car.

The drive home was quiet. Well, other than the loud music that was rupturing Ann's eardrums. She made a mental note to wear earplugs next time.

Ann wasn't sure what to say, if anything. *Do I tell him I had a good time,* she thought, *or is that too lame? No it's too lame, I could just say thanks. Or maybe I shouldn't say anything and let him do the talking.* Jacob pulled up to Ann's house and turned the car off. Without thinking Ann lurched from the vehicle and to her front door. Jacob followed her.

"I had a good time tonight." Saying it out loud sounded even lamer then in her head.

"Good," Jacob said smiling as he began standing *really* close to Ann. She wished if he were going to kiss her that he would do it already, so she didn't have to stand there feeling self-conscious. Jacob wrapped his arms around her waist and pulled her closer; his lips were inches away from hers.

"Is this okay?" he asked.

Ann couldn't answer. She was thinking about her pizza breath. Jacob didn't wait for her to respond as his lips seized hers. Ann expected her whole body to start surging like it had with Danny, but for some reason, it didn't. She thought that maybe it was because she was too nervous kissing Jacob because he was like a teen god or something. (Really, she said "teen god." I'm not even going to comment.)

Their lips moved in sync with each other. Jacob with his lips wrapped around Ann's bottom lip, nibbling on it. Ann nibbled his top lip and he kissed her with more intensity. They kissed for a few minutes before Jacob pulled away.

"See ya at school tomorrow, Grey," he whispered in her ear.

"Uh, y-yeah okay," she stammered.

Jacob jogged to his car, not looking back as Ann stood on the porch, finding her composure. For the first time in a long time, Ann was looking forward to tomorrow.

Surviving being friends with the T.F.P. clique.

Ann thought going back to school after her father's death would be awful. She worried that everyone would look at her and see the girl with the dead father, but she discovered it could be worse: No one could look at her and nobody did. She thought there would be at least a few random sympathizers who'd approach her and say, "I'm sorry," even if she couldn't stand to hear it. She soon learned that if people were talking about her father's death, they weren't talking about it to her. One of the downsides of attending a big school, having a dead father wasn't enough to get attention.

What does get you attention in a big school? Going out on a date with Jacob Waters. Ann went to school the next day, expecting to be ignored by Jacob and the rest of the T.F.P. clique. She figured the weekend had wiped the slate clean and she'd go back to being nothing. To her surprise, Jacob approached her in the hall before the first bell and gave her a hug. She was getting acknowledged in Chem class now. She may not have been invited to the conversation, but Krissy and Maggie were at least saying hi to her. Ann went from invisible loser to exciting new girl. Members of the T.F.P. clan were saying hi to her in the halls. Most called her "Little Grey," but she didn't mind. She was having notable conversations with T.F.P. insiders, one being Krissy Stevenson. "Omigod, Ann can I totally say that I didn't want to even talk to you because of what Jacob did to Pam." Ann tried to figure out what that had to do with her, but nodded instead. "But you seem so sweet," Krissy rattled on. "And I'm totally excited to hang with you. Are you planning on going to winter formal?"

"Isn't it, like, in two months?"

"Yeah. You should definitely come."

Ann nodded and smiled, unsure of what to say beyond that.

Singleton also seemed to have had a change of heart in math. He chose to sit next to her, even though she was trying to sit away from him. Danny sat in the back left corner, ignoring her. (It was more like her ignoring him).

Bryce apologized for calling Ann a lesbian, stating, "Ya know I'm just kidding around, right?"

Ann wanted to say, "No, I just think you're being a self-centered prick," but didn't. Instead she took the peace offering, nodded and smiled. She was doing that a lot. Rather than the eye-rolling, it had become a wide-eyed unsure smile with a head nod. What else was she expected to do? She was in unexplored territory here. Completely out of her normal routine.

Jacob invited her out that next Friday and picked her up in his convertible. They went to a home football game where Terrell, Bryce, and the rest of the guys she didn't know yet were playing. Pam, Maggie, and Krissy were cheering. Only Ann, Jacob, and a few others were left watching the game together.

Jacob told Ann he was too old to play this year because he was nineteen. Not sure if that was a real excuse or a cop-out, Ann didn't ask why he had been held back. There were a slew of rumors ranging from his starting school late because he had a pants-wetting problem to his being expelled after he seduced a teacher. Ann figured they couldn't possibly be true and ignored the subject entirely. (I'd put my money on the bed-wetting rumor, but that's just me.) Ann didn't see Jacob as the jock type. Ya know, the kind that doesn't have a neck? Jacob definitely had a neck. That Ann gently kissed after the game in Jacob's car.

Later, she and Jacob met up with everyone at a friend's house. They were standing on the back porch when Ann texted Lisa to come over. Lisa said she couldn't, that she was busy. Ann rolled her eyes, hurt that Lisa was lying to her. She slipped her phone into her back pocket and Jacob extended a large plastic bottle filled with water and smoke. It took her a minute to realize it was a homemade bong.

Ann looked at it unsure.

"I already started it for you. Just take a long drag, get as much smoke in as you can, and hold it for as long as you can," Jacob instructed.

Without thinking Ann sucked the smoke into her lungs and held her breath. Her lungs shrieked as they caught fire, she exhaled the smoke with a hoarse cough and collapsed to the ground. "Am I already supposed to be feeling it?" Ann asked, her words spinning around her.

They all laughed. "This batch is strong," someone remarked.

"You gave her too much."

She wasn't sure if she was feeling it. All she knew was that her lungs and throat burned and she felt like her body was too heavy to lift. The emptiness expanded around her like a black hole sucking her into a cold universe.

"Guys, help her up," she heard a girl say. It sounded like Krissy, but she wasn't sure; everything sounded different.

A pair of strong arms carried her into the house and laid her on the couch.

"Don't close your eyes," Jacob said. "It makes it worse."

Ann peeled her eyelids open and Jacob was gone. She repositioned her body toward the voices. Minutes passed like hours. She saw Jacob playing a game of foosball with Bryce.

"It was like this the first time I smoked." Krissy stood over Ann. Her hair seemed bigger than usual. Ann feared if she didn't close her mouth that Krissy's hair would climb in it and strangle her.

Krissy sat next to Ann and ran her fake fingernails through her hair and scratched her scalp. Ann focused on the sensation as she stared blankly ahead and tried to forget her paranoia. She eventually closed her eyes and spun out into the universe. Krissy stayed next to her, but was a hundred miles away. Suddenly she found herself clinging to Jacob. He set her in his car and drove her home. The sharp wind against her face brought her back to earth.

Jacob pulled into her driveway. "Can you walk?"

She shook her head. "Everything feels so heavy, I can barely move."

Jacob helped her to the front door and kissed her goodnight. He opened the door for her and she crawled upstairs and into bed.

She awoke the next day feeling raw and sick. All she could think about was how gross she felt and how dry her mouth was, but reasoned it was better than thinking about Meredith and everything she'd lost. At least she was thinking about herself for once.

She adjusted to her new status seamlessly. She happily noted that she managed to enter and exit senior hallway completely unscathed. No elbow to the clavicle, no unfortunate kidnapping, not even a hazing, just mindless chatter while lost in a sea of muscled jocks and scented male body spray. She also ate lunch at the HEAD table, called this because it was the table at the north end of the cafeteria and it ran east to west while the smaller tables ran north to south in a sort of checker board pattern. The layout was ridiculous and nonsensical. But that's a different story, one involving Fran the jilted lunch lady in a love tryst with OCD Hall Monitor, Jackson, who appreciates long lines and cringes at disorder, and the front desk secretary, Bethany, who eventually won his love. But I digress.

Ann had been walking down the hall with Lisa ready to ditch and get lunch off campus, as they often did, when Jacob threw his arm around her and herded her into the cafeteria. She looked back and saw Lisa dart out the side door. Lisa wasn't there after school to give Ann a ride home. She called her and got her voicemail, and immediately started apologizing but knew it was no use. When Lisa gave someone the silent treatment, it meant she was categorically angry. The only thing Ann could do was give Lisa time to cool off.

She walked outside, regretting she didn't have the courage to ask Jacob for a ride. She didn't want to take the bus home, but it was her last option. She stepped around the school corner in time to see the buses leaving. *Shit.* She dreaded the idea of walking home but didn't have any other choice. She was on the verge of an internal meltdown when she heard "Need a ride?"

She turned around to see Danny jingling his keys. Humiliation aside, she did need a ride and if he was willing to offer...

She nodded her head and followed him to his car. She slid into the passenger's seat and remembered the familiarity of his car and the pleasing scent of faux leather seats.

"You've been avoiding me," he said.

She blanched. "No I haven't."

Danny looked at her, unconvinced.

She looked away, embarrassed. "Okay. Yeah, I have been... avoiding you."

One thing she loathed about being with Danny was how everything real came bubbling to the surface and could no longer be denied or ignored, only acknowledged. So many conflicting emotions bombarded her at once, pulling her in opposite directions. Sometimes it felt like her head was going to explode.

"Where are you going?" Ann asked when he pulled off Main Street onto a random side road.

"I want to take you somewhere."

Ann huffed.

Danny smiled ruefully. "Come on," he laughed, "It won't be that bad."

Ann said nothing as they rode the rest of the way, listening to the stereo. When Danny pulled into the park, that familiar knot in her stomach deepened its grip.

"I don't want to be here," she said shaking her head.

Danny took her hand in his, and she relaxed. "Trust me," he said. Ann took a breath but didn't move. Danny let go of her hand and got out of the car. He went around to her side, opened the door, and again extended his hand. "You're going to be okay," he assured her. She took his hand and he helped her out of the car and led her to a secluded area dense with trees.

"You used to come here with your dad?" Danny guessed by her

earlier reaction.

"Yeah," Ann said.

"I come here to…" Danny paused searching for the right word, "remember."

"Remember what?" Ann asked.

Danny shook his head. "I don't know. What's real, I guess. What's important to me. "

Ann tucked her hair behind her ears and muttered, "To know what's real."

" 'Be it life or death, we crave only reality,' " Danny said.

"Thoreau?" Ann guessed.

"From *Walden*."

"Why are you so into him?"

"I guess I understand him," Danny said. "What about you?"

Ann shrugged, "I don't know. My brother told me to read it. I guess I started to read it to try to understand my brother."

"Do you?"

She shook her head, "Not really."

"I know what we should do!" Danny said, squeezing Ann's hand and pulling her up the path.

"What?" Ann laughed.

"We should climb a tree."

Ann's eyebrows rose. "Really?"

"Yeah, I know a good one too. Don't worry, I'll help you."

Ann laughed. "I don't need your help, I know how to climb a tree. I just haven't done it since I was ten."

"Really? That's too bad." Danny commiserated. He led her to a tree with low-lying thick branches that were easy to climb. He guided her forward and helped her up. He placed his hands on her waist, and she remembered the feeling of his breath tickling the back of her neck and how her body grew hungry for his touch in a way it never did with Jacob. She tensed, nervous but excited.

"It's okay. I've got you," Danny whispered in her ear, misreading. Ann nervously grabbed the first branch above her head, secured her foot on a lower branch, and with Danny's hands secure on her hips, she pulled herself up. She didn't need Danny's help, but his hands didn't leave her waist until she'd reached the higher branch. She could still feel the warmth of where his hands had been touching her and she wondered if that's what was making her heart pound, or if it was the climb. Once she was settled on a high branch, he came up after her. They ascended as high as they could go before the branches grew thin and unstable.

When Danny reached the top, he was surprised to see Ann smiling at him. Not a wistful smile either; it was a genuinely euphoric smile. That was perhaps the moment Ann fell in love with Danny. Nothing monumental happened, the earth didn't shake, and lightning didn't strike. There was just a simple moment of raw emotion, unbridled and exposed to the daylight. She never said as much, but it was obvious in the way she looked at him. The emotion shone behind her silky blue eyes. Then a sudden panic crawled up her spine, making her shiver and she looked away. Her smile faded.

Whatever reasons people have, logical or not, to shut themselves off from love, Ann had hers. Her fear of loss consumed the details of her true feelings and morphed them into something unrecognizable that drew her away from all she loved and into the arms of Jacob Waters. Jacob was a carefree bohemian light to her, an escape and a breath of air under water. Danny was more like rain: beautiful, romantic, peaceful, but also capable of washing away the fiery exterior and leaving her drenched and exposed.

The park lost some of its light around five o'clock and that's when Danny decided to take her home. The drive back to her house was silent. What little she did say was polite, which made Danny suspicious.

"Did I do something wrong?" Danny asked.

"No." She fiddled with a small hole in the knee of her jeans. "Thanks for the ride and the visit to the park. It was nice."

Again, suspicious.

"I'm glad you came with me," he said.

Ann pulled at the small fibers in her jeans, making the hole in her knee unravel and grow bigger.

Danny pulled into the driveway and before the car was in park Ann reached for the door handle. Danny couldn't let her leave, not like this. He grabbed her hand, intertwining his fingers with hers. Startled, Ann looked at Danny's hand holding hers. His body was tense and his soft eyes had grown serious. When his eyes met hers, her heart pounded against her ribs as if trying to break free from its cage.

"Ann, I need to tell you something. "He licked his lips and hungrily stared at hers.

"Don't," she murmured.

Danny unbuckled his seatbelt. "Then I'll show you," he said launching over the stick shift and seizing Ann's lips with his. Ann grabbed the collar of his shirt to push him away but instead drew him closer. He cradled her face in his hands kissing her top lip then seizing her bottom lip and sucking gently. Her mouth opened in response with a soft moan and his tongue stroked hers, sending a tingling vibration through her body. He kissed her slowly, exploring her lips as he traced their plush curve with his tongue. Still cradling her face in his hands, he planted two soft kisses on her lips and pulled back just enough to see a sadness grow in her eyes, deeper then any sadness he'd ever seen. It made him want to kiss her again, but as he leaned in to touch her lips, Ann pushed him back. "What is it?" he asked. "Tell me what's wrong?"

Ann bit her lip. "I'm sorry," she said, pushing the car door open. She felt Danny's hands sliding off her as she stood. She told herself not to turn back as she entered the house, shaking.

The slamming of the front door behind her sent an ominous echo through the empty house. She made sure to lock the door as an anxious heat rose from her heart and constricted her airway. She tore off her jacket and t-shirt in an attempt to alleviate the heaviness from her chest. It didn't help. Dizzy, she turned on the air and stumbled towards the nearest vent in the living room. Dropping to her knees, she tried not to move as her heart thudded in her ears and her vision began to tunnel. She closed her eyes and focused on the sensation of the cool air hitting her face and tried to think of nothing else as her breathing slowed. Soon, her heart calmed and the heaviness lifted. She opened her eyes and the tunnel was gone. She slithered to the floor, exhausted.

She replayed the kiss in her mind. She knew it was a kiss she'd think about for years to come. Never had a kiss made her feel so safe and scared at the same time.

An exercise in sanity.

Most weekends hanging with the T.F.P. crew involved a casual party. At least twenty people showed up at various times of the evening. Some people had sex behind closed doors, or made out on the couch, and drinks and drugs were always available. Every weekend she invited Lisa, and Lisa declined. Ann tried again on the way home from school that Friday.

"I really wish you'd come to the kickback tonight," Ann had said, staring out the passenger window as the world swept by her. When Lisa didn't respond, Ann turned to see her laughing inaudibly. "What?" Ann asked.

"Honestly," Lisa shook her head, "I can't believe you're actually hanging out with them."

Ann rolled her eyes. "Why can't you just be happy for me."

"I'll be happy for you when it's real," Lisa said tersely.

Ann wasn't sure what she meant by that. She'd be happy when Ann's happiness was real or when her relationship was? Ann climbed out of Lisa's car without saying goodbye. She sulked to the door and up to her bedroom. She later emerged from her cave to eat and get ready for her date. Around eight o'clock she heard Jacob's honk in the driveway, and she was on her way out when she saw the door to her dad's office was open. Her heart pounded as she peered into the room.

When Ann's father died every room in the house was haunted by memories of him. After the funeral, Ann walked into his office half expecting to see him at his desk reading. Him squinting his face when he couldn't make out the words, then donning his glasses and opening his eyes wide to read. He used to call her Annie Babe: "Hey, Annie Babe what's up?" "Hey, Annie Babe, are there any boys at your school I need to take care of?" he'd say, flexing his biceps. Ann rolled her eyes. "No, Dad."

Those memories flitted away and turned into the dust covering the desk and bookshelves of her father's office.

She missed her dad, but not as much as she missed her mom. Her dad had worked a lot. He had used Meredith's inheritance to start a Thai food restaurant. Soon his restaurant had two locations, one in Glenwood and one in Cloverdale. When her father died, Meredith sold the businesses and made enough money from the sale and his life insurance policy to drink herself into an early grave.

Ann shuddered, feeling sick, before squaring her shoulders and shutting the door. She wished there was a way to lock it permanently.

"Tommy," Ann called. He appeared at the top of the stairs. "I'm going out. Call my cell if you need anything, okay?"

"Yep."

"Hey, were you in Dad's office?"

Tommy shrugged.

"Why?"

"I needed a stamp."

"What for?"

"To mail something."

Tommy walked away and shut his door. Jacob honked from the driveway again and Ann forgot everything else, plastered a smile on her face and headed out the door.

The gathering was at Pam's house this weekend. Her house was so big, with its indoor tennis court and three living rooms, that Ann's house could easily fit inside. After being there five minutes, Jacob offered Ann pot, this time from a bowl. She shook her head no.

"You gotta keep doing it and eventually it will start to feel good, and your body will adapt," he encouraged. It was the same thing her mom's yoga instructor had said to her once and her answer was the same both times.

"No, thanks." She grabbed a beer to show she was still participating.

She quickly drank the beer and discovered it had a very pleasing effect on her nerves. She started to feel more at ease and in the moment. She wanted the feeling to stay with her, so she grabbed another beer and drank it faster than she should have. The savory liquid coursed through her; she felt her body loosen as it hummed. Ann began to feel more comfortable at the party. Everything that had been weighing her down seemed to disappear. Her emotions dulled and she was able to presence herself in the moment. For a moment she wondered if this was why her mother drank. So she could numb the pain?

That's not why I'm doing it, Ann argued. *And even if I am, I'll never be like her.* On this, she was resolute.

HALLOWEEN CAME AND WENT. Ann hadn't even remembered it was Halloween until she answered a knock at the door and saw three munchkins dressed as princesses asking for candy. Ann cursed and the princess' parents glared and covered their children's ears. Ann knew of an old bag of candy left in the pantry. She threw it in a bowl and set it on the front porch. Then she turned out the lights so her house stood dark and vacant to deter future trick-or-treaters. At one point she thought she heard Danny Feller calling to her. She crept to her window and saw a shadowy figure walking down the street. She wasn't sure if it was him or not (it was) and she was glad he left (he was sad he didn't stay).

Finally, her life was turning around for her. The only frustrating thing was that she never knew when Jacob was going to call. She hated not knowing. She wondered if he ever hung out with other girls. He didn't say and it was obvious he didn't feel he owed her an explanation, and she was too afraid to ask. What if she questioned him and he dumped her? Her new status would abruptly end.

She sat in her English class listening to Mrs. Forchester drone on about deforestation and how all their essays would be handed in electronically from then on. Ann rolled her eyes as she sketched Mrs. Forchester's Sainthood and her own eventual doom.

She was beginning to remember why she wanted to hang with the T.F.P. crew in the first place. And it wasn't because she was jealous and hated them (although that was true), and it wasn't because she wanted to forget how much her life sucked (which was also true), but it was because they didn't seem to care. About anything. Well, at least not anything that mattered. The cheerleading sub-clique focused on dances and dresses and make-up, and the guys didn't seem to take anything seriously except football.

Morals weren't a big deal either, which seemed a strange relief. Although she was still a tad unsure by what Jacob had said to her on their first date, about not having sex, just having fun. But it was not like she was guarding her virginity or anything. She had been ready to give it up for Danny Feller. Impulsive, detention-delinquent Danny Feller, Jacob seemed like an upgrade from that. But Danny was undeniably sexy, which Lisa, bless her heart, continued to remind Ann of every time they were together.

AFTER SCHOOL ANN STOPPED by her locker. She didn't need to go there, but she hoped to run into Jacob before she went home. She pulled some books out and stuffed them in her backpack before heading over to senior hallway. Just as she was glancing down the hall in search of Jacob, she heard Danny's voice from behind.

"Ann, wait up," he called.

Ann sighed, turned around and smiled. "Hey," she said.

"Did you drop math?" he asked.

She nodded. "I'm too far behind to catch up, so, looks like summer school for me."

"I could help you," Danny offered.

"Help with what?" Jacob interrupted.

Ann cringed; she hadn't wanted to be seen talking to Danny, especially not by Jacob. "I'm failing math, he was offering to help," she explained. She turned her full attention to Jacob and hoped Danny would leave.

"So Friday night, Nikki's party, you're going to be there?" Jacob asked.

Ann nodded even though it sounded more like a command then a question.

"Yeah, we were talking," Danny interrupted.

"Well, I think you're done now." Jacob smiled and waved him off. "Bye."

"How 'bout you let me finish talking to Ann and then you guys can resume talking about your lame-ass party plans."

Jacob looked at Danny, agitated. Danny meant nothing to Jacob. That was made clear in one simple look. "Whatever," Jacob shrugged and laughed. "I got better things to do," he said, looking at Ann before turning to leave. With that one look, both Danny and Ann saw how little Jacob cared for her. How easy it would be for Jacob to throw her out once she became a nuisance and Danny's presence was making her into a nuisance.

Ann grabbed Jacob by the wrist, desperate to keep him. "Jacob, wait," she pleaded.

"Ann," Danny said, fuming.

"Please go," Ann said stepping between him and Jacob. Danny's eyes softened when he looked into hers. There was a momentary flash of pity in his expression before he spun on his heel and left.

"Sorry, about that," Ann said to Jacob.

"It's fine," he said curtly, pulling away from her.

"Can you pick me up for school tomorrow?" Ann wanted to pull Jacob back in, to know he was still interested in her. She thought this was the perfect excuse since Lisa was going out of town with her dad on another trip.

"Sure." He shrugged. "Later." He turned his back on her and walked away.

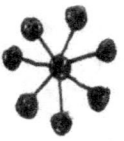

"WHY DID YOU CHOOSE BOY BAND JACOB over rock star musician Danny Feller?" Lisa said on their drive home from school. Ann was still reeling from the encounter in the hall. She hadn't told Lisa about it yet. She wasn't sure if she wanted to.

"Lisa, Danny rejected me. Besides, Danny is weird."

"Annie, you're weird."

"I'm not weird, and why did you call me Annie?"

Lisa's face fell. "Oh sorry, I forgot. Anyway ANN, you are weird and in total denial, which is kind of cute, but mostly EXAAAAASPERATING."

"Lisa, can I just be screwed up without you calling me weird and being a bitch to me?"

"Yeah," Lisa conceded with a weary sigh. "So how's hanging with your favorite Bryce Singleton?"

"Oh, he's pretty much leaving me alone now."

"Really?"

"Yeah, plus he's really into his football so he's not around when I'm with Jacob."

"He plays football, huh?"

"Yeah he's like the quarterback or something." Ann chuckled, thinking it was funny she didn't know or really care, even though everyone else in the T.F.P. crowd seemed to think it was a big deal.

"Grease-ball Singleton? Really? So is Maggie Shirvey preying on him like a piranha?"

"Why would Maggie be doing that?"

"Because she's head cheerleader, and he's like the star football player. It's like every teen girl's orgasmic fantasy."

"Seriously? You're being so stereotypical right now."

"I know. But it's fun."

"Maggie isn't even interested in Bryce. If anything he seems to make her uncomfortable."

"Playing hard to get."

"Can we not talk about them, it's irritating," Ann said.

"You're the one hanging out with them."

"Not because I don't invite you."

The silence fell between them and Lisa cranked up the music. Ann thought about how Maggie was still pleasant towards her, but always seemed to be giving her a weird look like she wanted to rip her hair out. Ann did her best to ignore it, rather than saying anything and having it turn into a hair-pulling cat fight in the hallway, which would likely never happen, but you never know.

"So are you hanging out with Jacob tonight?"

"No."

"Why not?"

Ann sighed with obvious irritation. "It's not like we hang out all the time. We've only been seeing each other for a few weeks."

"Right. Ya know if you wanted to get laid, I could have hooked you up with one of the guys from the drum line."

"This isn't about sex and I'm not into your sloppy seconds anyways."

"What? Drummers are hot."

"True," Ann said, slapping away the Danny-Feller-rock-star fantasy. Why did he say that in the hallway to Jacob? What was he thinking?

Lisa looked at Ann and managed a smile. Ann was glad they were at least getting along. Sort of. Even though they weren't hanging out as much because Lisa refused to be acculturated into the T.F.P. clique.

"You know, you probably shouldn't be having sex right now anyway. It's not like it's going to make life any easier," Lisa said.

"Yeah," Ann agreed, thinking she might not have a choice if she were going to keep hanging out with Jacob. Even though Jacob said they didn't have to do anything, Ann knew he wasn't satisfied with just making out. She never told me the details of their physical encounters (really, I don't need or want the imagery), but I can assume their kissing went beyond second base.

Lisa, having lost her virginity when she was fourteen to a drummer, and had only been with drummers since, also said it was a bad idea to get serious. Now was the time to just have fun without all the attachment. Ann saw her point, but also thought it was messed up. She wondered how you could not be attached to someone you were having sex with?

"Oh!" Lisa started. "So I'm walking down the hall today in between first and second and the second bell's already rung so I'm pretty much alone except for Mike."

"School-shooting-Mike?" Ann clarified.

"Yeah, and he's about fifteen feet ahead of me, he turns the corner at the end of junior hallway and I'm right behind him, but when I turn the corner, he's vanished." Lisa's eyes grow wide.

"So?" Ann said, "He probably went into his classroom."

Lisa scoffed. "Except for the fact that there are no classrooms at that end of the hallway, just lockers."

"And..." Ann already knew what was coming.

"And I think Mike's an alien," Lisa said.

"I've suspected him for awhile now," Ann admitted.

Lisa nodded, "Can I ask you a serious question?"

"Yeah."

"Why Jacob Waters? Really?"

"Because I'm pretty sure he's not an alien," Ann joked.

"Psht," Lisa gave Ann a disbelieving look, "that's what you think. But, seriously, why hang out with all of them? We've always made fun of them in the past."

Ann figured this question would come up at some point. "Honestly, I always made fun of them because you made fun of them, but, I don't know...those were William's friends, and I get tired of..." *being...nothing*. Those were the only words that came to her. But she couldn't say that to Lisa. So she searched for better words. "I just want to get out, ya know, party and have fun, meet people, not think about consequences, have mindless relationships...I don't know...ya know?"

"Um, okay? Guess I'll visit you in rehab." Lisa laughed at her own joke.

Ann wanted to tell her the truth, what she was *really* feeling, but didn't. She wondered if Lisa would understand, then decided it didn't matter. Ann wasn't even sure if she understood herself. She just knew that for now it made her happy, and that's all that mattered. Lisa pulled into the driveway and left the car running.

"Hey, don't you want to come in and hang out?" Ann asked.

"No. I'm helping my dad with some...um...cleaning so..."

"Okay. Well, I'll see you later." Ann paused with her hand on the door handle.

"What's up?" Lisa asked, sensing something was off.

Ann considered, "You know I'm not like Stacey what's-her-face from detention."

"Okay. Where did that come from?"

"I don't want you to think I'm hanging with Jacob because I'm a slut, or easy or whatever."

"You're worried I'm going to call you a slut?" Lisa asked, confused. "Do you think I'm a slut?"

"No, of course not." Ann said.

"Why do you think Stacey Milano's a slut?"

"Err. Isn't it obvious?" Ann asked. "She's always dressing provocatively and flirting with everyone. It's why she's always in detention."

"No it's not." Lisa said. "She gets detention because she smokes in the girls bathroom. She's just comfortable with her body, unlike you, who is always trying to hide everything."

"That's not why I dress like this," Ann argued.

"You dress like that because your older bother tells you to because he's not comfortable with your sexuality either."

Ann started rubbing her forehead. "Um, okay. How do you even know Stacey?" Ann wanted to change the subject.

"She tutored me in math. She's just got a smoking problem. She started when she was thirteen because both her parents smoke. She's tried to quit, but says it's really hard."

Ann suddenly felt sick. Like her world was slipping away from her.

"Why didn't you tell me you knew her?"

"It was after the accident," Lisa said, softly.

Ann bit the inside of her cheek. "You know you can still talk to me."

Lisa didn't say anything.

Ann sighed and climbed out of the car, slinging her backpack over her shoulder and slamming the door shut.

Ann entered her house and saw a dark haze coming from the kitchen. Her mom had taken to smoking inside the house more and more now. It stunk. Literally. Ann hated it. She rolled her eyes, dropped her backpack on the floor, and opened the windows in the living room, then entered the kitchen. She tried to forget about her conversation with Lisa as she looked in the fridge, not feeling hungry. Her mom sat at the counter looking dead. The Antabuse she was on lasted a week before she became violently ill and went off it. That worked like a charm.

"Hungry, Ann?"

"No I'm fine, I'll fix something for myself."

Meredith puffed on her cigarette. Ann opened the kitchen windows and obnoxiously sprayed an air freshener into the air around her mom, making it obvious she didn't want her smoking, especially not in the house. Ann also started coughing as she continued to saturate the smoke-filled air with lavender-smelling fragrance. Meredith finally took the hint and flicked her cigarette out the sliding glass door that Ann had previously opened to waft the smoke out of the kitchen. Then Meredith turned towards Ann and smiled pitifully.

"I love you," she said, hugging Ann. Ann awkwardly patted her mother on the back, but when her mother didn't let go, Ann's eyes grew hot with tears. She buried her face into her mother's shoulder and swallowed her tears. She was so angry with her mother, because she missed her. Missed this.

It had been so long since her mother had touched her. Too long. Meredith pulled away and not looking at Ann walked over to the staircase, up the stairs, and into her bedroom. Ann heard the door shut behind her.

Ann rubbed the tears from her eyes and ran to her room.

She was sick of not hearing from William. So, she determined to send a *real* e-mail this time. Telling him exactly what was up. Maybe then he would respond.

To: brother_who_abandoned_his_family@collegerules.com
From: desperate_sister@lifesucks.com
Subject: i hate you

okay, so i don't really hate you. but you have seriously been giving me the cold shoulder. i am sure you can understand, that although we haven't technically mentioned it to each other, life at the grey household sucks. mom tried to quit drinking, which worked until she began vomiting uncontrollably from whatever the doctor put her on. i think it's supposed to make you sick if you drink. so that was super special. that's why i'm angry with you. ever since you left for college you don't seem too interested in my life anymore, and i'm considering writing you off as a brother. so are you coming home for thanksgiving or what?

-ann

P.S. PLEASE COME!!!!!!!!!!!
P.S.S. i may lose my virginity to jacob waters. friend of yours, right?

Ann clicked "send," feeling pleased. If the badgering didn't get to William, the last line would, and Ann was counting on it. She stretched in her chair and heard a rap at the door.

"Come in, toad."

Tommy entered holding his skateboard. "I'm going skating."

"Not until you finish your homework."

Tommy sighed and rolled his eyes. "I already did."

"Then let me see it," she demanded.

Tommy walked away and came back a few moments later with homework in hand. Ann snatched it and gave it the once-over. "When did you do this?"

"When I got home."

"But you haven't been home very long."

"I know."

"And you finished your math homework already?" Ann glared at Tommy, she knew he was cheating.

"Yeah, Big A, I actually do my homework, not buy it off the Internet."

"The difference between you and me Tommy, is that I actually am smart and don't need to work at it." Ouch. That wasn't meant to sting like it did. She knew he didn't deserve it. Oddly enough he wasn't mad. His eyes simply softened.

"I'm not lying to you, Ann." He grabbed the skateboard he had propped against the doorframe and disappeared. Ann shook her head, feeling cruel. She wondered if Tommy was serious. Was he some sort of genius who whipped out math assignments and English papers without any effort? Doubtful. He had to be cheating. But so was she.

She wanted to apologize, and resolved she would as soon as he got home. For now, she had her own homework to attend to and she planned on doing it—by herself.

The imaginings of a
storybook dinner,
or something like that.

Ann was bored with her homework. She sat at her desk scribbling math equations and glancing over at *Walden*. She leaned back in her chair and sighed, rubbing her forehead before reaching for *Walden* and flipping through its pages. She hadn't finished the book yet. She had a hard time reading books from start to finish and had a tendency to jump around. It made it a little confusing, but she didn't care. *Walden* was already confusing to her. She stopped at a page with an underlined passage.

I never found a companion that was so companionable as

solitude. We are for the most part more lonely when we go abroad among men than when we stay in our chambers.

Ann thought, *Why would you feel lonelier among people, and why would William underline this passage? Is that why he never came home?* Ann racked her brain before throwing the book down and giving up.

Ann's experiences of solitude were like a haunting. Feelings became unwelcome guests and tormentors that she could neither see nor touch. She did her best to exorcise the loneliness before returning to her homework.

A couple of hours later, Tommy still hadn't returned and Ann was getting hungry and chilled. She went to grab a jacket from her closet and remembered the one she'd left at the Gibbs's house.

She decided to take a break from her studies and run over there to grab it. She knew it was lame, but she was also hoping to get dinner out of it. Dumpling something or other soup, or whatever they were having. She wasn't trying to be a food squatter or anything, she just thought it might be nice to hang out with them.

She grabbed a different jacket and headed out the door towards the Gibbs'. She thought about her storybook dinner with Mr. and Mrs. Gibbs, their laughing and being jovial. Her petting the stupid dog while it licked her face. Them having deep philosophical discussions about Thoreau over the damned finest home-cooked meal that Ann had had since the accident.

And of course that's the exact opposite of what happened.

Ann could have concluded that after the reality of her previous Jacob Waters fantasy. But, whatever. A girl can dream.

Things were going as planned when Mr. Gibbs answered the door and Ann mentioned that she had left her jacket there. Before Mr. Gibbs could retrieve it from the closet, Ann's stomach growled practically on cue, and Mr. Gibbs invited her to stay for dinner. The one thing that could ruin this perfect moment was Danny Feller. And before she got into the Gibbs's house, she spotted him and Tommy climbing out of Danny's car and moving toward her own house.

Damn that sexy *bastard.* (These were the exact words she used when later recounting this event to me. She said them with a mischievous smile. Although I'm sure, at the time, what she was really thinking was *BASTARD.*)

"Uh, excuse me Mr. Gibbs, there is an intruder at my house," she said.

Concerned, Mr. Gibbs trailed behind Ann as she stormed home.

"The new version of that game is ten times better..." Ann heard Tommy say as she grew closer. *Great,* Ann thought, *now they're like video game buddies or something?*

"Can I help you?" Ann blurted.

"Oh Ann, hey, I was just dropping Tommy off, thought I would come say hi."

"Why were you with Tommy?"

"I wasn't *with* Tommy, I was just giving him a lift. I saw him walking from the gas station where I was filling up."

"Oh. Thanks," Ann said.

"He did invite me in to play video games," Danny said.

Ann glared at Tommy.

"What? He can be my friend if I want," Tommy countered.

"Whatever, doesn't matter, I'm not going to be here anyway so, knock yourself out," Ann said, slapping Danny's arm. The touch was awkward and Ann stepped backward, embarrassed, as Danny smiled. Ann turned to leave and ran into Mr. Gibbs' arm.

"Oh, excuse me, Ann," Mr. Gibbs apologized. "Danny, how are you? I didn't know you knew Ann."

"Yeah, we're acquainted."

Ann ground her teeth. *Figures that stupid Danny would know Mr. Gibbs*, she thought.

"So, I was just inviting Ann over for dinner. You two boys are welcome to come."

Ann gave Mr. Gibbs that "don't do it" look, but then realized he wouldn't get it and would think she was being weird. So she quickly hid her face with her hair and grumbled when Danny and Tommy accepted the invitation.

So there was her storybook friggin dinner ruined by Danny freakin Feller. Sexy and mysterious don't mix with storybook. They mix with fatal attraction movies, *not* an evening of sanity with the Gibbs's perfect existence. Warm fuzzies out the window. Ann seethed as she sipped every last bit of the damned stew that Mrs. Gibbs prepared.

Stupid Danny Feller. Ann stewed on those words as if they were her personal mantra.

Then, of course, Danny went on and on about how wonderful the food was and how awesome the Gibbs were for inviting him over. His overt sweetness was making Ann nauseous.

Danny was there for one reason: to be with Ann. He was having a hard time stomaching her obvious resentment toward him. All he wanted was to be close to her, but every time he drew closer she pulled away. Every time he tried to make eye contact she ignored his gaze. He wasn't sorry for what he had done, not about stopping them from having sex, or standing up to Jacob. He knew he had done the right thing. If only he could make Ann understand.

The only thing that kept Ann's attention during dinner was the bowl of stew. She addressed Danny once. "Hey Fanny, do you think you could pass me the rolls?" Danny smiled and handed her one and Ann went back to ignoring him. Later, she shot him a glare when he started drumming his hands on the table, and he quit. Ann was glad when her empty dish clinked in the sink. She finally felt like she could excuse herself to leave and hoped that Tommy and his new lemming wouldn't follow.

But Danny did follow her home with Tommy on the pretense that they—he and Tommy—were going to play video games. But as soon as they returned home, Tommy made up some lame excuse of a school project he needed to finish before they could play video games. He said he'd be done with it in a jiffy.

Jiffy.

That was his exact wordage. And Ann and Danny were conveniently left alone in the sitting room.

Stupid Tommy, Ann thought.

"So are you going to stay mad at me?" Danny asked.

"I'm not mad," she lied. "I just don't want to talk right now."

Danny nodded and scooted closer to her on the couch. She didn't pull away this time; she got that familiar feeling of butterflies and numb knees that she always got with Danny.

"Ann, I'd like to say I don't get you. But I do. I get you so much. It irritates me what you're doing," he groaned, then sighed. "Still, I just want to be near you."

"Yeah it sure seemed like you wanted to be near me when you were shoving me off you."

"You're still mad about that?" Danny asked, reaching for her hand. She pulled away.

"It wasn't like that, Annie."

"Why did you just call me that?" she said, angry.

Danny held her gaze. "It wasn't like that. I just, this..." he motioned to the space in between them. "Whatever this is, is more than that."

Ann looked at him, confused.

"What I'm trying to say is I like you too much to have sex with you."

Ann rolled her eyes.

"To *just* have sex with you," he corrected. "And don't roll your eyes at me Ann, that's how I really feel," he said tersely.

Ann believed him. She clenched her jaw and gazed at the floor. The space between them seemed to melt together until it was gone. Ann's head felt racked with confusion. The heart palpitations and weak knees were returning. Danny Feller or Jacob Waters? She never thought she'd have to choose between the two. But was there really a choice? "It's too late," she murmured.

"Why? Because you're Jacob Waters' new toy?"

Ouch.

"Get out of my house," Ann said, jumping off the couch and marching to the door.

Danny followed. "Do you really think you and Jacob are going to last?"

"No. I don't," Ann said.

"Then why?" Danny asked.

"Because."

"Because why?"

"Ugh. Just go away." She opened the door. "I don't even get why you're interested in me. You don't even know me."

"I know you better than you think."

Ann scoffed. "How's that?"

"Because I pay attention."

"What the hell is that supposed to mean?"

"I notice you when you think no one's watching. When you don't have this hard shell up. When you're just Annie."

"Don't call me that! I'm not Annie!" She said pushing him out the door.

"Then who are you?" He stood his ground.

"It doesn't matter." She turned away, embarrassed that she'd lost her cool.

"Why does your name bother you so much?"

She turned to face him. "Are we really going to have this conversation on my doorstep?"

"Only because you're kicking me out."

"I don't want you here!"

"Fine."

"Fine."

Pause.

"But..." Danny started, "Tommy already invited me over to play video games. So..."

"Are you serious?" Ann looked into Danny's brown eyes and saw by his hard expression that he was *very* serious. "I don't care what Tommy said, you can't be here."

"Ann, just one game," Tommy pleaded, from behind her. "Please. I'll do my homework for real."

"I knew you were cheating."

Tommy rolled his eyes. "Let him stay, Ann."

Ann grumbled.

"I'll be out in a minute," Tommy assured Danny before disappearing into his room again.

Danny stepped inside and shut the door behind him.

Ann turned toward the staircase and figured she'd lock herself in her room and focus on finishing her homework. Danny grabbed her hand. "Can I just talk to you for a second?"

She looked into his beautiful eyes and forgot she was angry with him. "About what?" She took her hand back.

"Look, I..." He looked up at the ceiling, then down at the ground. "I..." he looked at her.

She raised her eyebrows. *Spit it out,* she thought.

"I used to be a jock."

Ann laughed, "What?"

"At my old school I was freshman playing Junior Varsity. I was having a tough time adjusting and I started hanging out with some seniors."

"Okay." Ann wondered where this was going.

"So, one night I'm at a party with them and this girl I know, she was kind of a friend, I guess, and she got drunk and passed out. And we thought it would be funny to..." He stammered.

God he was beautiful, Ann thought. "What?"

He took a breath, "We wrote stuff on her body, like, with permanent marker as a joke," he paused. "Except..." He closed his eyes mustering the strength. "Except she never woke up."

"She...?" Ann's eyebrows rose.

Danny nodded and bit his lip, ashamed. "We should have taken care of her...and her parents had to see her with everything written on her, and some people wrote some...pretty heinous stuff." He shook his head and walked away from Ann running his fingers through his hair. "Then two weeks later," he sighed and faced her, "I'm looking through pictures on my phone and I see this picture." He paused. "I don't even remember taking it. It's of April lying there passed out while Bobby *dickface* Lowrie draws a penis on her face." He turned away from her. "When I saw that I just smashed my phone into a million pieces."

"That's why you don't have a phone," Ann muttered. "I'm sorry." She didn't know what else to say.

He stood with his back to her. It was silent for a moment.

Danny turned to face her. "I'm not telling you this for you to feel bad; I have to live with what I did. I'm telling you this so you don't get hurt."

"What?" She took an unconscious step back. "You think that's going to happen to me?"

"Not that exactly, but something, yeah."

Ann shook her head and folded her arms. "Not all jocks are stereotypical frat-boy douchebags, you know."

"You're right, they're not. I just—"

"That was your old school, Danny. That's not Glenwood, and it's not Jacob, and it's not me."

Danny laughed, almost an angry laugh, as if he was mocking her for being senseless. In a way he was, but only because he cared for her.

Ann became defensive. She was seconds away from giving Danny an economy-sized piece of her mind when Meredith Grey, drunk and disorderly, came on the scene like a tornado, making sure to destroy everything in its path.

Stupid Meredith.

Remember Meredith's five stages of drunk? Well this was one Ann hadn't seen before. She wasn't desperate, laughing uncontrollably, acting like Audrey Hepburn, she wasn't even crying.

She was insane.

"What are you saying about me?" Meredith screamed as she arched over the staircase.

"Mom?" It was all Ann could muster in her shocked state.

"You think I don't hear you! You think I don't know what you're saying about me behind my back! I hear everything!"

"Mom," Tommy stood in the doorway to his room, "we weren't even talking about you."

"I can hear it, Tommy, I know what you think about me!"

Meredith clumsily descended the stairs. Tommy and Ann exchanged looks of horror. This was uncharted territory and neither knew what to do.

Ann wished Danny had left. She glanced at him out of the corner of her eye. He seemed to be as astonished as they were. It figures that on the night her mom decided to go completely mental she'd have an audience.

"Mom, let's talk about it upstairs. Not in front of our guest." Ann thought perhaps if she made Meredith aware that she had a spectator that she'd stop flaunting her crazy.

Wrong.

"Who the fuck is this?"

"Mom. Stop." Ann's voice was like a whimper.

"Why are you letting strangers into my house?!"

"Mom, he's a friend of Tommy's...and mine."

"You don't have any friends, Annie," Meredith started. "You're too busy being better than me. Thinking that I can't do this on my own. Well, you're wrong. I don't need you, Ann! You're pathetic. You. Are. Pathetic!" Meredith spat.

Ann stood stunned, avoiding Meredith's frozen glare. Meredith turned on her heel and skirted toward the kitchen. They heard her rummaging through the pantry. Ann wanted to stay strong but her heart began to crumble.

"Ann, you know she doesn't mean it." Tommy walked down the stairs.

"Yeah, I know, Tommy." It didn't matter whether Meredith meant it or not, Ann still felt it was true. "I just...I don't know what to do with her."

"I don't know if there is anything you can do," Danny chimed in.

"Is this your house? Your family? Were you invited to the

family meeting? No. So leave already." Ann never said this out loud, because she knew Danny was right. And even though it mortified her to have him there, it also comforted her. She wasn't alone.

An abrupt crashing echoed from the kitchen. They ran to find Meredith lying on the floor verging on unconsciousness with shattered glass strewn around her.

"Do you think she hit her head?" Ann asked.

"I don't know," Danny said.

Ann felt the back of her mom's head for swelling or blood. Meredith's eyes closed.

"I don't feel anything," Ann said.

"She'll be fine."

"Are you sure?" Tommy was worried.

"Yeah," Danny tried to reassure them. "My mom used to do this all the time." He hoped his own experience would make him an expert on the subject. He would have done anything to be able to wipe the pain and worry from their faces. "Let's just get her to her room," he suggested, bending over to scoop her up in his arms.

Danny carried Meredith to her bedroom while Ann and Tommy trailed behind. He laid her on the bed, propped her head with a pillow and covered her with a blanket. Ann watched amazed at how gentle and caring Danny was, as if it were his own mother he was tucking into bed and not some crazy drunk lady that he'd only met one other time.

"Thanks," Ann mumbled, trying not to cry as she shut the door to her mom's bedroom. Danny wrapped his arms around Ann, holding her close to his chest. Her eyes began to fill with tears. She hated crying. She told herself to pull it together.

"I'm sorry," Danny said. "I didn't know your mom was like this."

"She usually isn't," Ann managed to choke out. "I mean, she's usually drunk and unavailable but she's not mean like that."

Danny said nothing but held her close to him, not letting her move. Tommy excused himself to clean up the glass.

"Do you want me to stay?" Danny asked. "I'd like to stay," he quickly added.

No. Don't stay, she thought. The only thing worse than his not staying would be his staying. She was too vulnerable, too humiliated, and too fucking pathetic, just like her mom said.

"No. Go," she said, pulling away. "I appreciate your helping, but you should go. We'll be fine."

Danny reached down and kissed Ann on the forehead. She wasn't sure if this was real, or just Danny feeling sorry for her again. Either way it didn't matter. She was with Jacob, right?

Danny continued to hold her, not letting go. Ann told herself she was strong. She swallowed her tears and pulled away from him. He let her go. She couldn't look him in the eye. She knew she wasn't strong enough for that. She turned away from him and walked into her bedroom and shut the door behind her. Letting her legs collapse beneath her, she slid to the floor.

She heard Danny hesitate outside her door. After a minute he descended the stairs and said something to Tommy. Then after about ten minutes she heard him leave. A few tears escaped her eyes, but she was too exhausted to cry. A chill of loneliness tickled her spine. With all her defenses down, she wasn't able to hide from the feelings that plagued her.

She knew she had homework to do, but did it matter? She might fail, and not get into college, but if that happened, she would run away. She didn't care how she got out of the house, just as long as she did. But she knew she never would. She could never leave Tommy here alone.

Ann undressed as if in a conscious coma. She crawled to her bed, and sank her head in the pillow. She lay under a blanket of darkness with today's events on replay.

A while later she heard a light knock on the door. "Come in," she called and Tommy slid in.

"You okay?"

Ann sat up on her bed. "Yeah. I'm fine." It was a lie, but she wanted to stay strong for Tommy and appear unaffected.

Tommy stood staring at the floor.

"Do you want to talk about something?"

"No. Maybe later. I just—I love you, Ann."

"I love you too, Tommy."

Great. Tears again. But this time she didn't hide them. She reached out for Tommy and he sat on her bed as they embraced. At least she knew she'd always have Tommy. Even if her mom was crazy and her dad was dead and her older brother was gone, she'd always have Tommy.

Humiliation can make a person do strange things.

Ann woke on the wrong side of the bed the next morning. Perhaps it was the dream of the plane crash she'd had. It was full of twisted metal, fire, and dead bodies.

She was done feeling angry, hurt, and sad. She was done with Meredith. Done with waiting around for Jacob Waters to drop her. Done hating herself for being a bad friend to Lisa. Done with Danny Feller trying to fix her and feeling sorry for her. Done with hoping for a better life. In short, she'd given up completely.

She went through the motions that morning as she waited for Jacob to pick her up for school. He never showed. Luckily, she managed to catch the bus.

When Danny approached Ann in the hall she knew it was over between her and Danny. No sense in dragging this on and getting hurt later on.

"Hey, Ann, I wanted to talk to you about tonight. My band's playing a show and I thought maybe you could come see it?"

"I can't make it," she said.

"Why?"

"Because I have plans."

"Plans?"

"With Jacob."

"Oh right. Waters. So nothing's changed."

Ann shook her head.

"I was hoping..."

Ann looked away.

"I thought maybe Thoreau had inspired you to live your life to the fullest." He cringed after he said it. That wasn't what he'd wanted to say.

Ann sighed. "I am living my life to the fullest, just not with you." She wanted it to hurt. And it did.

Danny didn't have a smart remark or teasing comeback. Ann could see that he'd given up. Finally. His shoulders fell, his head sank down. "I'm sorry," he said.

"For what?" Ann shot back.

He shook his head. "For thinking you were someone else." Then he looked up at Ann, smiled just a little, and grabbed her hand. Ann didn't pull away this time. "Well, my dearest Annie Grey, I hope you find what you're looking for." He kissed the back of her hand.

Of course he would do something like that, she thought.

But now was *not* the time for one of her fantasies. In fact, she'd decided she was altogether done with being a dreamer of any sort.

"Why do you keep calling me Annie?" She took her hand back from Danny's grasp.

"Because you are an Annie, and I'm not going to keep calling you something you're not."

Ann stood there a little confused as Danny turned his back and walked away. He didn't look back at her. Her eyes followed him down the hall, until he got lost in a sea of faces.

She felt nothing.

"Hey, Babe."

Ann jumped, startled by Jacob's sudden presence. She smiled. So what if he forgot to pick her up this morning? He was there now, and she convinced herself that that was enough.

"Hey, I won't be able to take you home after school since I need to figure out a way to get some alcohol for tonight's party."

"You were supposed to pick me up, not take me home."

"Oops." He laughed.

She smiled and relaxed. Maybe Jacob did like her after all. He hadn't forgotten her, just misunderstood her. She started to feel better and was looking forward to tonight.

"Hey, I can bring some liquor that we have at home," Ann offered.

"Serious? That would be awesome, your parents won't notice?"

"No," she lied. "They don't drink often." She wasn't sure why she was saying 'they' as if she still had two parents.

"Great, Babe," he said, hugging her. "I'll pick you up at eight, okay?"

" 'Kay. Text me on your way?"

"Yep." He turned to walk away. Ann turned the other way towards her class when Terrell stopped her.

"Hi," she said, looking at him, confused as to why he was blocking her path.

"Hey. Can we talk?" His gaze was intense.

"Sure," Ann said, feeling uneasy. She liked Terrell the most out of the group, but he was acting strange.

Terrell glanced around the once crowded hallway, now thinning as students entered their classrooms. "Ann..." he said, shaking his head as he searched for the right words.

Ann waited, her eyebrows lifted.

"You need to be careful with Jacob. He's not exactly..."

"Reputable?" Ann said, finishing his sentence.

"Safe, was the word I was looking for," Terrell finished.

Ann looked at him, confused. Terrell looked over Ann's shoulder. She followed his gaze to Maggie. *Oh*, she thought, *this is Maggie's last-ditch effort to steal my boyfriend. Wow.* "I'll keep that in mind," Ann said, closing off.

"Ann, seriously," Terrell said pulling her back in with his intensity. "Call me anytime, night or day, if you ever need anything."

"Okay," Ann conceded.

Terrell nodded and walked away. Just as Ann thought it was safe to go to class she was, again, bombarded.

"Omigod, we are going to have so much fun tonight! You're not wearing that to the party are you?" Ann tried smiling at Krissy, and then glanced down at her outfit. She was wearing a baby blue tee that brought out her eyes, and a pair of black pants. Krissy was wearing an olive green short-skirt and white tank with a cardigan. *She looked cute, but really? It's school*, Ann thought. She didn't see anything wrong with her own outfit but replied. "I guess not."

"Let's totally go to the mall after school today and get new clothes! It will be so much fun. I have been dying to go shopping."

"Okay," Ann hesitated. She wondered if she and Krissy were to become friends if she could still call her String Bean behind her back. Either way, Ann figured it would be a good idea to get some new clothes. She would just have to make sure she swiped her mother's credit card before heading to the mall.

"Great. I'll see you after school then."

Ann nodded and then had a better idea.

"Hey, how about we ditch fourth period. That way we can avoid the crowds."

"Fabulous idea. Meet me in the girl's bathroom by senior hallway before the fourth period bell and we will totally ditch. It will be awesome."

Ann smiled and nodded as she waited for Krissy to leave. Once again, Ann had weaseled out of gym class. She savored these small accomplishments.

AFTER THIRD PERIOD, Ann hid out in the bathroom as planned. The fourth period bell rang and still Krissy hadn't shown up. She waited five more minutes, before realizing that they could be waiting in different bathrooms. There were two girls' bathrooms at either end of senior hallway.

Ann peeked her head out of the door. The hall was empty. She began walking to the other bathroom when she heard a banging. It was coming from the maintenance closet. She wondered if someone had been stuffed in there by a senior and now couldn't get out. She cautiously walked to the door. The pounding didn't sound like a cry for help but more a plea for sanity.

Ann reached for the doorknob, but before her hand could clasp the cold metal the door swung out and open, smacking Ann's hand.

Startled, she took a step back, holding her hand to her chest. Her eyes glanced up to see Mike.

Yeah.

As in school-shooting Mike.

As in likely-to-be-an-alien Mike.

Ann averted her eyes and her legs froze in place.

"Did I hurt you?" Mike asked with genuine concern.

Ann didn't speak.

"Sorry," he muttered and walked away.

Ann's eyes followed him. She watched as he slid his shaky hands into his pockets. A wadded piece of paper fell from one of his jean pockets. Ann waited for him to round the corner before she picked it off the floor.

The paper crinkled as she opened it. The handwriting was difficult to make out. She began reading.

The hole in my heart burns my chest,
Leaving nothing behind but your duress.
The blackened chars that once held light,
The person I once was now lies in the ashes.
How do I forgive and forget?
How do I move on from here?

The words shook Ann to the core. She knew the feeling.

She tucked the note into her pocket with the intent of keeping it. She never mentioned it to anyone. Except me, of course.

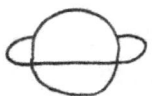

ANN MET KRISSY in the *other* bathroom as planned. They sneaked out to Krissy's car, careful to avoid being caught by Mr. Jackson. The last thing Ann wanted was to have to talk to *Bob*.

She wasn't a big shopper. She used to love shopping with Lisa before the accident, but then food became more important than clothes and most of her shopping trips were to the grocery store. Now she was painfully behind the times in fashion, which Krissy lovingly pointed out to Ann as she began throwing hanger after hanger of clothes into Ann's arms for her to try on.

After the millionth outfit in the seventh store, Ann wanted to hide under a rock. She was used to being insecure, but Krissy took it to a new level. *"Does my butt look big in this?"* Krissy asked. *"Do my boobs look okay? Does this color make my skin look weird? Do these shoes make my feet look big? Should I get a spray tan? Do these pants make me look like I have cankles?"* By the end of it, Ann decided to skip the plastic surgery and go straight for a lobotomy.

Ann didn't care anymore what she was wearing for the party so long as the torture ended. She bought whatever Krissy put on the counter for her and handed over her mom's credit card that she'd swiped on her way to the mall. She glanced at the clock behind the counter and saw it was after six. Her stomach grumbled. That might explain partly why her mood had turned sour.

Ann talked Krissy into stopping at the food court before they left so she could get a slice of pizza. Krissy conceded, but swore she wasn't hungry herself.

Ann's stomach growled as they approached the food court. The smells wafted to her nose and she was ready to devour the first thing in sight. She entered with her handful of sacks and glanced around for a pizza place.

Out of the corner of her eye she saw a couple making out. *Ugh.*

She thought. *Save it for later.* She was about to make a snide remark to Krissy before she remembered that she and Greg were the masters of sucking face in public.

Then something hit Ann in the deepest pit of her stomach like a bowling ball being slung into her bowels: as the couple parted, she recognized one of the instigators.

Lisa.

Betrayal #1.

Ann's feet carried her to the table across the food court as Krissy dawdled behind, clicking her heals against the hard flooring. Ann didn't know what to say to Lisa. "How's the business trip going?" "Who are you sucking face with?" Or a simple "What the hell?"

"Hi!" was all she could muster.

Lisa looked stunned for a moment and then quickly regained her composure.

"Geez, Ann, did you and String Bean clear out the mall?" Lisa was referring to the caseloads of bags that Ann and Krissy were hauling.

Krissy didn't seem to notice that String Bean was referring to her. She just smiled at Lisa like this was some sort of game.

"Why are you being like this?" Ann asked.

"Ann, why do you care? You've got the life you've always wanted and you don't need me anymore."

"Lisa, you're my best friend. Why would you think that? I have wanted you to be a part of all of this with me."

"But I can't follow you around, Ann, I've got my own life."

"So I see," Ann said looking at the unidentified guest sitting next to Lisa. She didn't recognize him from school. "Why didn't you just tell me?"

"Because you were so...pathetic...I couldn't. I didn't want to hurt you."

"Pathetic?" There was that word again. Falling from the lips of her best friend. "You know what I mean," Lisa back-pedaled once she saw Ann's pained expression.

"Apparently, I don't," Ann spat. Her pain turned to anger.

"You couldn't see anything that was going on outside of you. You only see you and how much you hate your life now that it's not perfect anymore," Lisa charged.

Kay. True, Ann thought. "Why didn't you just tell me?"

"How could you not have noticed?" Lisa said, incensed.

"Oh, I'm supposed to read your mind now?"

"Look, maybe I didn't tell you, but we've been friends for a long time and...it's not like there weren't plenty of signs. You just stopped paying attention. I mean, one day I told you that I had to go home to help my dad clean."

"And that's supposed to be code for 'I'm ditching you to hang out with some guy.'"

"No, It's just that you didn't even question it. I mean, Ann, you know that we have a cleaning service. We used to steal their cleaning supplies just to be funny."

Lisa was right. She also knew Lisa hated going on business trips with her dad. But instead of asking her about it, she just

214

assumed Lisa hated Ann. Ann made everything about her. She stopped noticing Lisa.

But what had Lisa expected? Ann's dad died, her life was falling apart. Did Lisa want Ann to trace Lisa's every move so that Ann could know Lisa was hiding something from her? It was bullshit.

"Look, I'm going to Nikki's party tonight with Jacob. If you want to still be friends with me, bring your boyfriend and meet me there. We can hang out, with our boyfriends together, like friends do. If not, I'll assume it's over and you can go live whatever life you want to."

"Ann, really?" Lisa looked confused. Like she wasn't getting the test. Yes, this was a test. Whether Lisa was going to show up and be a friend to Ann, or continue to keep secrets and ditch her. The choice was hers. Ann said nothing more. She just shook her head, rolled her eyes, and walked away.

She walked away.

With three bags of clothes she hated.

A pseudo-friend with big hair.

An aching stomach.

An aching heart.

No food.

No Lisa.

Betrayal #2. Life is pain.

When Krissy dropped Ann off it was already seven o'clock. Ann chucked her infinite quantity of clothes on her bed. She had an hour before Jacob would get there. In the meantime she needed to replace her mom's credit card, slip into what she was now calling her new "skank" clothes, and acquire large quantities of alcohol.

Luckily Krissy already picked out the outfit Ann would be wearing tonight, so that was one less thing she needed to think about. Stealing her mom's liquor supply might be a tad more difficult.

Wasn't this fun, fun, fun?

Ann would check in with Tommy first. Make sure he had something to do tonight and let him know she wasn't going to be home till late. Ann never went into Tommy's room but figured she'd check there first before looking in the backyard for him.

He wasn't in his room, but his textbook was spread open on his desk. *Maybe he's been doing his homework,* she thought as she slid the rest of the way into his room and approached his messy workstation. On his desk she saw a flip notebook that had a small stick figure cartoon drawn on the bottom page. She flipped the pages with her thumb and saw the images move together. She watched as the stick figure leapt from a bicycle to a skateboard, flipped upside down and landed on his head, which broke off. She flipped the booklet around and watched as the stick figure fumbled to find his head and instead accidentally stepped on it, smashing it into a bloody inky mess.

Ann smirked. *Typical Tommy*, she thought. She tossed the book down and saw his textbook splayed out on his desk with math equations scribbled on his notebook. The equations looked like they were beyond junior high math. In fact they looked like they were beyond the kind of math Ann was studying. Ann wasn't sure what to make of it.

She knew she shouldn't be snooping, but she figured it was harmless. It's not like Tommy had anything to hide. She saw a letter stuffed under some papers. Ann slid it out from underneath them; it was addressed to her mom.

Dear Mrs. Grey,

We are pleased to let you know that Thomas tested in the exceptional range in his math and verbal reasoning skills in our talent search and testing program through John Hopkins University. Due to your son's exceptional abilities we are accepting him into our Center for Talented Youth program beginning next term.

The letter went on. It requested an acceptance letter and a down payment for the residence.

What was this? Ann thought it might be a joke. Something that Tommy had made up to...to what? Get back at their mother? Threaten her with moving away to some school for kids with special talents?

"What are you doing in my room?"

Ann gaped at Tommy, still holding the letter.

"What is this?" She held up the letter

Tommy groaned.

"Tommy you aren't even good at math. You cheat. Do they know you're a cheater?"

"I'm not a cheater, Ann."

"Then why were you failing math last term? Did you actually think that mom was going to fall for this?"

Tommy stayed silent and stared at the floor.

"Answer me!"

"You don't want the answer, Annie."

She cringed. "Tell me what this letter is?"

Tommy sighed. "Look Ann, I am good at math. The reason I failed last semester was because they *thought* I was cheating."

"You were cheating!"

"Do you want to hear the truth or not?" Tommy yelled and chucked his skateboard to the floor.

Ann jumped back, startled.

"I wasn't cheating, okay!" Tommy glared at Ann to gauge her reaction. She stayed quiet. "I hate school, Ann. I hate it. I see the answer in my head and they want me to write out some stupid equation to prove that I'm actually doing the work. That's why they thought I was cheating. Because I could get to the answer without the equation."

Ann held her breath. *Could this be true?*

"Finally, my teacher this semester believed me. Believed that maybe I was just bored, that maybe I was smart. So she had me tested."

"But, Mom..."

"I forged her signature," Tommy explained.

Ann paused to digest. "Okay, so you're gifted. Whatever. Now you're leaving?"

"No."

"But this letter."

"Yeah, that school's in Baltimore."

Oh, she thought. *He would have to leave me. It would be Meredith and me. Alone.*

"You're staying?"

"Look, we both want to get out of here. I hate Mom, I hate William for leaving, and I hate school. But I'm not going to leave you."

Leave me? This whole time she had been watching out for Tommy, she never thought Tommy had been watching out for her. No wonder he kept pushing Danny on her. So she wouldn't be alone.

Arf.

Ann couldn't look at Tommy. He looked so serious. Old. Adult. He was only thirteen. Almost fourteen. He was just a kid. When had he grown up? And how had Ann missed it?

"How could I not have known?" she said, mostly to herself.

"I'm not mad at you, Ann. I'm grateful that you've done what you've done for me," Tommy said.

Ann dropped the letter and rubbed her eyes. This was too surreal for her. She felt so foolish. First Lisa and now Tommy. Last night she had thought she would always have Tommy, no matter what, and now he was slipping away from her. The only reason Tommy was sticking around was because he felt sorry for her.

"Leave, Tommy. Go to your gifted school and have a nice life," she said, pushing past him. He called after her and she slammed her bedroom door and locked it. She knew she had no right to be so livid. She didn't want Tommy to leave but she didn't want him sticking around ruining his life because she was pathetic and couldn't take care of herself. Besides, she could take care of herself. She didn't need William or Danny or Lisa and especially not Tommy looking after her. She wasn't a child.

She shook her anger off with a grunt and shoved everything else from her mind. She had a party to get ready for.

When life gives you lemons, smash them in the face of the nearest victim.

Ann had asked Jacob to text her before he showed up at her house so she'd be ready. She knew by now that whatever time Jacob said he would be there wasn't always the time he was going to show up.

She was just slipping into the outfit of Krissy's choice, a black strapless cocktail dress, when she heard a car pull into her driveway.

Great. She thought. *Guess he forgot to text me when he was on his way.*

Ann remembered the plane crash dream from last night. She never did look up the foreboding omen (overcoming obstacles and a lack in self confidence), and Ann ironically assumed that the rest of the day was going to be stellar, as it had already exceeded her expectations of greatness!

Ann sifted through the piles of clothes and plastic shopping bags on her bed for her phone and called Jacob's cell. He answered on the third ring. Ann figured he couldn't hear the phone ring over the music he was playing loud enough for it to feel there was a concert happening in her driveway.

"Hello?"

"Hey, I see that you're in my driveway," she said, her voice cracking a little as she choked on tears from her encounter with Tommy.

"That is very observant of you."

"Well." She hesitated, wondering if she should bitch him out for not texting her, like he had said. "I'll be out in a second," she relented.

" 'Kay. Hurry up." He didn't bother to ask if she was okay. Or apologize for not texting her. Instead, he acted like he was annoyed with her.

Whatever, she thought.

She pulled on the rest of her outfit, applied lots of makeup, also compliments of Krissy, and did her hair in a quick up-do that Krissy had coached her on earlier. She stashed some money, her phone, and lip-gloss in her bra (yep, all fit). Then she remembered the promise she had made to Jacob about the liquor.

The good stash was kept in her mom's closet. Her mom didn't think she knew where it was. But Ann had discovered it one day while grabbing her mother's pajamas to help her change after she had puked on herself.

Ann wondered if she should deliberately barge into the room and grab the alcohol in a show of dramatic mutiny or be more covert about it. She quickly realized she needn't do either as her mom was in the shower.

Good for her. Ann thought. *She was starting to stink.*

Ann stuffed her backpack with bottles. When that was full, she grabbed two more, one for each hand. And there was still some to spare for Meredith's binge later. Geez, this woman could drink.

Before Ann ran out to meet Jacob, smuggling her contraband, she caught a glimpse of herself in the bathroom mirror. She stepped inside and flipped the light on. For a second she almost didn't recognize herself. She looked good. Not that she didn't before, it was just different. She admitted that dressing up like this was more fun than she thought it would be. For the first time in her life she felt sexy. She thanked Krissy for the new clothes and decided she was done being the sad girl. Tonight she was going to have fun.

Her new high-heeled shoes clanked against the tile in the entryway as she carried her loot.

"What are you doing?" Tommy asked. Ann hesitated for a moment. But she didn't turn to look or even respond, she just left.

Ann hurried to the car and slid inside. Jacob gave Ann a hungry look when he saw her, looking her up and down. She briefly worried he may get the wrong idea about the dress and think she was wearing it because she wanted something from him and not because she simply liked wearing it. "Damn, girl," Jacob finally said. "You clean up good." She knew he meant it as a compliment, but the way he said it bugged her.

She wore a ski cap for the drive, since it was getting colder now, with Thanksgiving around the corner. Plus she didn't need her new up-do to be wrangled in a snarl by the time they reached the party. Jacob gave a bit of a disapproving look when he saw the cap.

Whatever, Ann thought. Why he insisted on driving with the top down despite it almost being winter was beyond her. He also didn't thank her when he saw the excessive amount of hard liquor she was packing. He was being an ass.

Finally his car pulled up to the house and he turned toward her and smiled. "Ready for this?" and charming Jacob was back.

THE ALCOHOL TOOK AFFECT on Ann's senses faster than she had anticipated. What the hell had she been drinking? She knew it wasn't beer, but it looked like lemonade except there was a bite to it that shivered down her throat. *Fuck it,* she thought. I deserve this.

She continued to drink, hoping that maybe if she got drunk enough she would be able to figure out the answer to world hunger or global warming. Yes. She could feel herself getting smarter. Then she could feel the world tilting a little to the left, and consequently forgot about global warming.

Music was going and the lights were dim. Bodies were vibrating together while others lounged on the sofas talking, smoking pot and exchanging pills. Ann no longer remembered whose house she was at. Nor was she curious as to why there were so many unfamiliar faces.

She stopped caring.

Ann learned that night that she also had several stages of drunk. The first was mere apathy accompanied with a general feeling of self-loathing, hatred of life, and wanting to give up. This initiated the drinking. Shortly after the grandiose thinking stage, she fell into the next stage of incessant giggling in which *everything* was funny. When her hair came undone? Funny. When the heel of her shoe broke off while she was drunkenly prancing? Funnier. When she chucked her broken shoe across the room and hit Bryce Singleton in the head? Downright hilarious. (Oh, how Bryce loved those heels!)

This was followed by the need to be the life of the party. She joined the vibrating bodies and began throwing herself around like a whip. But there were too many bodies and not enough room, so she climbed on a table and danced until she danced herself right off the table and on top of the vibrating bodies.

She wasn't sure if she hit the ground or not. Her body didn't hurt. Usually this kind of behavior would have embarrassed her, but since she was feeling smarter, it didn't bother her an iota.

"Ann are you okay?" she heard someone say.

"How much has she had to drink?" someone else asked.

"I should take her home." Another female voice said that sounded like Maggie. Of course Maggie would want her to go home. Maggie hated her and wanted her gone so she could make a pass at Jacob.

Then entered Ann's next stage of drunkenness. "Get the fuck off of me, Maggie. I don't need your sympathy."

"Ann, you're drunk. Let's go." Maggie grabbed Ann's arm and she jerked it away.

"Maggie, do you see how pathetic you are? Do you think I can't see the way you look at Jacob, and how he doesn't look back? You want to know why? It's because he's with me now, Maggie. Me!"

Maggie tensed but brushed off the remark. "Please Ann, trust me. I need to get you home."

"I don't have a home!" Ann screamed.

And then she vomited.

THE LAST OF THE VOMIT made it into the toilet. She wasn't sure how long she had been there, or how long she had been partying. She couldn't think about that now. All she could think about was the fact that she felt like she was going to die. This didn't feel like the projectile vomiting she had had when she got drunk with Lisa. She didn't know the meaning of projectile vomiting until this night.

She hugged the toilet seat, knowing she had nothing left to puke, but still feeling the urge. She sat there for a while, willing herself to be sober. Her hair had come partially undone and fell into the toilet bowl water and puke. Ann wondered where her so-called boyfriend was. Obviously not present to hold her hair back while she barfed.

Ann pulled herself up to the sink, turned on the faucet, and rinsed her hair under the cool running water. When she thought she had gotten it all out, she steadied herself against the counter.

She told herself she was with Jacob because he was the light and Danny was the rain. She saw the truth now. Jacob wasn't the light, the Bohemian, carefree light. Jacob simply didn't care. About her, or anyone. And sure, Krissy was a lot nicer than she had thought, but she would prefer *not* to pal around with her as her best friend. And Danny...

Fuck, she thought.

Ann looked up and remembered the familiar list she'd made only weeks earlier about the cheerleading sub-clique in chemistry class while gazing at String Bean's yellow hair nest. *Annoying, self-absorbed, stupid hair, fake, pathetic.* The words swirled through her thoughts, except this time she wasn't staring at the back of Krissy Stevenson's head, she was looking in the mirror. Hours before she'd felt sexy, confident, new. Now she looked as if that perfect self she had tried to create was melting off her to expose an ugly truth behind it.

Who had she become in just a few short weeks? Everything she thought she had always wanted. And now? It felt more hollow and empty than anything ever had. Ann couldn't understand how she had changed so much. Not just in the last few weeks, but in the last year. She knew she could never go back to the innocent, happy girl she once was; all she could do was move forward.

An internal switch flipped and Ann saw herself for the first time. *Really* saw herself, with all the complex layers of her emotions, the great wall of protection, the pretending, the denial and the façade. She knew she couldn't live like this anymore. This was the end. The realization was simple and devastating at the same time.

The answer to her problems was easy, but she'd made so many mistakes, and hurt so many people getting to this point. What if Lisa didn't want her friendship back? What if Tommy never forgave her? What if Danny was finished with her?

As much as she wanted to unleash her self-loathing, she knew she couldn't continue to hate herself for the mistakes she had made. She had lived, she had learned, she was done with it. She would rather embrace the pain of her former reality than run from it and create this new world of pain. That's what Thoreau had been telling her. What Danny had been telling her, but she hadn't got it until now. No regrets. She was moving on. Now she just needed to get out of this place, right now and for good.

If I could kill one person...

"There you are, Babe. I was just coming to check on you."

The hot/cold thing with Jacob was getting old. Ann seriously doubted he was coming to check on her, since he had been standing at the top of the stairway flirting with some blonde Barbie she didn't recognize.

"I want to go home," Ann said. *I want you to get me out of here. I want to apologize to Tommy and to Lisa and I want you to take me home, now!*

"What?" He said pretending not to hear her over the music.

"Take me home, Jacob."

"What?" He said again, acting like he couldn't hear her before ushering her to a nearby bedroom, and shutting the door.

"Sorry I couldn't hear you very well," Jacob said. "The music was too loud. I thought we could talk."

Ann folded her arms. Talk? Did Jacob think she was an airheaded bimbo? That she didn't know that "talk" was code for sex. Ann still felt dizzy and worried she might pass out before she could get home. She had to get out of there. She marched toward the door.

"Hey, wait up, you're drunk, you shouldn't leave." Jacob grabbed her arm and pulled her toward him. "Babe, tell me what's going on?"

Ann didn't want to explain, but Jacob deserved at least that much.

"Jacob, I don't want to be with you anymore."

His eyebrows furrowed. "You're dumping me?" he said in disbelief.

Ann slowly nodded.

Jacob laughed.

"What?" Ann asked.

Jacob said nothing, but laughed even harder. Ann rolled her eyes and went to leave. Jacob grabbed her forcefully by the arm and pulled her back. When she tried to protest, he covered her lips with his hand.

"My little firecracker," Jacob said. His demeanor had quickly changed. He removed his hand and plunged his lips onto hers. She tried to pull away, or push him off her, but he had her pinned against the wall with his body weight. Her head hurt as it pushed into the wall. He held her there, hands clenched tightly around her arms, his body pushing and rubbing against hers.

Ann knew she had to get away from him, but he was so strong. She bit his lip that was pressed against hers and he pulled back seemingly unaffected even though she could taste his blood in her mouth. He pushed her against the wall harder and her head hit, making her feel dizzier.

Then Jacob flung her on the bed, pressing his body against hers, pulling down her top, and rubbing her breasts. He covered her mouth with his hand when she tried to scream. His other hand pushed her skirt up and then he unzipped his pants.

Ann heard banging on the door.

Please help, she cried inside.

"Jacob, are you in there?"

It was Maggie.

"Jacob!"

She yelled, banging on the door. It must be locked. Jacob ripped off Ann's underwear. She tried to scream, flail around, pull his hair, hit him, knee him in the groin. Anything. But she was so dizzy and he was so strong, and she felt so helpless. All she could think about was how stupid she was for drinking, and getting involved with Jacob in the first place. She knew better. And this was all her fucking fault.

It wasn't true! If I could have been there I would have yelled, "It's not your fault, Ann!" I would have told her how amazing she is, and I would have beat Waters into a wheelchair.

"Ann! Are you in there?" She heard Maggie call before the door burst open and Jacob was pulled off Ann. Shaken, she scrambled to the head of the bed, as Terrell pounded his fist into Jacob's skull.

Maggie went to Ann. "Are you okay?"

Ann grabbed the back of her pounding head, on the verge of tears. Maggie pulled Ann's top over her exposed breasts and grabbed her now shredded panties, which clung to her left thigh. Terrell beat Jacob till he was moaning and unmoving. Then he threw his letterman jacket over Ann's shoulders and escorted her out of the party and to his car.

Ann heard a few people ask, "What the hell happened?" But Terrell and Maggie ignored them and kept walking on either side of Ann, arms around her, protecting her until they scooted her into the back seat of the car.

"Ann did he rape you?" Maggie asked.

"No," Ann croaked. Then she lost control at last. The tears came pouring out of her like a broken faucet. Her whole body trembled as she sobbed. Maggie held onto Ann as they sat in the back seat of the car and Terrell drove away from the party.

"Where are we going, Maggie?" Terrell asked from the front seat. Maggie didn't answer right away and Ann jumped in to answer through her sobs.

"Cloverdale. I need to go to Cloverdale.

Secret spies and other surprises.

Ann gained enough control of her crying to give Terrell directions to Uncle Joe's house. He was the only person left she could turn to right now. She hoped he would be home. The ride didn't take long. Terrell parked in the driveway and Ann leaped from the car.

All the lights in the house were off. She banged on the front door. She wanted to wake him if he was asleep. No answer. Ann banged on the door again, choking on her tears, faintly aware of Maggie and Terrell behind her.

Ann worried that Joe might not be home and started crying. He might not even live there anymore. What if she had to go back home?

The porch light turned on and the door crept open. Joe stood with his sandy blonde hair in a messy mop, just like her father's.

"Annie?" He rubbed his eyes.

Sobbing, Ann flung herself into Joe's arms. He held her tight, "What is it? What's wrong?" He looked to Ann for answers. She just shook her head. He invited them in and helped Ann to the couch.

"What happened?" Joe said addressing the question to Maggie and Terrell this time.

"She was..." Terrell started, then looked to Maggie for help

"...sexually assaulted, tonight, at a party. She asked us to bring her here." Maggie finished.

"Oh my god. Are you okay?" He looked at Ann.

She cried and clung tighter to him.

Joe looked at Maggie and Terrell. "Thank you. I guess you don't have to stay, unless Annie wants you to." Joe's soft hazel eyes seemed torn and confused. He didn't know what was best for Ann.

"I called Will," Terrell responded.

When did Terrell *call William?* Ann thought. She didn't even know they were friends.

"He said he is on his way, I texted him that we were coming here. He said he would be here soon, maybe an hour or so."

"Good, good," Joe said, hugging Ann to his chest.

The heaviness of Ann's emotions weighted her to the couch. As she sunk deeper into the cushions, she didn't noticed Terrell turning to leave. She heard Maggie tell Terrell that she was going to stay, even before she had checked to see if that was okay. Joe must have nodded his head, because she didn't hear him say anything. She heard the front door shut and Maggie sat on the couch across from them.

Ann wondered why Maggie, the girl who always looked at Ann like she wanted to scratch her eyes out, would stay. But she couldn't wonder about that now. She could only gasp for air as her lungs threatened to collapse. Her world crumbled into rubble and ash. Joe held her tight as everything inside her savagely ripped apart. She cried for her dad and Meredith and Lisa and Tommy. And. And.

ANN DIDN'T REMEMBER FALLING ASLEEP, but remembered faintly waking when someone scooted a pillow under her head and draped a blanket over her body as she lay curled up on the couch. There was a dim light coming from the kitchen and she heard voices.

"You knew he was dangerous and you didn't say anything?" Joe said, trying to whisper as his anger grew.

"That's why I called Terrell. I wasn't sure." Ann heard William say. Her heart leaped when she heard his voice. She tried to peel her eyelids open, but exhaustion paralyzed her.

"It's my fault. I should have said something," Ann heard Maggie say before it got quiet and Ann was asleep again.

Ann awoke a little later to a hand on her face. She wanted to say something, but was so sleepy she couldn't will herself to respond.

"Thanks for watching out for her, Danny," she heard William say from across the room.

"I care about her," she heard Danny respond, hovering over her.

Ann later admitted that if she had been slightly more awake she would have assumed that William had formed a spy patrol to watch out for her. But because she was only marginally awake, she just felt warm, comfortable, and safe as she fell back asleep.

ANN FINALLY WOKE feeling as if her head was splitting in two. She wasn't sure if that was from the drinking or from her head being bashed into the wall by dickhole earlier.

She grabbed her head, willing the splitting to stop, making sure the two halves of her brain weren't going to literally tear apart.

"There's aspirin there for you," Ann heard Joe say from the kitchen adjacent to the living room.

"Thanks," she said, noticing how dry her mouth felt. She grabbed the white pills on the table and swallowed them with a gulp of water from the glass that Joe handed her.

"How are you feeling?"

"Like shit."

Joe nodded.

"Is William here?"

"Yeah. He and Maggie are curled up on my bed asleep."

Oh right. Ann thought. She assumed Maggie was using Ann to get to her brother. *Nice tactic,* she thought.

But Maggie had saved her from...Ann forced the memory from her mind, just feeling grateful that nothing more had happened.

"Was anyone else here?" Ann asked, wondering if her memory of Danny was a pleasant hallucination or an even more pleasant reality.

"Yeah. Your friend Danny stopped by to see you. I guess

Tommy let him know you were here. He had to leave."

"How did Tommy know I was here?"

"I called your home, to speak with Meredith, I thought she would be worried that you hadn't come home."

Ann rolled her eyes. Meredith didn't notice.

"And you talked to Tommy?"

"Yeah."

"What did he say?"

"Just that, um. Well, he tried to cover for your mom. But I could tell something was up. He was refusing to put her on the phone. And then finally, he told me. I'm so sorry Annie. If I had known, I never would have stayed away."

"So you've been staying away on purpose?"

"Only at your mother's request. But if I had known she wasn't taking care of you...you know I would have been there."

Ann stayed quiet. She focused on the throbbing and the splitting and the tightening of her chest.

"Annie, I'm so sorry, about your dad. You have to know that I never..."

"It's not your fault, Uncle Joe. Yeah, you were the reason he was out that night...but..." *just because he was out picking up your sorry drunk ass from a bar because your wife left you doesn't mean a driver hitting his car was your doing...*

"I quit drinking. I want you to know that," Uncle Joe said.

Ann nodded. She didn't need his apologies or explanations. Yeah he'd been a screw-up sometimes, but he was always good to Ann and she never had blamed him for anything. That was all Meredith's doing.

"I've been in AA for the past year. I've been stuck on step nine." He rubbed his forehead. "I've been writing letters, thinking I might mail them to you, all of you, someday, but..."

"It's okay," Ann said shaking her head. She didn't need to hear any more.

William entered the room. "Annie."

Ann sprang from the couch and wrapped her arms around William. "William you asshole," she said, burying her head into his chest. She wasn't expecting those to be the first words to come out of her mouth. Maybe "it's good to see you" and save the name-calling for later.

William didn't seem to mind. He just laughed and said, "I know" as he held her. "I'm so sorry, Annie."

Ann pulled away, "Why didn't..." She didn't know where to begin. *Why didn't you call, return my e-mails, warn me about Jacob or let me know that you had a set of spies looking after me?*

"Mom asked me to stay away."

"Why would Mom do that?"

"She said it would be too hard for you having me around, she said a bunch of other bullshit too," he said running his fingers through his hair. "The real reason is that I reminded her of Dad, and she didn't want me around. So I just..."

"Gave up on us?"

"I'm sorry."

Ann didn't want to fight with him, at least not now. She hadn't seen him in almost a year. Nevertheless it slipped out. "I cannot believe you are using that as an excuse! You could have at least called or responded to my e-mails, or something."

"I know. I know. I've been an asshole. I'm not denying it. I just was confused. I didn't know what to do so I just tried to ignore everything. Dive into my life at college, ya know?"

Ann rolled her eyes.

"But once, again, as I said. Me. Asshole. I know. No more excuses. I'm going to stop being an asshole."

Ann hugged him again, willing him to shut up now. She'd heard enough and was glad she had her brother back.

Thoreau is the shit.

After dropping Maggie off, Ann asked William to swing by Lisa's house. William asked why and Ann told him everything: how she had stopped paying attention to Lisa's needs because she was too focused on her own.

"It's funny that you recommended I read Thoreau," Ann said, "because what he was telling me was exactly what I needed to hear, but still I wasn't paying attention. I read every underlined passage of yours, hoping to understand why you left," she admitted.

"I really am sorry, Annie."

"I didn't bring it up so you'd apologize again," she said.

He cleared his throat. "Ya know, it's interesting that you did that, with *Walden*, because I did the same thing, except I was trying to find Dad."

"What do you mean?" Ann asked.

"That was Dad's book, those passages were things he underlined, not me. When he died, I realized I hardly knew him. So, when I found *Walden* in his office, I read it, hoping to understand him better, I guess."

Ann nodded and smiled. It wasn't just William she had found, she also found her dad. She realized that he'd been with her all along, even when she'd sealed him off and refused to talk about him. And Danny... had he really shown up last night, after everything?

"Did Danny show up last night? Do you know him? And what's with you and Maggie? And why did Terrell have your number?"

The barrage of questions took William aback. "Well." He cleared his throat. "First off I, uh, I didn't think you were serious when you sent me that e-mail about Jacob. But then I called Maggie just to be sure, because I knew Maggie knew what Jacob was capable of."

"What do you mean Maggie knew what Jacob was capable of? I thought she hated me because she wanted to hook up with him."

William scoffed. "Maggie hates Jacob Waters."

Ann looked surprised. "Why?"

"Look, if I tell you, you can't mention this to anyone. All right?"

"All right."

"Well, when I was a junior, and Jacob and Maggie were sophomores she and Jacob sort of hooked up, they were dating. Maggie and I were really good friends by this point and one night she came over in the middle of the night and told me Jacob did something to her. She was bawling, and she didn't really say what it was, but I just figured maybe things had gotten hot and heavy and out of hand and now Maggie was feeling guilty about it and..."

"And?"

"Well, I guess he...raped her."

"Oh," Ann said, alarmed. No wonder Maggie had been giving her disapproving looks. It was because she was worried about her. *Why didn't she just say something?* Ann wondered. Then again, would Ann have believed her? Could she blame her for not wanting to talk about it?

"Wait, what do you mean 'you guess'?" Ann said accusatorially.

"Well, I didn't really believe her when she told me. Jacob might be a little cocky and have a certain spark with the ladies."

"Is that how you describe man-whores?"

"You know what I mean. I just didn't believe that Jacob would do something like that. I just figured she felt guilty or something...I know, I know," he said, waving his hand in surrender. "I was being an asshole, I've been on a streak of assholiness for awhile now, I get it."

Ann laughed, which seemed odd since her insides felt like they were on the outside.

"Are you okay?" Will glanced her way.

"I honestly don't know," she said, studying her hands. "I feel like shit, but I also feel...." What was the word? Peace? It sounded so trite, but did it matter? It was true. "I'm sad...angry—mostly at myself—but grateful. It could have been much worse."

William heaved a sigh of disappointment.

"You were there for me," she reassured him.

"Not like I should have been."

She smiled. "Yeah, okay, I'll let you feel bad about that."

He looked at her.

She laughed again, wiping a few tears from her eyes. "Assholiness, huh? I like that. It's like your holiness, except it's in honor of your being a total ass."

William smiled, but she wasn't going to get a laugh out of him. She wiped away the tears that refused to stop pouring. She didn't understand how she could cry and laugh at the same time. It felt so inappropriate to laugh, but it was either that or collapse into a puddle of tears.

"So did Maggie tell anyone else, or report it or..."

"No. She didn't know what to do. Figured no one would believe her. So she just did nothing. And now there's really nothing she can do. It's her word against his."

"That's awful." Her hand moved to her stomach where a deep pit of sadness, twisted rage, and revulsion seemed to settle. "How can she stand to be around him?"

"Well, she kind of disappeared last year, but no one knew why, except me."

"Disappeared? How? She's head cheerleader?"

"She just said she was always busy with something. Had an excuse for everything. Why she couldn't hang out or go to lunch with us."

"Wow," Ann said, trying to fathom how hard it must have been for her. "So did you apologize to her?"

"Yeah."

"Did you grovel?"

"Sort of."

"Not good enough," Ann said. William nodded in agreement. "Actually...I kind of feel like everything that happened with Jacob was my fault," Ann continued. "I was so stupid to drink and dress like this. I knew he had a reputation."

"Ann," William said through clenched teeth. "I've been to a lot of parties with girls dressed like that and never once had an inkling to rape one of them."

"I know," Ann sighed. "But I knew Jacob had a reputation."

"Yeah, as a serial dater. Not a serial rapist."

Ann cringed. "I guess," she said, unconvinced.

William swerved to the side of the road and slammed on the brakes. Ann lurched forward, alarmed. "What are you doing?" William snapped the parking brake into place and looked at Ann, fuming.

Her only thought was, *I know. Look at everything I've done wrong.*

"I could kill him."

"William." Ann said calmly, trying to snap him out the rage that suddenly engrossed him. A rage that had been inside him all along that he could no longer contain.

"This is not your fault, Ann. This is not your fault. I need you to understand that."

Ann wanted to believe him, especially since he was saying it with such intensity, but she didn't. Tears spilled from her eyes and William unlatched his seatbelt and reached over to hug her. She nuzzled her head into his shoulder and cried. The tears felt good this time, bringing a wash of relief.

"I'm so sorry," he whispered in her ear.

"It's not your fault," she choked.

"It's not yours, either."

ANN DIDN'T KNOW HOW LONG WILLIAM HELD HER while she cried. She just knew, that after awhile, the tears stopped and she pulled away. William offered her some napkins he had in his glove compartment to wipe her face.

"I'm coming home on the weekends. I can't commute to class everyday. But it would be easy to come home for the weekends and that way I can screen the guys you're dating."

Ann rolled her eyes, secretly happy with the thought of having an overprotective brother around. But there was only one person Ann wanted to be dating and she hoped it wasn't too late.

WILLIAM'S CAR PULLED INTO THE DRIVEWAY of Lisa's two-story home and Ann was *so* ready to grovel. She stood on the doorstep reciting what she might say before she rang the doorbell.

After a minute the door opened. "What happened to you? You look like shit."

Lisa always did have a way with words.

"We can talk about that later." She didn't want to get Lisa's friendship back out of pity. "I just came over to say that I'm really sorry that I've been such a self-absorbed bitch."

"Wow. Nicely put."

"Yeah. I stood on your doorstep for five minutes thinking about the perfect words."

"They were perfect." Lisa smiled. "So. Is that it?"

"Well, yeah, I figure that would pretty much sum it up." Ann worried this wasn't going to work.

"And it did," Lisa reassured.

"So, friends?"

"Are you still hanging out with the cheerleading trio?"

Ann considered. "Yeah."

"Okay. Friends." Lisa nodded. "And I'm sorry too. I should have just talked to you."

"Thanks." Ann smiled.

"Are you okay?" Lisa stepped closer and put her hand to Ann's cheek. "Your eyes are all puffy. You look like you've been crying."

"I have." Ann nodded. "It was only a matter of time until I started feeling something."

Lisa nodded, she understood. Of course she did. "Is that William in the car?" Lisa waved.

"Yeah," Ann said, smiling.

"Good. Someone else that can put up with your shit." She smiled. "I'm just kidding. Come here and give me a hug." She pulled Ann into her. "Call me later?"

Ann pulled away, wiping away tears and nodding.

Lisa smiled and winked.

Before Ann left she asked Lisa what she was doing for Thanksgiving break in two weeks.

"I dunno."

"Well, I'll call you. Let's hang, okay?"

" 'Kay, as long as you explain to me why you're dressed like that."

Ann made a face.

"It's not bad." Lisa defended, throwing her hands up. "You look super hot. It's just different is all I'm saying."

Ann laughed,"Thanks. We have a lot to talk about," she assured her.

ANN LEFT LISA'S FEELING LIKE A WEIGHT had finally lifted from her shoulders, but there was still more to do, and more to know. She got the rest of the story about Danny and Terrell from William on the drive home. Apparently, after William called Maggie and apologized, he asked Terrell to keep an eye on Ann. Then last night when Ann was plastered, Terrell overhead Jacob say that tonight was going to be his night with Ann. So Terrell called William.

William also swore that he'd never met Danny before last night, and the fact that it had sounded like they were talking like old friends was just a coincidence.

When they approached the Grey house, William opted to stay in the car. Not ready to face Meredith. Ann's body started buzzing and she considered what she might say to her mother, but first, there was more groveling to do.

The final confrontation.

Before Ann could even get to the front door, Tommy opened it and flung himself at her. Grabbing hold of her shoulders. "Are you okay?"

"Yeah. I'm okay," she managed to say.

She felt so guilty. She had been awful to Tommy and he didn't even care. He was only worried about her. Looking out for her.

"Tommy, we need to talk."

"Why, what's wrong?" he said, pulling away. He didn't look like the grown-up he had yesterday. He looked like a frightened child.

"Nothing's wrong, I just need to talk to you. To apologize."

"Ann, you don't have to say anything."

"No, Tommy. I can't do this anymore," she said, stepping back from him and turning away to gather the strength she needed.

"Tommy, I want you to go. I'll hate your guts if you don't," she said, crying. Damn tears. She didn't think Tommy would take her seriously if she were crying. So she looked away. She heard a sniffle from behind her. Tommy was crying too. "You're a good sister, Ann." He hugged her.

Ann didn't care if she was crying anymore; she let go and so did Tommy. Finally they were completely open, sobbing in each other's arms. Neither was alone and they knew they never would be.

"Thanks for looking after me, Tommy."

"Thanks for looking after me, Annie."

He called her Annie and for the first time in a long time, she didn't mind.

AFTER TOMMY AND ANN'S FRONT PORCH SOB SESSION, Tommy went to see William, who was still hiding in the car. Ann was humming as she entered the house. She determined that Meredith was not downstairs, so she snaked her way up the stairs to her mom's bedroom. The door was open and her mom was sitting at her vanity. Ann hesitantly stepped inside and Meredith spun around to face her. "Did you steal my liquor?" Meredith spat. Her hair was a nappy snarl and she was still in her pajamas. She had clearly been drunk last night and probably didn't even know about what had happened with Ann.

Ann bit her lip and drew a deep breath of courage while Meredith's eyes burned into her skin. (You can see where Ann picked up that little technique.)

Ann was so ready to unleash wrath on her mom, but didn't know where to start. She knew the typical "You're ruining my life" teenage rage, although true, just wasn't going to work. Besides, her mom wasn't ruining her life, or at least not meaning to. No more than her dad meant to get in a car accident and die.

Ann knew all this, but could she say it and mean it without having all the anger and hatred that lived inside her spew out as well? Either way, she knew she wanted Meredith, or Mom, to take her seriously.

Meredith stayed silent, but continued to burn holes with her eyes in Ann's skin, while Ann continued to take deep breaths, gaining the courage to speak.

"Mom you're an alcoholic." She said the words with disgust and angry tears followed. She brushed them away.

Meredith stopped the eye-hole-burning thing, but stayed quiet.

"And you're not taking care of us."

Silence.

Okay, let it rip, Ann.

"Look, here's the deal. Your son Tommy is going to some super duper smart school, because he's some weird genius, and he's had to forge your signatures to even get accepted and you can't even support him in this because you're such a stupid drunk. And I don't want to hate you because you're my mom, and you used to be a good mom, but now… there's no point in having you around because you don't give a shit about us.

"Tommy is going away and Will is not going to stay away just because he reminds you of Dad. And I can't believe you actually said that to him! Are you really that selfish? Honestly, if you choose to keep dealing with your problems by drinking then I am moving in with Uncle Joe and there's not a damn thing you can do about it! I'll call child protective services if I have to, as long as I can get away from you!" Tears flowed. She didn't really mean it. Or did she? Maybe that's what was so heartbreaking about it. She had reached her limit.

"I was almost raped last night!" she wailed. "And I can't even come home and have you take care of me. I have to go to Uncle Joe's because you're completely unavailable!" She was sobbing now.

Meredith rushed to her and tried to hold her.

"Don't touch me!" Ann screamed. "You don't get to touch me! I don't want your help now. It's too late!" She said it but didn't mean it. All she had really wanted was her mom's help, but she wanted to know first that she could trust her mom. She wanted to know that look of remorse on her mom's face was real and lasting, and not going to disappear with the next drink.

"Annie," Meredith finally croaked. "You're right."

Ann rolled her eyes. It was another one of those speeches from Meredith that never amounted to a damned thing.

Meredith began, "When I realized you had probably been drinking last night I—well I was angry, at myself mostly. And I decided I wanted to stop, that I needed to stop, but I didn't know how, I started drinking more until finally... I knew I couldn't anymore. I'm not going back. I started taking my Antabuse again. I swear this time it's real. I'm so sorry for what I've done."

"Well no offense, Mom, but I don't believe you. You've said that so many times, your word doesn't mean anything. Apologies mean nothing. You have to prove it. I can't...do this if..."

Do what? Trust, love, rely on Meredith?

"I can't do this if it's not real. If you're not really ready to quit. I just...I can't do it anymore. I'm exhausted."

"I know and you don't have to. If it's better, you can..." Meredith choked on her words, "you can stay with your uncle Joe if it would make it easier on you."

Ann, crying again, didn't know if this was true, if it could be true; she hoped it was the beginning of the end, but knew it wasn't going to be easy. Either way, this time when Meredith approached her she didn't shut her down. She let Meredith hold her, and she cried.

She didn't know how long they'd been standing there when William entered the bedroom.

"Hi, Mom."

"William." Meredith pulled away from Ann and they both wiped their faces.

"Can we talk?" William asked.

"Of course," Meredith said.

Ann walked past William to the door. William put his hand on her shoulder, and that's when she saw that she was shaking. She drew a breath and sighed a few more tears.

"Nicely done," he whispered.

She smiled wondering how much of the lecture he'd heard.

"You're friend Danny is here."

Ann managed a smile. Maybe she hadn't ruined her chances with him completely. Then a wave of fear crashed into her. What if she had and he was here out of concern and nothing more? Whatever the truth was, she wasn't ready for it. She felt wrecked. She was so raw and still likely to break down into heaving sobs at a moment's notice. Plus, she was still wearing the black dress from the night before. The only thing she wanted to do right then was rip off the dress, burn it, and then take a shower and wash the night off her.

She slid into her bedroom to change her clothes, quietly shutting the door behind her. She moved to her closet next to the door and pulled the top of her dress down to her waist and began pulling stuff out of the strapless bra she was wearing when she heard Danny's voice, "Oh, sorry."

She flung herself into the closet and pulled a t-shirt across her chest as she turned to see Danny sitting on her bed.

Shit. Shit. Shit. Shit, they both thought.

"Sorry. I'm not looking," he said as he stood and turned around. He seemed embarrassed but Ann could see the smile in the corner of his lips. "You probably didn't know I was here, I uh, I'll just look away and you can change. Sorry. It's, ya know. I didn't see. I mean I did see, but not really."

Ann rolled her eyes and Danny kept talking. She shimmied the rest of the way out of her dress and quickly threw on a new t-shirt and jeans.

"I mean I really barely saw. It was kind of, ya know, far away, my eyes aren't what they used to be. I had 20/20 vision as a kid, but it's not so good now. I mean not that I wear glasses, obviously, you know that."

Ann glanced in the mirror as Danny carried on. Her eyes were swollen and red, and her face was blotchy, mascara had blurred around her eyes, and her hair was a snarl. She tried licking her fingers and cleaning up the mascara. It was the least she could do.

"I don't wear contacts either, but I probably should. I mean that tree across the street kind of looks like a green blob. Seriously, it's bad."

"I'm done."

Danny cautiously turned around to look at Ann. She tried to conceal her face as much as possible by letting her messy hair fall over it as she studied the floor.

"Hi," Danny said.

"Hi."

"Are you okay?"

"Fine."

A few moments of awkward silence passed.

"Look, Ann, I don't know how to say this, so I'm just going to say it."

Ann flinched, waiting for the rejection.

"I like you, Annie, and when I heard about what Jacob did to you, I wanted to kill him. I did. But I...I know why you thought Jacob Waters and that superficial crap would make you feel better. I thought like that at one point too. So I get that. But I can't keep having you push me away. If you don't want me after this, that's it, ya know. It's just...like I'm the mouse and you're the cat, and I want to be friends, but you keep digging in the claws, not in a bad way. No that was wrong. Scratch that." He shook his head. "Whenever I'm around you I feel like I can't talk right and I start sounding like an idiot."

Ann stared at him, gaping. Not only was he into her but he *also* had recurring speech impediments when they were in close proximity.

"O-Oh," she stuttered and turned away.

"You know, when you said I wasn't the girl you thought I was..." She bit her lip but it didn't stop the few tears from escaping.

"Yeah," he said softly.

"Well, I am that girl. At least, I want to be. I don't know what happened to her or where she went. And after all that's happened I don't know if she's still...here," she sobbed.

"She is." He walked toward her.

She shook her head. "Everything that happened with Jacob."

"So?"

"I feel so..." She couldn't find the words. She only knew it as a feeling, a hollow and empty feeling of being defiled, less than worthy, undeserving. Of feeling like the trauma she received was exactly what she deserved.

"What is it?" Danny was careful in touching her. He wished to scoop her into his arms. Instead, he gently placed his hands on her shoulders.

"I can't..." she cried, shrugging him off. Can't what? Love? Be loved? Be happy? Or was it more that she didn't know how to disassemble the wall she had lived with for the past year. She didn't know how to let someone in, even when she wanted to.

"Don't do that, Ann!"

She wasn't exactly sure what she was doing. So she didn't know how to stop.

"Don't you see how beautiful and amazing you are?"

Ann shook her head without even realizing it.

"It's fucking Waters."

"You tried to warn me and I wouldn't listen," she said.

"If I knew he was going to do this to you, I would have locked you in your house," Danny said. "Scratch that, I would have locked him up. You deserve to be free."

Ann bit the inside of her cheek, unconvinced.

"Would you have dated him knowing what he did to Maggie, knowing what he was about to do to you—what he did do to you?!"

She shook her head but couldn't find the words to say "no."

"You didn't do anything Ann, Jacob did. Don't you ever blame yourself for his fucked up behavior."

After all the crying she'd already done, she was surprised she still had so many tears left.

"Ann, don't feel like you don't deserve better. Just because of your mom and your situation...I know it hurts. It sucks, but it doesn't change how amazing you are."

Ann melted. For once she let herself believe that what he was saying was true, and she fell into his arms and sobbed.

She cried for everything she had lost and everything she had found. She found herself, the one true thing she had been looking for. And even though the process hurt, hurt was an understatement. It had been miserable. Even so, she knew she would never wish to change it, and through her sobs, she felt peace.

WHEN NO MORE TEARS COULD POSSIBLY BE SHED, Danny took off his shirt for her to wipe her wet face with. It was strange, but seemed right. He hugged her head to his bare chest. He caressed her cheek with his hand until Ann fell into the most blissful sleep she ever remembered having, and when she dreamed she dreamed of an apple orchard full of fresh green apples. She was suddenly dying of hunger; she could feel her mouth water as she plucked an apple from a tree.

ANN WOKE TO DANNY tacking a Led Zeppelin poster to her wall.

"Where did you get that?"

"Oh you're awake."

"What time is it?" she said, not waiting for him to answer her first question.

"Five o'clock."

"Wow."

"Feeling any better?" Danny asked.

"Yeah, my head doesn't feel like it's splitting anymore."

"William."

"What?" Ann asked.

"He brought in the poster," Danny said.

She looked at the placement. He'd hung the poster over the word "suffering" that she'd recently etched onto her wall.

"Love equals Zeppelin." Was now what it said.

"Yeah, I hope that's okay."

"I love it." She smiled. "So where's Will?"

"He had to leave, but said he would call you tonight and he would try and be back before Thanksgiving. He didn't want to wake you."

Ann's heart sank, but she had to believe things were different, that William was coming back.

"He gave me the poster?" she asked.

"Yeah. I thought it would look good here." He finished putting in the final tack.

"It's definitely an improvement."

"Are you hungry?"

"Starving." Had she really not eaten since lunch yesterday?

"Let's go out and get some food."

" 'Kay."

"Do you have a shirt I could wear, since mine's kind of..."

"Covered in my snot."

"I'll never wash it," he joked.

"Very sweet of you. I only have girl clothes."

"Whatever you have's fine."

Ann laughed and loved that he didn't care. She grabbed a hooded sweatshirt from her closet and figured it was the least feminine looking thing she had that was clean, even though it was bright pink.

She looked in the mirror. Yep, still looked like she'd stepped out of tornado wreckage. She didn't care. She grabbed a ski cap and tucked her chaotic hair underneath it. Danny grabbed her hand and smiled adoringly at her before kissing her gently on the lips.

"Ready?" He asked.

"Ready."

AFTER DINNER ANN SHOWERED. Then she and Danny burned the dress she'd been wearing the night before. Ann also noticed her mom was sober, a small victory. She and Tommy were filling out entrance papers for his new school so he could start after Christmas break.

William even fulfilled his promise to call later and see how she was doing. Danny flipped through Thoreau as Ann talked to William, who promised he'd be there for Thanksgiving, but he couldn't come home any earlier since he needed to finish some paper he had due in his anthropology class. Maybe things were really changing this time, Ann hoped. She knew it wouldn't be perfect, but she could accept that now.

Danny stuck around and they read Thoreau and hung out in her bedroom. Danny found his favorite passages and underlined them for Ann.

"Here, listen to this one," he said excitedly. Ann laughed at what a dork he was. (She loved it.) " 'Not till we have lost the world, do we begin to find ourselves, and realize where we are and the infinite extent of our relations.' "

"Wow." Ann was impressed. That's kind of what she felt she had just gone through. "Or lose yourself in the world and find out that it's completely fucked up, and then back track from there," she said, laughing. She ripped the page from the book and tacked it to the wall as a reminder of where she'd been, what she'd learned, and where she was going.

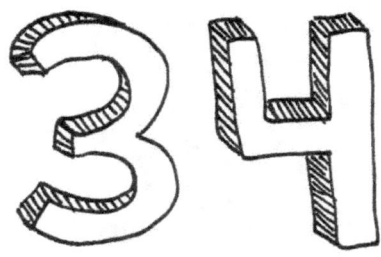

Home.

Ann had wanted to avoid school that next Monday, but Danny said she needed to face her fears, saying if she didn't go it would only make it harder later. Ann knew he was right (as he often was) so she sucked it up and went. To her surprise it was pretty much the same old stuff.

Avoiding senior hallway, drifting off in a world of doodles in her classes. The difference was Danny waiting by her locker between classes and Lisa telling Ann about her drummer boyfriend named Glass, whom Ann mercilessly goaded Lisa about.

"Seriously who calls themselves Glass?"

There was no stint in detention or a trip to *Bob's* or the allure of the T.F.P. group and Jacob Waters. There were Terrell and Maggie who invited her and Lisa to sit with them at lunch. Ann nervously glanced to the HEAD table looking for Jacob, but learned he wasn't in school because he was waiting for his face to heal. The rumor going around school was that he'd been in a fist fight with another girl's boyfriend from a rival school. Most party participants were so drunk or high they didn't argue, but instead created elaborate fight stories that they swore they witnessed. The few people who knew the truth eventually splintered from the group.

I later asked Ann why she never reported the assault. She answered honestly and said, "Because it never occurred to me that I should. I just figured these things happen and there is nothing the police can do and reporting it would only make it worse. I didn't want to bring up the past. I just wanted to move on."

It wasn't until Ann's freshman year of college that she came forward with her story. She had learned that one of Jacob's college girlfriends had filed multiple rape charges against him. Maggie decided to come forward too. Ann visited Pam during this time and asked her to share her story with the police. Pam scoffed. "He never raped me," she said, playing with the ends of her lavender pixie cut. Ann speculated that if she were to put an old high school photograph of Pam next to a more recent one, no one would believe they were the same person.

"He never hurt you?" Ann asked, disbelieving. She remembered Pam in the bathroom sobbing on the same day Jacob asked Ann on a date. The whole incident now made her nauseous.

"I never said that." Pam looked to the floor.

Ann and Pam had become friendly in high school, but were never close like Ann and Krissy.

"I told him I wouldn't sleep with him unless he was wearing a condom," Pam said. "I saw him put one on, but then after a minute he covertly took it off. I could tell something was wrong so I asked him about it and he assured me everything was fine. The pregnancy test revealed otherwise. That's when he dumped me."

Ann hugged Pam and told her it wasn't too late to hold him responsible, but Pam didn't agree. She said she didn't want everyone knowing that she'd had an abortion. Her family was religious and she didn't want to hurt them. Ann understood. Three months later Jacob was found guilty of rape and sexual assault. He served half of a two year sentence. He died six months after he was released from jail of sceptic pneumonia.

That was the end of Jacob's story, but not of the pain he had dealt to his victims. You can survive a spiritual wound but there will always be a scar. I guess what you do with the scar is up to you. Fight it? Embrace it as part of the meanness of life, like Thoreau talked about? Or try and forget and move forward as best you can? I've never been in that position so I couldn't say. I watched Ann do all three as she picked up the pieces of her life. She cried a lot and she laughed a lot. She seized the day by learning to live in every moment with an open heart.

She started telling her story. First to Lisa who hugged her while they both sobbed. Then to Krissy who fawned all over Ann, hugging her repeatedly, asking her again and again if she was okay and swearing she would never speak to Jacob again (she didn't). Ann and Krissy remained friends throughout high school and college. Ann continued to let Krissy pick out clothes for her when they went shopping and Ann enjoyed getting dressed up when she wanted to. When William first saw Ann wearing a pink mini skirt and make-up he asked, "Why are you dressed like that?"

Ann laughed, "Because I like it."

William harrumphed and turned back to his text book.

Ann knew she would never feel like her old self. Her old self had died. She grieved the losses of her old self and her old life sometimes. But now she had a new self and a new life, and she was happy with that. She missed her father and knew she always would. Some days that realization hurt more than others. But still, she carried on. She made new friends and kept old ones and watched her mother heal and become present with her again.

Ann learned a lot during this time. One thing that she admittedly learned was that cheerleading is quite hard. Ann hates explaining how she found this out, because it lead to her getting a black eye. But let's just say that one night while at a sleepover at Pam's house with the rest of the gang they tried to convince Ann to try out for cheerleading the following year. Ann scoffed, but went along with learning a few moves. Ann quickly learned, after Maggie and Krissy tried to unsuccessfully base her, that she has a fear of standing on people's hands. After a screaming/clawing dismount, Ann's head met the coffee table. (I may or may not have laughed for a week straight).

At one point Ann remarked on how she had looked at herself in the mirror and noticed that her countenance had changed. She was able to look beyond her round nose, thin lips, mute-brown hair and complacent eyebrows into what made her beautiful as she saw her father's soft blue eyes and her mother's radiant smile.

She remembered a time when she was sitting on her father's lap and she had said something funny. Her father had laughed and said, "You're too cute," and she didn't object, she simply squeezed him and smiled. She thought of that memory and what her father had said exactly. "Annie Babe, you are too cute."

Annie.

NOW THANKSGIVING WAS FAST APPROACHING and Ann was looking forward to it this year. She used to hate Thanksgiving, mostly because she loved eating and always got a stomachache. Then while she was passed out on the couch, hugging her stomach, William and Tommy always finished off the pies before she ever had a single bite. It always made her livid. One year, when her grandparents visited, Ann hid one of their pies in her room and ate it by herself. These were fond memories.

The first Thanksgiving they had without their father was like being wrapped up and mummified in a tomb. They didn't even bother to celebrate it. Ann spent most the day locked in her bedroom.

This year would be different. This year light was breaking through the branches and illuminating the dark spaces. There were people, there was understanding, there was hope, there was love, and it was getting easier for Ann to lose herself to fits of laughter.

The first time she found herself truly laughing was the Monday before Thanksgiving. Meredith absentmindedly made a sandwich and halfway through had changed her mind as to what she wanted. So one side was slathered with jelly, the other side was garnished with lunchmeat and mayonnaise. When Ann and Tommy saw what she'd done, instead of feeling sorry, or worried for her, they started laughing at her. And Meredith laughed with them.

When Ann laughed she felt it flow up from somewhere deep inside her, and it was as if she were experiencing life for the first time.

THE NIGHT BEFORE THANKSGIVING William returned home. Ann found him and Uncle Joe sitting in the old office talking, while her mom was in the kitchen smoking. The office door was ajar and Ann approached cautiously. She kind of wanted to eavesdrop, but also wanted to say hello. It had been so long since anyone had been in her dad's office. She approached the door and heard nothing. She wondered if they had stopped talking because they had heard her. She stepped inside and found them hugging. She paused. Uncle Joe pulled away. "Hi sweetheart." He said it just like her dad used to.

"Hi," she stumbled toward him. His big arms wrapped around her and she breathed the smell of cotton.

"We're just talking, going through some of your dad's old stuff," Joe said.

"Have you seen Mom?" Ann asked.

"Not yet," Joe said. "I'm going to talk to her about AA." Ann looked surprised.

"I already mentioned it to her," William said. "She seemed… open to the idea."

"That's great," Ann said.

"Whatever happens, your mom still has a long road ahead of her in her recovery. But, I just want you to know that I'm not going anywhere," Uncle Joe said.

The floor squeaked outside the door and Meredith stood before them, her face blanched, her posture stooped as if a heavy weight lay on her shoulders. She stepped into the room, as if she were waiting for the floor to turn to molten lava and devour her. She walked to Joe and hugged him. He held her as they cried. Then she pulled away, kept eye contact with the ground, and went back to the kitchen.

"I'm going to go talk to her." Joe excused himself.

It was quiet for a minute. "I already got rid of all the alcohol," William reported

"Did you check the shoe box under her bed? Or behind the garbage in her bathroom."

"I haven't, but I will. Here, I found this, thought you might want it." William handed a picture to Ann.

It was a photograph of her with her father sitting on the front steps of their house. The picture had been taken a few years ago. They were both grinning like idiots. She remembered now. They had been watching Tommy skateboard in the driveway for the first time. Her dad had called for Tommy, and when he looked up he accidentally ran into the back of the car and that's when Meredith snapped the picture of them. Tommy was fine. The memory of it still made her laugh.

"Thanks," she said. She didn't look up from the picture, her eyes transfixed.

William excused himself to look for Meredith's hidden alcohol stashes. He ended up finding only one bottle crammed between her dresser and the wall. She said she didn't remember ever putting it there. They all hoped she was telling the truth.

Ann took the picture of her with her father upstairs and pinned it to her wall, just above her headboard. She picked up *Walden* from her desk and plopped on her bed as she flipped to a random page near the end. She stopped and read a highlighted sentence. It brought a joyous curve to her lips. She smiled wistfully through losses and fears as she experienced a deep river of peace flowing through her.

She glanced around her room. The neglected plant was still barely surviving on the windowsill. The excerpt from *Walden* that Danny had torn out was pinned near it…Ann chuckled as she looked at the bleeding wall. The picture of her and Lisa together, smiling, unaware bad things could ever happen to them. The quotes on the wall from *Walden* that Danny had written…the hash marks representing Meredith's false promises. Each told a different story and held a memory for her, some pleasant, some not. Still, they were reminders of her life. She stood and swiped the black marker from her desk. Next to the picture of her father she scrawled the underlined quote she had just read from *Walden*:

However mean your life is, meet it and live it.

"Thanks, Dad," she whispered.

The end of the story.

That night I stopped by to see Ann. I brought the *Classifieds* sketch that I had found seven months earlier. She laughed and told me to keep it. We made homemade macaroni and cheese for dinner (I showed her my special recipe), and later she told me everything, just as I've told you (without *any* embellishments, of course). We sat on her bedroom floor under a dim lamplight, listening to Zeppelin. I held her hand, while her other hand fiddled with *Walden,* drawing her thumb across the pages and tracing the image of the trees and cabin on the cover as she spoke. As I heard her story, I felt the pain of her sorrows with her and together we celebrated the good moments. I knew then that I loved her and had for some time. I'm glad I worked up the courage to pass her that note in detention.

We spent all night talking, and as the sun began to rise, I kissed her and called her Ann and she corrected me: "Annie."

Snowflake

Obsidian

memoir of a

"FUNNY, HEART-WRENCHING, REAL."
—FREDA'S VOICE

CUTTER

written by

Sage Steadman

the hippie with ANGER issues

another day begins

I was a naïve, bleached blonde, white, ignorant, Mormon, suburban girl living in a Mormon bubble right in the gosh dang heart of Utah. (No, not Provo. Provo is the bubble inside the bubble and once you get two bubbles deep things start to get really weird. Like, substitute swear words such as gosh and dang are considered inappropriate. So, fuck that).

And I was asleep.

The only thing I didn't have at the moment was a set of hideous fake acrylic nails because when I did have them they interfered with my guitar playing.

And, okay, I lied. I was no longer a magnificent bleached blonde. I had recently owned my rightful place as a brunette, because, and I can only assume, whoever said blondes had more fun was likely referring to Marilyn Monroe and a steam vent, not to me. Hence I became a brunette, but truth be told, I wasn't sure what my natural hair color was since I hadn't seen it in such a long time. And, as I said, I was asleep. Literally.

The alarm went off, and I woke with a start.

Like a zombie I swung my legs out of bed and shuffled them across the wooden floor. My mismatched white and blue socks barely clung to my feet as I peered, eyes half-opened, at the alarm clock. The time read seven o'clock.

The blare of the alarm assaulted my ears, and I blindly stabbed the clock with my forefinger until the noise stopped. Then I immediately crawled back into bed and wondered why the hell I was awake.

I eventually opened my eyes to the morning summer sun shining through the slats in the blinds above my bed. The clock on my dresser now read ten a.m. That was more like it.

The sun's piercing rays shone vibrantly into my half-opened eyes, sending a headache to my brain. I blinked in an effort to dampen the pain. It didn't work. I gave up and closed my eyes, letting them rest before beginning my daily chores.

Yep, I had chores, seeing as I still lived at home and went to the local university. Yeah, I'm *that* cool. In my defense, I wasn't the only one. Many of my friends were working, living at home and going to school, except I hadn't gotten a summer job either. So I owned my rightful place as a brunette *and* a slacker that summer. Really, I had every intention of living life to the fullest, just as soon as I finished my chores.

Today's chore was to clean the bathroom. Not necessarily for my sake, but for visitors who fell upon it in a moment of desperation and were forced to use it or lose it. Especially those who had to coat the toilet seat layer upon layer with toilet paper for fear they might catch some horrid disease. So, I decided to save them the trouble, as well as a few trees.

I trudged into the bathroom with the cleaning supplies, thinking it didn't look so bad if you were able to overlook the fact that it was developing its own animal life because everything was covered with stray strands of my long hair.

I slipped into my yellow rubber cleaning gloves like an old person slips into their first adult diaper. It was comfortable, yet alien. I began scrubbing the dried toothpaste that clung to the counter. The sponge died from asphyxiation sooner than I had anticipated from the amount of hair clinging to it. I rinsed it off and continued to the toilet, followed by the bathtub, and then I decided to finish with a bang and tackle my Beloved Sink. That's not a typo. It's the name of my sink. The man who provided me exactly twenty-three of his chromosomes and not much else frequently complained about Beloved because she was spotted with dried paint. We'll call this man Bill since it's a nice round and sturdy name that can also be used synonymously with money without having to call him something hip, like Cash, or something dignified like Benjamin, because I've known too many Benjamins in my life and my father was definitely *not* a Benjamin.

"Willow, why don't you clean this sink? It's filthy," Bill had said to me the other day.

"Bill, if you don't like it, you don't have to look at it," I replied.

He was missing the chaotic beauty of it, the way the colors had splattered with random perfection. Blues, greens and reds covered the faucet and were dashed onto the ivory white of the sink. She was truly a work of art all her own. Still, I scrubbed, apologizing and reassuring her that everything would be okay.

As I scrubbed I noticed my arms had their own streaks of color from painting the night before. I hesitated briefly before I turned the sponge on myself. I figured if Beloved could withstand the pain of losing her individuality, so could I.

When I was done I said goodbye to Beloved. I patted her shimmering faucet and returned to my room. The time read noon. I opened the blinds to allow more daylight into my dim palace and flopped on the bed.

My bed was adorned with patchwork pillows that shimmered with sequins, and was complemented by a drooping cloth canopy. I liked to think that it was plush enough for a sultan, or at least one of his wives.

My bare walls were screaming for décor. I had painted each of them a different color. The strawberry red wall was where my easel sat, beckoning me to paint. The window was carved out of the pumpkin orange wall that also played backdrop to my bed. The bright purple wall held the door to my walk-in closet. The fourth wall was green and had been nicknamed the "baby poop" wall by my older sister, who had two young children at the time. Despite the nickname, I found the tone inviting.

The basic style of my room was organized clutter with my least favorite paintings shoved in cracks between furniture pieces, while my favorites stood propped around my easel. This group included a painting of a woman falling backwards in a delicate arc onto thick grass, her chest emitted a stream of light. It was my image for happiness. But everyone else who saw it thought it looked like an alien abduction. Some suggested I had been watching too many of my father's much loved sci-fi shows. Shows I pretended I didn't watch, or like, or know anything about. Like how I don't know that the Nexus is an energy ribbon that James T. Kirk disappeared into during his rescue mission of the USS Enterprise-B, and that the Nexus is a place where all of one's desires become a reality. I liked to think that my palace was my own little Nexus, my refuge from the storm, a place where anything was possible.

With that thought, I grabbed my sketchbook from its usual spot on the chair in the corner of the room and began sketching. The pencil did all the work drawing as I observed. My goal was to somehow capture the complexity of what I was feeling at that moment and then turn it over to the acrylics.

Once I finished the sketch I donned my coveralls that had layer upon layer of dried paint coating the legs, making them stiff but still comfortable. I pulled them over my legs and tied the arms around my waist. I turned on the stereo and let the dull whine of Billy Corgan's voice lure me into the painting.

After thirty minutes of dabbing, stroking, and smearing, I was stuck. The image in my mind was grossly different from the one that stared back at me. It always was.

I quickly got over this fact and let my fingers wander to the canvas. There was something soothing about paint between my fingers. I added more blue paint, and ran my fingers across the canvas, until all the colors mixed together to make a muddy brown. I stopped to examine the brown glaze of paint on my hands, and went to the closet on the other side of the room.

My friend Trinity and I had previously left ass prints in the form of red acrylic paint on the blank wall just inside the doorway of the walk-in closet. Mine were bigger than hers. (In case you were wondering).

I squatted down and pressed my paint-covered hands against the wall, next to the two red round smears of paint. Above it I scrawled the words "live freely."

Satisfied with my impromptu closet masterpiece, I rubbed the hinges of my knees that ached from squatting. Then, I succumbed to the music and danced.

The rhythm harmonized with the beat of my heart and emptied out of my toes and fingertips. Eyes closed, I let myself go. The music penetrated every cell of my body. My spine started to tingle, my hands reached out and—

Bang!

The slamming thud of the bedroom door being flung open caused my heart to leap, quickly reaching the confines of its place in my chest. My arms pulled themselves back in so quickly the back of my brown hand collided with my chin, leaving its mark. I felt embarrassed to be seen in my moment of abandoned exhibition, and I whirled around to see who had interrupted me.

It was Jo.

Jo

Josephine. Jo. She had a heart attack in fifth grade. After riding her bicycle up a hill to a friend's house, she passed out and was taken by helicopter to the hospital. She had a weak heart. It always made her unique. Her damaged heart claimed celebrity status in a group of fifth graders. Somehow, maybe because I didn't treat her any differently than I had before her newfound fame, we became friends. And once we did, our lives fused together.

It wasn't our similarities that made us friends, but our differences. Like yin and yang, we functioned as one unit, and could carry on conversations without the use of words.

Growing up, I made fun of her for her big rabbit teeth and buggy eyes, which, as she matured, turned into a full voluptuous smile and bright, perfect eyes. Add her long legs and she was nothing less than stunning. I envied her for those perfect features that used to make her look so ridiculous.

Jo entered the room with a slightly confused look on her face. She already thought I was crazy, so I knew she wasn't surprised.

Before she said anything, Jo leaned her head to one side and squirted eyedrops into one of her bloodshot eyes. The left over drops streamed down her face like tears. Then she medicated the other eye.

Eyedrops were Jo's closest companion when allergy season rolled around. For Jo, that began in March and ended in October. The few things you would always find in Jo's purse were lipstick and eyedrops, and on a good day, cash. On a bad day, tampons.

"Willow, are ya done yet? I've been upstairs watching scorpions on the Discovery channel with your dad for an hour," Jo said.

I laughed because I knew it was true.

"I wanted to come down earlier but I figured you were painting and I know how you *get* when you're *disturbed*," she added.

That was one major difference between Jo and me. I could stay shut away for hours or days at a time without social interaction and be fine. Jo never understood that. She was a social butterfly and I was a caterpillar.

"Hey. I resemble that," I responded dryly.

She laughed at the lame joke that I had said to her a million times before. I loved that about Jo. Her ability to find everything funny.

I reached down to gather up my paintbrushes and dirty water while Jo lay on my bed texting. I noticed my hands were still covered in paint so I went to grab the clean towel that Jo was lying on, despite the fact that my parents wouldn't be too pleased to know I was using it as a painting rag.

I grabbed the corner of the towel and began yanking on it while Jo texted, hoping that she would get the hint that I needed her to move. She didn't.

"Dude, could you move already?" I said.

"You shut your mouth," Jo responded. Not skipping a beat in her text.

I gave up on the towel and returned to gathering up my brushes. Jo was the kind of girl who knew how to talk trash, which was something that I always loved about her. Especially since on the inside I knew Jo was a big softy. It was a refreshing combination that I found endearing.

She finished texting and tucked her phone in her pocket. "I came over because I need you to help me get my yellow jacket back."

I immediately knew what jacket she was talking about. The jacket she had bought at a thrift store when we were in the eighth grade. It came with a rainbow pin that said "Ann." It was the jacket she always threw on, come snow, rain or shine, it was her trademark.

"You don't have it?" I asked.

"Yeah isn't it an outrage?" she said flippantly and began rubbing her eyes.

"Where is it?"

"Jake has it," she said with a sigh. "He stole it from me when we were dating last summer."

"Stop rubbing your eyes," I insisted knowing they would turn red and puffy if she kept at it. "Or am I going to have to put socks on your hands?"

"Gross. I *will* not have your nasty socks on my hands."

"Why not?" I said, teasing her. "I bet they're nice and moist."

Jo hated the word "moist." I took pleasure in watching her cringe after I said it.

"Okay I'm done," she said, sitting on her hands to keep from rubbing her eyes.

"Ya know Jake has one of my skirts," I said.

"Weird. Why?"

"Because he's an in-the-closet cross-dresser."

"Please. There's nothing in the closet about his cross-dressing. Didn't he wear your skirt to the grocery store once?"

"Yeah," I admitted. "Ya wanna go over to his house and get them?"

"Hold on," she said pulling her cell phone out of her pocket and dialing. "Hi, where are you?" she waited only a moment before hanging up, presumably before the conversation had ended. "Jake is golfing."

"Was that him?"

"YYYYYep," she said with a devious smile.

"I'll clean up."

I carried my paint-soaked brushes to my newly cleaned Beloved. I paused half a second, before turning on the faucet with my paint-covered hands and emptying out the jar of dirty water into Beloved and washing my hands, observing the new splattered paint design.

jekyll, meet hyde

Before we continue, there is something you have to understand about my relationship with my friends. First of all, I considered my friends to be more like family, people destined to share at least a fragment of their existence in relationship with me. Sometimes I felt that my friends knew me better than I knew myself. But there was a part of me I kept concealed from them and from everyone really. That beautiful part of me I was afraid would be judged, misunderstood or hurt. That's why when I was among friends I was personal without having to actually share anything truly personal. I vacillated between outgoing irreverence and deep silence. I was open, yet secretive. My friends saw me as laid back, but they couldn't see the stirring inside. I kept myself hidden, hoping one day I would have the courage to risk showing someone my concealed self. My imperfect and beautiful self. My friends, they saw my fire, but they didn't see my passion.

in search of the yellow jacket

Jo knocked on the front door of Jake's house. I stared off into the distance and pretended I wasn't there. It was something I had learned to do in high school, disappear among the crowd of faces. It wasn't as easy as you might think, considering who my friends were. They belonged to one of the "hot girl" cliques.

My friends were gorgeous, and I always considered myself plain in comparison to their stunning beauty. Although my utterly beautiful friends received most of the attention from the opposite sex, I received some flattering attention, but I always assumed it was only by status default. It came in the form of a shoulder-rub by a creepy social climbing sophomore, or someone reminiscing about how they used to date one of my friends.

We were nicknamed the Blonde Squad on account of our all having blonde hair. Of course half of us were only pretending to be blonde, myself included until I took my rightful place in the sea of unnoticed brunettes.

I look back on my high school years with fondness, not because of all the social torture that accompanied it, but because everything was simple. Once I started college, the social torture ended, but the complications of life began. That's when I started to feel that the decisions I made would affect my happiness for the rest of my life. This internal pressure I put on myself was at times mind-numbing. That's why I was looking forward to a summer vacation without any commitments to school or work.

No one had come to the door since Jo knocked. She sighed and rang the doorbell a couple of times, then crossed her arms and waited. I let my thoughts drift as I waited with her. I thought about high school, my favorite teacher Mr. Zaborski. He was my favorite not because I learned anything from him, but because he was skittish and paranoid and it made me laugh. That was also the class I had with Shawn. He sat on the back row, always wore black, and for the most part kept to himself.

Shawn and I didn't become friends in that class. He sat directly behind me for most of the semester and we never talked. He later explained to me that he thought I was annoying. The first time we actually talked was when my friend Adam unexpectedly dropped by with Shawn six months ago. Once Shawn and I actually talked we clicked right away, and Adam was left out of the conversation most of the night. Occasionally Adam would pipe in with a, "Hey, Five Hours Ago called and said it was time to leave." But Shawn and I just ignored him and kept talking.

Things had changed a lot since then. My shoulders tensed as I thought about the phone conversation Shawn and I had last night. I shouldn't have mentioned my plans to hang out with Mike because that's when Shawn hung up on me, and now we were in another fight.

I told myself I should have called him back when he hung up on me. I guess I wasn't expected to since we were in a fight, but I didn't want him to feel that I didn't care either, since I was the one who had got us into this whole mess in the first place. I knew we needed to talk about it, but the thought of speaking to him brought a lump to my throat. I had really messed things up this time. I shook the thought from my mind when the front door to Jake's house finally swung open. Jake's mom stood behind the door smiling.

"Hi," she said.

Jake's mom had long red hair and a pointy nose, as did all Jake's sisters. Jake looked nothing like that. Jake's hair was sandy blond with loose curls, and he had a long round nose and a pointy chin. I sometimes wondered if he was adopted.

"Hi, is Jake here?" Jo said, playing dumb.

"Ya know what, he's not," Jake's mom answered.

Of course, that was the answer we were expecting.

"Yeah, we left some stuff here," Jo said. "Can we just go down to his room and get it real quick?"

"Yeah, come on in." She stepped to one side, letting us pass.

Of course the truth was that we hadn't left it there. Jake tended to wear our clothes home when he came to visit. He pulled off the cross-dressing bit with real class, to the point that I believed my clothes were better suited for him than they were for me.

We entered Jake's room with anxious excitement. His bed was covered with guitars and the walls were covered with random drawings and band posters. We began searching through his closet and drawers. I envied his clothes sometimes. I was sure most of them came from a thrift store or band concert. Except for his pants, which had small stuffed animals glued all over them that were inspired by Flea, the bassist from Red Hot Chili Peppers. Classic. I saw them lying on the floor near his bed. I picked them up, grinning.

"Seriously! Who does that?" I said, showing Jo the pants. Jo turned toward me and busted up laughing.

We had first noticed Jake as he was passing by our locker in high school, wearing these stuffed animal pants that he could barely walk in. His curly locks, dyed blue, looked all too attractive on him, and we couldn't help but stare. The difference between our stares and everyone else's though, is that ours were in complete admiration, instead of ridicule, which is what you got when you didn't conform to high school protocol: always smile, look pretty, be friendly, talk too much, wear name brand clothes, flirt, act dumb...the list went on. I realized in that moment how grateful I was those days were over.

Jo grabbed the pants from my hands and slipped them on over her clothes. She couldn't stop laughing and neither could I. Her laugh was truly contagious.

Laughing, we continued looking for our confiscated items. Jo turned towards the dresser and began opening drawers and shuffling under clothes, while I gravitated towards the closet and flung open the doors. As I began to sift through the hangers it was as if I were shopping at a second hand store called "Jake's Closet."

"Oooo! I like this shirt," I said. "Do you think it would fit me?"

Jo turned from the dresser she was searching, leaving clothes carelessly dangling from inside the drawer, to look while I held the shirt up to my chest. It was a faded black t-shirt that had a hot-pink star scribbled carelessly on the front center of the shirt.

"Probably," she said with a shrug.

I contemplated taking it, and then decided against it.

"Here's my skirt," I said, picking it up from a pile of clothes lying on the closet floor. The skirt was one I had made when I was a sophomore. It was one of the many reasons why my friends sometimes referred to me as "the hippie." It had a tie-dye design and it hung from my hips to the floor. The hem was dirty from dragging on the ground. Jo walked up beside me and began thumbing through the hangers.

"I don't see the yellow jacket, Jo."

"Oh look! His Seattle shirt! He loves this shirt." She pulled it from the hanger. "I'm takin' it."

Jake's Seattle shirt had long blue sleeves and a picture of downtown Seattle on it, and we took it. In place of the Seattle shirt we left a note:

Bring the Yellow Jacket to Willow's house or the Seattle shirt gets it!

the hippie

Hippie. A label that's associated with my very presence like a peace sign at a Vietnam protest. Being a Mormon and a hippie is sort of a contradiction. As a Mormon my life plan included staying a virgin until marriage, marrying a return missionary in the Mormon Temple and propagating the species while "magnifying" my church callings. Which, by the way, many Utah Mormons don't even *like* church callings. A lot of us pray that when the bishop calls that we'll be asked to do an easy job like work in the church library. Anyway, the whole thing doesn't really jive with being a hippie. Although, I admit I do have things in common with hippies, and it's not just the scent of patchouli that seems to follow me, or my secret desire to always be naked in nature. Or the fact that I'm a tree hugger, literally and metaphorically speaking. It's because I believe in a little thing that Jesus Christ spoke of called love.

Okay, it's not just that.

It's because I say things like "good energy" and "bad vibes," and I wear tie-dye skirts with no shoes, while simultaneously crying over caged puppies and the destruction of Mother Earth, and conservative Mormon's know no other word for what I am, except for hippie. The word is sometimes spoken with adoration, and other times in damnation. Either way, it's always entertaining. Like when I was seventeen and treated like a reality TV star by some stoners at a Dave Matthews concert in Colorado.

Stoner One: "Hey meet my new friend. She's a Mormon dude!"

Stoner Two: "Whoa! No way! Nice to meet you!"

He shook my hand while I checked out his shirtless tanned body then we danced our hearts out to Dancing Nancies.

So aside from the fact that I was drug free, and tried to obtain higher consciousness at 4:20 through meditation instead of marijuana, and didn't worship the Grateful Dead, I guess you could say I was a bit of a hippie. A tree hugging, peace-keeping hippie, with some deep seated anger problems that my six-year-old self used to manage by stabbing my mother's kitchen stools. Now, that fiery rankling was tantamount to a ticking time bomb on the verge of explosion.

And I wasn't the only one.

shawn

It only took a couple of hours of holding the Seattle shirt ransom before Jake and the clan of skaters ended up in my basement. The middle-class neighborhood I lived in called them delinquents. I called them friends. One evening a neighbor actually called my mother to tell her that vandals were lurking outside her home. My mother politely thanked the neighbor for her watchfulness, but didn't tell her those vandals were, in fact, her daughter and friends.

The group lounged in my father's office near the pool table, while I sat on my bed, alone, feeling sick.

I didn't know if I was ready to see Shawn, but I had no choice because Jake had invited him over. Everything had become so dramatic between Shawn and me. I hated drama! I didn't know why I needed some more of it in my life. Maybe I was bored.

I always told myself that drama was something teenagers created to make their dull lives interesting. Drama was the one thing I hoped to rid my life of once I graduated high school, and here I was diving into the pool of drama and making waves like the fat kid at the public pool.

But I did want to talk to Shawn and set things straight.

Except, he told Jo he *hated* me. He hated me because he liked me, and he *thought* I didn't want anything to do with him. Not true! Minus all evidence to the contrary that clearly showed that I was the one constantly pulling him forward and then pushing him away.

DRAMA! Dumb. Dumb. Dumb.

Growing frustrated, I bent over and tugged at clumps of my hair, wondering if I should scream. I scratched my head frantically trying to make sense of what I had done. I knew that I loved Shawn, and was attracted to him, but I wasn't *in* love with him.

The only reason why this got so crazy in the first place was because Shawn had dropped the "M" bomb. I wasn't ready for marriage! I had just graduated from high school a year earlier. I still thought I might join the Peace Corps or live in France or study abroad, but I never wanted to be married at nineteen. I didn't fully understand the mess I had gotten myself into. But I knew where it started. With a four-letter word: Mike.

mike

Mike. He was a cowboy for hells sake, on the brink of either being a jock or a redneck, the exact opposite of my type. He was a friend of my cousin's. The only thing that impressed me at first was that he made me laugh, and that was all it took for me to start liking him. Only to find out he wanted Jo. It was the classic story played out in countless teen movies. The girl falls in love with the shallow guy who is really more interested in her best friend, and then the girl realizes the real "man of her dreams" had been there all along. Shawn. Except...it couldn't be Shawn. I wasn't in love with Shawn.

Ugh! And besides, even if I were in love with him, it wouldn't change the fact that Shawn already had a girlfriend!

I pulled at my hair, tussling my long locks in all directions. Somehow it made me feel better, but my heart was still burning.

I had wanted Mike, but Mike was unreachable. Sometimes he would make me think I had a chance with him, other times he would bore me with stories about his ex-girlfriend and how he couldn't figure out why she dumped him. Meanwhile, I wondered why I hadn't remembered to bring some horse tranquilizers to get me through his droning on and on.

It was during this time I met Shawn. My feelings for Shawn were similar to a roller coaster. One minute I would truly feel that I was in love! Then suddenly Shawn would be the last person on earth that I could ever be with. One week we'd be together, the next week simply friends.

Despite this, I still loved him as a friend. Always. A month earlier, he had given up on us and gotten a girlfriend. I couldn't stand losing him, and it was easy to get him back. Two hours after I helped him decorate his girlfriend's car with hearts, we were making out on the couch.

I know. I'm a bitch.

What's worse is that when I had him wrapped around my finger, something didn't feel right, and it was one of those deep gut feelings that I probably should have listened to, but *really* didn't want to. And that's why I was so confused. I never knew which emotion I could really trust. Was it my passion or my gut?

I drove myself crazy with these thoughts until I finally told myself it was too late to worry. That was the past, what I had already done. I couldn't change any of it now.

I picked up my guitar and pretended to be relaxed as I strummed. It was at that moment, with my hair in a tussled mess, that Shawn entered my room. The lump I had in my throat dropped like a grand piano into my stomach. He sat next to me on the bed. I could smell him. I hated how he smelled. It reminded me of my first kiss with Gooey Mouth who wore the same cologne. He smiled slightly as his jet-black hair carelessly fell into his baby blue eyes. Those eyes could have hypnotized me if I let them.

His leg brushed against mine and the grand piano in my stomach burst into butterflies. A part of me wanted to jump on top of Shawn like I always had, kiss him and tell him I was sorry, and convince myself that we were meant to be together.

But we weren't meant to be together and I knew that. We were just too different.

"Hey," Shawn said as he used his fingers to comb his hair out of his eyes. I looked away from his hypnotic gaze.

"Hey…thanks for hanging up on me last night," I said sarcastically.

"Yeah, how was hanging out with Mike?" he retorted.

I went back to strumming the guitar. I kept repeating the same three chords over and over. I knew other chords, but I was too focused on pretending I was relaxed to fumble around with anything else. I didn't want to talk about Mike. I hated remembering how Mike was glued to Jo all night. He hung on her every word. There was no mundane droning on about ex-girlfriends, there was only her. And it had become painfully obvious that I had once again entered the "let's be friends" domain, while my former infatuation engaged in dating one of my friends. It felt like high school all over again.

Not that I could blame the men. When it came to good looks and the ability to flirt, I wasn't blessed with either. I was too tall, my skin was too pasty, I often had colonies of pimples living on my cheeks, which were simply too round, my feet were too big and my nose was too pointy.

After that night, Jo realized she'd hurt my feelings by flirting with the guy I was into all night and so she promised to stay away from him. I questioned her loyalty. She'd been acting weird lately. Like one of those goats you see on the Discovery Channel during mating season. They look deceivingly sweet just before they ram their horns into an innocent bystander's knobby knees.

"Oh," I said to Shawn, remembering the hurt. "It turns out he doesn't want me. He wants Jo."

"Well, sucks for you," Shawn said with bitter satisfaction.

My hands fell flat before I could complete the chord I was strumming. His words and the tone of his voice, so sarcastic, so pleased, crawled over my skin. The butterflies in my stomach fled for higher ground and lodged themselves in my throat. I was afraid of what I might say if I opened my mouth. I didn't want to say something I knew I would quickly regret. So, I calmly set down the guitar and got up to leave. I became extremely conscious of my movements, as I rigidly walked towards the door. I told myself it was finally time for me to say goodbye to Shawn and let him go. I was tired of hurting him.

"Nice talking to you, Shawn."

I said it sincerely, but he was used to my sarcasm and most likely took it offensively.

I left him sitting on the bed and couldn't decide if I was angry or sad. I rigidly walked down the hall holding my breath. The hallway ended as I entered the room where the pool table was adjacent to my father's office. Adam and some New Kid were playing pool. I decided to make it look like I was watching the game, when in reality I was thinking about Shawn. I briefly noticed that a bunch of people were crowded in my father's office. Some people I recognized, some I didn't. Jake and Jo were among the crowd. I heard them arguing about the jacket.

"I told you I don't have the yellow jacket," Jake insisted. "I think Aaron took it from me."

Jo threw on the Seattle shirt over her tank top. "Just my size!" she exclaimed.

"Noooo!" Jake yelled flirtatiously and Jo took off running.

The two whizzed past me as Jake chased Jo down the hall to where Shawn was. I heard Jo's laughter and was glad she was having a good time.

"Hey Will, come play pool," Adam said.

Will was what most people called me. The masculine nickname was very fitting, even though I had the biggest cup size of all the girls in our group, I was also seen as the biggest dude. Being "one of the guys" was something I heard frequently. I both dreaded and enjoyed it.

I grabbed the pool stick from the New Kid who joined the other guests in my father's dim office. The noise coming from the other room was so loud I didn't hear Shawn's footsteps until he was right behind me. I felt him gently brush past me as he walked by, and I shuddered. He hated me. He had every right to. As Shawn approached the office I heard him announce to the rest of the group that he wanted to leave. I told myself to focus on the game. I took aim and shot.

"Will shoots for the seven ball, which is mine, but who knows what the mastermind is up too," Adam said with an announcer voice.

I laughed, trying to forget the drama.

Adam circled the table looking for a shot. I glanced over at New

Kid's floppy, bleached blond hair as he took a seat in the corner of the poolroom. He didn't say much and looked content keeping to himself. I noticed him leaning over to look at the bottom of his bare feet. He was shoeless when he came in, and it appeared as if there might have been something interesting under there. His attitude was reserved and laid back, and there was something about him that caught my attention. It made me feel almost uncomfortable because of how it was distracting me entirely. I wondered if maybe it was his eyes. They seemed troubled. Wait. Maybe they were blank. I debated it. Blank eyes? Or troubled eyes? Maybe they were mysterious eyes. His eyes did have a hint of darkness to them, as if they were keeping secrets. I then wondered what mysterious eyes might look like before I could cast my final ballot. Then I voted to not vote, and instead pretend I hadn't noticed.

"Will!" Adam said.

I snapped back to reality.

"Huh?"

"It's your turn," he said.

"Oh," I said focusing my attention on the game.

"Hey Shawn wants to go home, can I drive him in your car?" Adam asked.

"Adam, it's a clutch," I said, raising my eyebrows.

"Come on. I'm real good at it now. I've been practicing," he said.

I looked at him half smiling and rolled my eyes. It was probably better if Shawn left, so I told myself to go along with it.

"Okay, but I'm coming," I said.

"You don't trust me?" he said, pretending to be offended.

I grabbed the keys from my pocket and handed them to Adam. "Is this news to you?"

snap

We were silent on the way to Shawn's house. Adam's cranking of the stick shift made me aware that he still couldn't drive a clutch. But with Adam driving, I was able to sit alone in the back seat while Shawn sat shotgun.

When we pulled up to Shawn's house I was feeling tense. The driveway was slanted and after Adam pulled onto it, the car began to roll backwards before Shawn could get out. His frame was stiff.

"Adam, you gotta leave your foot on the brake," I said from the back seat.

"Wait a second..." Adam said, looking for the emergency brake that was underneath and to the right of the steering wheel, instead of the usual place between the jump seats.

"No. Here..." I said, leaning forward to pull the emergency brake. Adam and I started laughing.

"Will, why the hell are you doing this?!" Shawn yelled, facing me.

Completely alarmed, I jumped back in my seat.

"Do you really want to talk about this right now?" I asked.

"Yes!" Shawn yelled.

That was the last thing I remember hearing him say before he lost it. I couldn't hear what he was saying exactly, I was too numb. I just know Shawn's face turned apple red as he screamed profanities coupled with feelings of hate.

I had never seen Shawn like this before. It was the strangest thing to love and fear somebody at the same time. Shawn wasn't foul like this, he was funny and sincere and inspiring. The only thing that made sense in that moment was that I was responsible for his anger.

As abruptly as it had started, Shawn's performance ended as he got out of the car and slammed the door.

I thought I should feel something, but I didn't feel anything. Maybe I was in shock. Definitely shock. I was still trying to figure out what had just happened.

Adam looked at me with wide eyes. "Oh my gosh! What was that?"

* * *

More books by this author:

The summer after graduation three teens living together in a small town reevaluate their lives as they question their respective futures. Jen reconsiders leaving for college as she battles to break free from her abusive relationships and pines after her emotionally distant and brooding best friend, Gabe. Gabe reels from the loss of his twin sister, Ginger, and struggles to keep the promises he made to her before she died. Noah looks for a new relationship as the secrets from his past begin tearing him apart at the seams. Paths cross and come to a head in this poignant drama about the struggles of breaking free.

Titles available through the same publisher.

Jenny Taylor has always wanted a simple, normal life. But when the dangers and secrets of a past she can't remember come hunting for her, she can no longer ignore the nightmares and her parents' overprotective natures. And her simple life doesn't just crumble—it shatters.

Thank You

The first time I wrote acknowledgments I think I thanked every living human being on the planet. So now I think it's time I thanked people not from this planet. So, aliens, I don't know you personally, but I don't think you've probed my brain yet and I'm pretty happy about that. Also, if you are influencing our government, you gotta up your game cuz shits getting real.

I'd also like to thank some people from this planet (although, that's yet to be confirmed). I'd like to thank Tyler Steadman for helping me find my voice and supporting me in my writing. Lauren T. Hart for always making me write better (by being fucking brutal. J/K. Or am I?), and thanks for the other ten thousand things that you and Trissa Fonnesbeck do for me. Trissa, thank you also for your keen editing eye. You haven't actually had your eyes on this document yet, but I'm sure you'll read it after it's published and point out all the spelling/grammar errors that were missed and I'll have to go in and fix them and republish it all and it will be a big hassle and I'll wonder why I didn't just have you read it in the first place. So, thanks.

Thanks Pop for feeding me, sheltering me, and watching *Barney* with my little babes. Thanks to my friend and editor extraordinaire Twila Van Leer. And to Jeff Karon for proofreading the final document and keeping his opinions about Almond Joys vs. Mounds to himself.

Discussion Guide

1. On page 186, we learn that Lisa stopped talking to Ann after the accident while Ann was grieving. Do you agree with her decision? Why or why not?

2. On page 102, Ann describes how her friends disappeared after her father's death. How do you think you would have responded in that situation if it was one of your friends who lost a parent?

3. On page 185, Ann tells Lisa she's not a slut, even though she is dating Jacob Waters. What is your experience with rules regarding female versus male sexuality? What are these, and how do they affect your every day life and decision making?

4. What were your feelings when you discovered that Ann wasn't the only person that Jacob had previously assaulted?

5. Ann told herself that her drinking was different from her mothers. Do you agree or disagree, and why?

6. Have you ever lost someone close to you and how did that affect you? What was the grieving process like? How did people around you respond to you during that time?

7. Ann tried to find happiness by pursuing things she deemed as "normal." Have you ever experienced the same desire? Why or why not? If yes, what did you learn from the experience?

8. Jacob Waters represents a typical alpha male stereotype of rape and rape culture. Do you think it's a fair stereotype? Why or why not?

9. Ann didn't report the assault when it initially happened. Do you agree with her decision? Why or why not?

Sage Steadman was awarded a master's degree in social work from the University of Utah. While pursuing her passion for writing, she worked as a licensed mental health therapist. She published her debut novel, *Snowflake Obsidian: Memoir of a Cutter*, in 2010 under her pen name, The Hippie, and since, re-released the second edition under her real name. The novel has been deemed an "idyllic" read, filled with love, humor, romance and heart. She is also the co-author of the gritty and inspiring historical fiction novel, *Upon Destiny's Song*, alongside classical guitarist, Mike Ericksen, and has penned an article on teen cutting for Canadian Magazine, *Edmonton's Child*. She is also the author of the stunning and thought-reflecting novella entitled, *The Waking Dream*. Sage is heralded as a talented writer who tackles her novels with a witty, raw and honest approach. She currently lives near Salt Lake City, Utah with her family. Visit her online at: www.SageSteadman.com.

www.ingramcontent.com/pod-product-compliance
Lightning Source LLC
Chambersburg PA
CBHW071301170626
46809CB00001B/309